SIT. STAY. LOVE.

What Reviewers Say
About Karis Walsh's Work

Love on Lavender Lane

"The writing was engaging and I enjoyed the slow burn attraction between the two leads."—Melina Bickard, Librarian, Waterloo Library (UK)

Seascape

"When I think of Karis Walsh novels, the two aspects that distinguish them from those of many authors are the interactions of the characters with their environment, both the scenery and the plants and animals that live in it. This book has all of that in abundance…"—*The Good, The Bad and The Unread*

Set the Stage

"I really adored this book. From the characters to the setting and the slow burn romance, I was in it for the long haul with this one. Karis Walsh to me is an expert in creating interesting characters that often have to face some type of adversity. While this book was no different, it felt like the author changed up her game a bit. There was something new, something fresh about this book from Walsh."
—*The Romantic Reader Blog*

You Make Me Tremble

"Another quality read from Karis Walsh. She is definitely a go-to for a heartwarming read."—*The Romantic Reader Blog*

Amounting to Nothing

"As always with Karis Walsh's books the characters are well drawn and the inter-relationships well developed."—*Lesbian Reading Room*

Tales From the Sea Glass Inn

"*Tales from Sea Glass Inn* is a lovely collection of stories about the women who visit the Inn and the relationships that they form with each other."—*Inked Rainbow Reads*

Love on Tap

"Karis Walsh writes excellent romances. They draw you in, engage your mind and capture your heart. …What really good romance writers do is make you dream of being that loved, that chosen. Love on Tap is exactly that novel—interesting characters, slightly different circumstances to anything you have read before, slightly different challenges. And although you KNOW the happy ending is coming, you still have that little bit of 'oooh—make it happen.' Loved it. Wish it was me. What more is there to say?"
—*The Lesbian Reading Room*

"This is the second book I have read by this author and it certainly won't be my last. Ms Walsh is one of the few authors who can write a truly great and interesting love story without the need of a secondary story line or plot."—*Inked Rainbow Reads*

Sweet Hearts: Romantic Novellas

"I was super excited when I saw this book was coming out, and it did not disappoint."—Danielle Kimerer, Librarian, Reading Public Library (MA)

Mounting Evidence

"[A]nother awesome Karis Walsh novel, and I have eternal hope that at some point there will be another book in this series. I liked the characters, the plot, the mystery and the romance so much." —Danielle Kimerer, Librarian, Reading Public Library (MA)

Mounting Danger

"A mystery, a woman in a uniform and horses. ...YES!!!!... This book is brilliant in my opinion. Very well written with great flow and a fantastic plot. I enjoyed the horses in this dramatic saga. There is so much information on training and riding, and polo. Very interesting things to know."—*Prism Book Alliance*

Blindsided

"Their slow-burn romance is a nuanced exploration of trust, desire, and negotiating boundaries, without a hint of schmaltz or pity. The sex scenes are sizzling hot, but it's the slow burn that really allows Walsh to shine... The deft dialogue and well-written characters make this a winner."—*Publishers Weekly*

"This is definitely a good read, and it's a good introduction to Karis Walsh and her books. The romance is good, the sex is hot, the dogs are endearing, and you finish the book feeling good. Why wouldn't you want all that?"—*The Lesbian Review*

Wingspan

"I really enjoy Karis Walsh's work. She writes wonderful novels that have interesting characters who aren't perfect, but they are likable. This book pulls you into the story right from the beginning.

The setting is the beautiful Olympic Peninsula and you can't help but want to go there as you read *Wingspan.*"—*The Romantic Reader Blog*

The Sea Glass Inn

"Karis Walsh's third book, excellently written and paced as always, takes us on a gentle but determined journey through two womens' awakening. ...Loved it, another great read that will stay on my re-visit shelf."—*Lesbian Reading Room*

Worth the Risk

"The setting of this novel is exquisite, based on Karis Walsh's own background in horsemanship and knowledge of showjumping. It provides a wonderful plot to the story, a great backdrop to the characters and an interesting insight for those of us who don't know that world. ...Another great book by Karis Walsh. Well written, well paced, amusing and warming. Definitely a hit for me."—*Lesbian Reading Room*

Improvisation

"Walsh tells this story in achingly beautiful words, phrases and paragraphs, building a tension that is bittersweet. As the two main characters sway through life to the music of their souls, the reader may think she hears the strains of Tina's violin. As the two women interact, there is always an undercurrent of sensuality buzzing around the edges of the pages, even while they exchange sometimes snappy, sometimes comic dialogue. *Improvisation* is a true romantic tale, Walsh's fourth book, and she's evolving into a master romantic storyteller."—*Lambda Literary*

Harmony

"This was Karis Walsh's first novel and what a great addition to the LesFic fold. It is very well written and flows effortlessly as it weaves together the story of Brooke and Andi's worlds and their intriguing journey together. Ms Walsh has given space to more than just the heroines and we come to know the quartet and their partners, all of whom are likeable and interesting."—*Lesbian Reading Room*

Risk Factor—Novella in Sweet Hearts

"Karis Walsh sensitively portrays the frustration of learning to live with a new disability through Ainslee, and the pain of living as a survivor of suicide loss through Myra."—*The Lesbian Review*

Visit us at www.boldstrokesbooks.com

By the Author

Harmony

Worth the Risk

Sea Glass Inn

Improvisation

Mounting Danger

Wingspan

Blindsided

Mounting Evidence

Love on Tap

Tales from Sea Glass Inn

Amounting to Nothing

You Make Me Tremble

Set the Stage

Seascape

Love on Lavender Lane

Sit. Stay. Love.

SIT. STAY. LOVE.

by

Karis Walsh

2019

SIT. STAY. LOVE.

ISBN 13: 978-1-63555-439-7

This Trade Paperback Original Is Published By
Bold Strokes Books, Inc.
P.O. Box 249
Valley Falls, NY 12185

First Edition: August 2019

CREDITS
EDITOR: RUTH STERNGLANTZ
PRODUCTION DESIGN: SUSAN RAMUNDO
COVER DESIGN BY JEANINE HENNING

CHAPTER ONE

Alana Brendt pulled her blue suitcase off the cart and snapped its handle into place before joining the rest of the passengers in the short walk across the tarmac to the terminal. She sighed as she looked around. Yakima, Washington. How the hell had she ended up here?

Okay, she knew exactly how she had ended up in this out-of-the-way town. Best not to dwell on the embarrassing past and focus instead on the future. This was merely one brief rung on the ladder that would get her career out of the hole she had dug and back on an upward trajectory. She would ignore the depressing details in her surroundings and only look at the positive ones.

Like the weather. She had landed in heavy rain in Seattle, where she had connected through to Yakima, and now was enjoying sun and reasonable temperatures in the midsixties. Exactly right for the T-shirt and light cardigan she was wearing. And her flight on the Dash 8 turboprop had been quick and comfortable. The plane had been less than half full—she wasn't going to consider what that statistic said about her destination— and once the passengers had been shuffled around for better weight distribution on the little plane, she had gotten a row all to herself. She searched her surroundings, looking for more positives. Those hills were a lovely yellow-brown. Not a color she would ever choose in clothes, upholstery, or paint, but nice, nonetheless. Sort of. If one was desperate to appreciate *something* about this town, she supposed.

She turned away from the bland vista and moved quickly through the small terminal, passing a wall of vending machines that hopefully wasn't indicative of Yakima's level of fine dining. She had flown over this area on the way into Seattle, before backtracking on the regional flight, and she hadn't paid much attention to the scenery. She had been more interested in the snowy ruggedness of the Cascades and the green beauty of the western coast, but the eastern side of the state had passed by in a blur of patchwork farms and barren, rounded hills. Before coming here, she had read about the agricultural industry in Yakima but had rapidly lost interest in the details about apple orchards and squash fields. There were vineyards and wineries, as well as hops aplenty for the ubiquitous Northwest microbreweries, and that was all she cared to know about produce and farming.

She emerged into the sunshine again and approached the first in a line of three taxis waiting outside the terminal doors. The driver jumped out of his car and opened the back door for her before stowing her suitcase in the trunk. He trotted around the car, seemingly trying to get her and her belongings locked in before she could change her mind and go back inside the airport. She doubted he had a lot of business in May, a month or so before the massive influx of a dozen tourists descended on Yakima.

"Where to?" he asked, pulling away from the curb and following the exit signs.

"High Ridge Ranch," Alana said, digging through her tote bag for the emails from the ranch's owner. "Do you need the address? It's a new place."

He shook his head and glanced in the rearview mirror at her. "I know the place. Out toward Selah. Don't think it's open yet, though."

"It's not. I'm going to be working there." God help her.

The cab driver apparently hadn't noticed her resigned tone because he grinned over his shoulder at her. "That's great. Welcome to Yakima. You'll love living here."

Staying here. Not living here. She didn't correct him, though, since a lifetime of working in the hospitality industry kicked in and triggered an answering smile. Like it or not, she was a representative of the ranch as long as she was employed there. Reputations were built on word-of-mouth—and lost the same way, as she knew far too well—and an amiable conversation with this cab driver could directly result in new bookings for the ranch the next time a fare asked his advice about where to stay while in the area.

"It already feels like a friendly and welcoming city. I'm sure I'll love it here." One truth and one laughably unlikely statement.

"Where are you from?"

"Philadelphia," Alana said, feeling a pang of homesickness even though she hadn't lived there long. She'd miss the museums and the nightlife, the symphony and the elegant restaurants. All she'd seen out the cab's window so far were tidy residential streets lined with Craftsman-style homes.

"Ah, a big city," the driver said, filling the simple sentence with a sense of pity for those who had to deal with crowds and didn't have the luxury of living in rural Yakima.

Alana changed the subject and asked a few polite questions about him and his family, but once they reached the highway, she fell silent and stared out the window at the unfamiliar world around her. Hotels, gas stations, fast food restaurants. A large yard filled with piles of bare tree trunks and heavy machinery. She knew there was a mall area with big box stores, and the downtown neighborhood with smaller, more unique shops, but she didn't see any of that, and soon they were leaving even the sparse elements of town behind.

They passed yet another white building with a huge *Fruit* sign on it. Every inch of wall space was covered with smaller signs with names of different fruits, as if passersby might not understand the more generic term. Apples, peaches, blackberries. Nonfruit items like asparagus and honey. All the enormous fruit stands were closed, and after passing the third one, Alana realized they were probably seasonal, opening only when the fresh produce was available. Fresh produce—another positive. She pulled out her phone, noticing with some surprise that she had cell service out here in the boonies, and searched to find out what local fruits or vegetables she could find in May.

Lettuces. Alana struggled to find a way to make a head of lettuce sound enticing, but she quickly gave up and scrolled through her email in case an amazing job offer had arrived in her inbox while she had been on the plane. Nothing, of course.

The cab turned off Highway 82 and headed into hills terraced with basalt ridges and sparsely covered with dry yellowish grasses. Alana wasn't sure where the produce for the stands was grown, but it obviously wasn't coming from the immediate area. The landscape had a certain minimalist appeal, but mostly it made her long for a glass of water. The road dipped into a narrow ravine, and her phone went offline.

Alana tossed it back into her bag and stared out the window, resigned to her immediate future. A brick gateway marked the entrance to the ranch, but the cab bounced along a pitted gravel road for another half mile before coming to a stop outside a large log building.

Home sweet home. For the next few months, at least. Alana got out of the car and stretched her back, taking a deep breath of pine-tinged fresh air. Even given her questionable attitude about being here, she had to admit that the setting was gorgeous. The logs making up the main building were a glossy red-brown, marked here and there with darker knots. A huge wraparound porch was filled with inviting chairs and hammocks in the corners. The central peak of the A-frame building had a pair of large triangular windows, and two wings constructed of brown-stained boards branched off to either side.

Alana thanked the cab driver and paid him before following a muted roaring sound to the edge of the parking lot. A steep drop-off was marked with a simple post-and-rail fence, and Alana rested her elbows on the top rail and gazed into the valley below where a river was barely visible through the tall, long-needled pines. She could see areas of small whitecaps where the river coursed around a bend and over some large basalt boulders.

"That's the Naches River. Beautiful, isn't it?"

Alana turned and smiled at the man standing a few yards behind her. Her new boss. He must be in his early thirties, but his face was already lined, probably both from spending plenty of time outdoors and from the easy-looking smile that creased his face. The sleeves of his navy chamois shirt were rolled up to reveal browned, muscular forearms, and his teeth were a startling bleached white against his tanned skin. She recognized him easily, even though their Skype interview had been plagued with pixelated images and distorted sound. She was certain that the reception issues had come from the Yakima end of the call, and not the Philadelphia side.

"It's lovely," she said, without needing to force her inner Pollyanna to the fore in order to agree with him. She could appreciate natural beauty. She might not prefer to live in the midst of it, but she could appreciate it. She'd have to be sure to take plenty of photos while she was here. The image spreading below her would make a great print to hang on the wall of her next big-city office space. "You must be Chip Sorenson. I'm—"

"Alana Brendt," he finished for her, shaking her hand. "You look much better in person than you did in our interview. Of course, then you were wavy and frozen on the screen."

He laughed and picked up her suitcase. "We can put this on the porch while I show you around. No one's here, so it'll be safe."

He didn't sound concerned about the lack of people at the ranch, Alana thought as she followed him across the parking lot. He had already delayed the grand opening three times, due to continued construction and personnel changes, and Alana had expected the lodge to be bustling with builders and staff members. His casual manner about the postponements had been a definite red flag to her during their interview. Another one had been the money he had sent to cover her flight and first month's salary, which had come in the form of a personal check and not off a business account. Still, he had constantly stressed the word *family* during their interview and in the job description. He was obviously the type who cared about the people he employed and would therefore be likely to write her a glowing recommendation when she left for another job, even if his own business venture didn't survive the year. And she needed a lot of glow to counteract the negative rumors her old boss had been spreading…

Alana firmly shut a mental door against those thoughts. She had raged about the injustice of it all, but the damage had been done. She was here for a fresh start. She climbed the steps and took a deep breath before walking into her new home.

She slowly turned in a circle and took in her surroundings. The inside of the lodge was as perfectly designed as the outside, although it was a bit too cliché-log-cabin for her personal taste. Still, it was probably exactly what the guests who chose this kind of vacation would expect and want. A long check-in desk was topped with a thick piece of wood that looked like it had come from a single tree, complete with bark on the guest side and varnished to a high sheen. A flagstone entryway led to a comfortable common room with log furniture covered with patterned wool blankets and two ornate and old-fashioned black woodstoves in opposite corners. Flat metal sculptures of various wildlife hung on the walls.

She walked over to a bronze moose and gently ran her fingertip over the smooth edge of its hoof. "These are amazing," she said, admiring the delicate work and continuing to plan the décor for her fantasy future office. The mental activity would help to keep her sane while she was here, since it reminded her that this wasn't forever. "Is the artist local?"

Chip grinned and raised his hand, as if he was in class. "Yep. My grandfather did a few of them, like the wolves over there by the woodstove and the heron here at the desk, but the others are mine. He taught me how to make them."

"Impressive," Alana said, stepping back to get a better view of the heron. Her grandparents had taught her to balance account books and make hospital corners on beds in their family-run hotel. Those were more mundane skills, nowhere near as artistic as this legacy, but they had left her with some good memories. She was firmly planted on the event side of the hospitality industry now and not interested in the day-to-day mechanics of running a hotel, but she could step in and turn out a spotless guest room if need be.

Hopefully, there would be no need for her to flex her cleaning muscles here, although given the way Chip had gone through employees before the ranch even opened, she wouldn't be shocked if he tried to open before he had full staffing. Alana would have to be firm about sticking to her role as Activity Coordinator, although she was desperate enough for a good reference that she knew she would do whatever it took to make a run for Employee of the Year.

She turned her attention back to Chip as he led her on the tour, pointing out the staff break room behind the front desk and the small gift shop.

"This is the dining room, where we serve breakfast every morning," he said, showing her the utilitarian room on the other side of the foyer from the office. Apparently whatever log-cabin catalog Chip had used to furnish the main room hadn't had a section for eating areas. The floor was speckled gray linoleum, and the tables were cafeteria-style white Formica. A stainless-steel counter for trays lined the food service area, where empty pans and caddies waited silently to be filled with scrambled eggs and tiny plastic tubs of creamer.

"It's very clean," Alana said, after searching in vain for a more flattering compliment. Chip seemed happy enough with her comment, even though it wasn't as enthusiastic as her appreciation of his artwork. Still, she'd prefer clean over other qualities when it came to her food.

"And here is your office," Chip said, opening the door next to the dining room with a flourish.

Alana hesitated in the doorway. Walking inside would cement the fact that it was *her* space, where she would spend the next however many weeks until she got a better offer. She exhaled and went into the little room. There wasn't much space for more than a plain desk, a brown metal file cabinet, and a bookcase, but it would do. A map of the property was tacked onto the wall, and a stack of chocolate-colored binders sat on the desk, but the rest of the decorating was obviously left for her to put her personal touches on the room. She was close to reception, where guests could find her easily. The work would be the same as she was used to doing, just in a different and less desirable setting. Whether she was called an event planner, a concierge, or activity coordinator, her job stayed consistent, and she was damned good at it.

Well, ignoring the slight hiccup that had gotten her sacked from her last job, even though it hadn't been entirely her fault.

Chip might be an entrepreneurial novice in a backwater town, but at least he didn't seem likely to throw her under the bus to save his own reputation, like her ex-employer had done. Alana turned to face him with what she hoped was an enthusiastic smile on her face, the same one she wore when greeting guests even if she was tired of them.

"This will be perfect," she said.

"Good," he said, sighing in apparent relief. "I'm glad you like it, even though you won't be spending much of your time in here. I know you'd hate being cooped up inside as much as I would."

Alana made a noncommittal mm-hmm of agreement. She might have exaggerated her interest in the great outdoors just a teensy bit on her résumé. In truth, her citified version of the outdoors meant the concourse outside the stores at a mall.

"The guest rooms are basically finished, except for the last-minute touches," he said, leading her back into the foyer and gesturing toward the two branching hallways with a waving motion. "Linens, paintings, furniture, that sort of thing. Getting rid of the dust from construction."

"Will you...*we* be able to open next month, as planned?" Alana asked, remembering at the last moment to include herself in the High Ridge family. Chip's list of last-minute touches seemed fairly extensive.

"Here's hoping," he said with a cheery grin, holding up his hands with fingers crossed, as if she needed an illustration of his sophisticated business practices. He pointed at a closed set of double doors at the beginning of the right-hand hallway. "That's the pool. It's not filled yet, but you're welcome to use it anytime once we get water in it."

"Thank you," Alana said, although she wondered if Chip's cash flow would last long enough for the ranch to see pool water and guest room bedspreads. Her stay in Yakima might be even briefer than she had expected.

He clapped his hands and rubbed them together vigorously, as if he was the cartoonish villain in a superhero movie. "Now for the best part. You've been acting patient, but I'm sure you're champing at the bit, so to speak, to meet the horses."

"Well, of course I am." What the hell? *Meet the horses?* Was this some sort of West Coast custom, or was it specific to Yakima? Alana shrugged and followed Chip out the lodge's back door and across a yard blanketed with dry grass and sporting an ill-advised fire pit that could potentially set the entire ranch ablaze.

A space twice the size of the lodge's footprint had been cleared of all but a few scrubby pines and sectioned into a series of paddocks, complete with three-sided shelters and water troughs. Two or three horses lounged in each enclosure, swatting at flies with their tails and looking supremely bored with their lives in Yakima.

"This is where the horses are saddled for the day's rides and where the guests mount up." Chip opened a wooden gate that led into a large open space with a series of hitching posts. "This part of the ranch has been here for a few years. The previous owners did trail rides and tubing excursions down the Naches, and I got the horses as part of the purchase."

"Very nice," Alana murmured, skirting around a pile of horse manure and wrinkling her nose at the smell.

"And this is the barn. We only have a few stalls, in case a horse is injured or sick, but the weather here is mild enough for them to be comfortable outside in general. The tack room is right over here. Did you bring your own saddle?"

Alana's first inclination was to wonder where he thought she could possibly have stashed a saddle in her carry-on, and belatedly she realized he thought she was more of a rider than she really was. Which was *not at all*. She might have mentioned liking horses in her cover letter, too.

"I didn't bring it. Too much to ship," she said vaguely, trying to look dejected since now she wouldn't be able to ride. She almost added a sad *darn it* but decided it would be overkill.

"No matter," Chip said, patting her on the shoulder and apparently misreading her look of resignation and regret. "You're free to use any of ours."

"Yay," she mumbled under her breath as he closed the tack room door and continued the tour.

"Here's the feed room, and hay is stored in the loft. Marcus is our groom and he does the feeding and stall cleaning, but I'll have him show you everything in case he's sick or misses a day."

Alana paused in the shady aisle of the barn and watched Chip as he went out the back door and into the sunshine. She had been worried about being asked to clean guest rooms and hadn't even considered taking over barn duties. Just how shorthanded was he? She was going to have to nip this new development in the bud.

She caught up with him at the first of the paddocks. He hadn't noticed her lagging behind, and she caught him midsentence. "… and the chestnut is Penny," he said, pointing at a reddish-brown horse. "Over here we have Mouse and Dancer."

He continued to lead her through the maze of enclosures, naming each horse. The names seemed random, and Alana couldn't tell one horse from another unless they were spotted or had unusual markings, so she promptly forgot each one as he told her. Unless she was expected to call them to dinner by name, she didn't think it mattered if she remembered or not, so she just let him work through the entire herd.

He stopped at a pen with only one horse in it. The animal was good-looking as far as Alana could tell. His hair was shiny and his teeth weren't bared in preparation for biting her, which was about all she cared about in a horse. He ambled over to them and arched his neck over the top rail, butting at her gently with his massive head. She reached out tentatively and patted him. Chip was smiling at her, obviously expecting some sort of reaction, although she wasn't sure what he was waiting for. Glee? An ecstatic fainting spell?

"He's soft," she said, rubbing the velvety fur on his nose. She winced. It was probably not a comment a serious horse rider would utter, but it was the only thing that came to mind.

"He's a good boy," Chip said, stroking the horse's neck. "His name is Fitz."

"Fitz?" Alana repeated with a laugh, jumping back and out of the way when the horse gave a loud and wet snort. "That's a weird name for a horse, isn't it?" Although she only had examples like Mouse and Penny as comparisons.

"It's short for Fitzpatrick. He's an Irish Thoroughbred, and he was a champion jumper before he was retired and sold as a trail horse."

"Oh," Alana said sadly, brushing the horse's bangs out of his eyes and commiserating with his fall from grace. Neither one of them thought they'd end up here, when he was enjoying the glory days of competitions and she was planning events at a five-star hotel.

"He's the fanciest horse we have here," Chip continued. "I figured he'd be the best choice to lead the trail rides with you."

Alana's hand stilled on the horse's forehead. The sentence had been comprehensible until the addition of *with you*. She stepped back and looked Chip directly in the eyes. She had been letting small questions slide because she didn't want to seem difficult, but she needed to make her position clear.

"I don't lead trail rides," she said, adding a shake of her head for emphasis. "I schedule activities and help guests plan their stays. From my desk. In the lodge."

"No," Chip said, lengthening the vowel for several beats. "You make sign-up sheets for trail rides, barbecues, and white-water rafting trips. And then you lead them. I know your experience is more with competitions rather than trail rides, but the basics are the same."

Alana desperately tried to recall details from the job posting and their Skype interview. How much had been overtly said about her duties here and how much had she assumed to be true, based on her past work experiences? She opened her mouth to ask, but Chip started talking in rapid-fire sentences before she could speak.

"You have to stay. You can't leave. You're the ideal person for this job, and I couldn't believe I found you. Especially after three other people quit. I thought I'd be able to open sooner, but there's so much to do. Do you realize how much there is to do with a place like this? And then the carpets were wrong, and the electrician left before he finished the wiring. And then you came along." He opened his arms in an expansive gesture, as if she'd been the answer to his prayers. "With your degree and experience. And you love horses and fishing and rafting."

Alana bit her lip. She had forgotten about the fishing part. She really had gone overboard with that dratted cover letter. She held up her hands to stop his flow of words. His voice was starting to sound panic-filled, and she realized he wasn't as cavalier about the grand-opening delays as she had thought.

"I'm happy to be here, really I am," she said. Which was not necessarily a lie since she had been relieved when someone seemed willing to take a chance on her, even without any work references. She realized now that she had been more focused on that relief than on the actual job at hand—it was just a way to start over, after all. Now she was beginning to see that Chip had been feeling the same way—relieved to have someone qualified who could fill a huge staff vacancy and not overly concerned about checking references or qualifications.

"I just…I'm not a good enough rider or…or rafter to be in charge of guests. I can stay if you want me to, but I really can only accept a desk job."

"A place like this won't have enough business at first—if ever—to justify a full-time concierge position. One or two trail rides a day, a few rafting trips a week. I've had to cancel reservations as it is, since I had planned to open months ago, so we won't be likely to have more than a dozen guests at a time until we get established." His face brightened at the thought. "So you don't have to worry. You'll be able to start with small groups and build your confidence before we have a full ranch. I read your application and I know you're just being modest about your abilities, but once you've led a couple of rides, you'll be fine. And Yakima Expeditions does all the work with the white-water rafting trips. All you have to do is go along and make sure everyone has a fun, safe time."

Alana looked at the horse standing quietly beside her. How hard could it be to lead a trail ride at a walk? Or sit on a raft? Probably a lot harder than it sounded, but she had always prided herself on her ability to quickly pick up new skills. And to bluff her way along until she was the expert she claimed to be. Like Chip said, the groups would be small at first, and she had at least a month to learn before any guests arrived.

She nodded. "All right, I'll do it. It isn't what I expected, but I won't let you down." *Or me.* The rules of the game might have changed, but her need to resuscitate her fading career hopes remained the same.

"Great," he said. He looked as if he was about to hug her in relief but settled instead for clapping her on both shoulders. "You're going to be great. You'll love it here, and so will the guests."

Apparently she wasn't the only one desperately clinging to any glimmer of positivity she could find.

"Now, I know I said you'd have this first weekend free to explore Yakima and get settled, but I could use a hand here for a couple hours if you don't mind. We'll get you working with the horses right away, so you can get a feel for their personalities."

"Oh, I'm not dressed for riding," Alana said, backing away from the fence.

"Not riding. You'll have all month to ride them. Today, they just need vaccines."

"You want me to give them *shots*?" She had no idea where she'd stick a needle, and she was sure that making the wrong decision would likely get her kicked or chomped on.

Chip laughed. "No. The vet will do the shots. You just need to halter the horses one at a time and hold them for her."

Halter and hold them. She could probably manage to do that, as long as she had a few minutes to use her phone to find a tutorial or diagram online. She was pretty sure the purple nylon thing hanging from Fitz's gate was a halter.

"Fine, no problem," she said in what she hoped was a breezy tone. She glanced at her phone's screen. "By the way, what's the lodge's Wi-Fi password? I just need to check something before I get started here."

"Chiperoo96."

"Is that the password the guests will use?"

"Sure." He shrugged, and she looked at him in silence for a few moments.

"Oh," he said. "I should make it something more professional, shouldn't I? See? You're already making the ranch better, and you just got here. Come on, I'll show you where we keep the horses' medical records."

Alana followed him back to the barn, keeping part of her attention focused on the ground in front of her and the rest on swiping through videos on her phone.

CHAPTER TWO

Tegan Evans glanced at the passenger next to her as she drove her Jeep along Highway 82. Desiree had been her assistant since the beginning of the year, acting as both receptionist and vet tech in Tegan's small practice, but Tegan still barely knew her. When she had first decided to hire a young intern, she had imagined herself in the role of mentor or older and wiser sister. Sharing her passion for her job and her wisdom as she nurtured a future vet. All she had learned so far could be found on Dez's résumé—she was a student at Yakima Valley Community College and lived with her family in the city. And she was obviously enthralled by her cell phone.

Tegan cleared her throat, but Dez merely sighed and continued to tap her screen. They spent most of their farm-call days driving through areas with poor or no cell reception, so she must have had a pile of games loaded on her phone to keep her occupied.

The subtle throat clearing was useless, so Tegan tried a more direct approach. "Why don't you put that thing down for a while? We could make it a work rule. No phones in the car, unless it's business related."

"Would you rather I just stared out the window while you drove?" Dez asked, not looking up or pausing in her eternal tapping.

Tegan glanced around them. *She* had no trouble spending hours admiring the million shades of reds, browns, and golds in the hills around Yakima, or interpreting the signs of past volcanic activity from the shape of the basalt formations thrust out of the ground. "You don't have to stare out the window in silence. I thought we could talk."

"Talk? To each other?" Dez looked at her as if she'd suggested they moon the people in the car next to them. "About what?"

Tegan ignored her incredulous tone. At least Dez was looking at her and not at the phone. "Well, we could discuss the Connors' gelding. Fascinating case. He looked dead lame in his near hind leg, but the X-rays were clean. Turned out, he was having back spasms and it had nothing to do with his leg at all."

"I know. I was there."

Tegan sighed. "Yes, I'm aware of that. But it's an interesting topic, don't you think? The way pain can present in unexpected ways, so we need to figure out the true cause."

"What else have you got?" Dez asked, her attention straying back to her phone.

"Well, when I was in vet school, we were treating a sheep that was losing weight for no obvious reason—"

Dez made a sound like a game show buzzer. "No work talk."

"Okay then, when I was young and being an obnoxious little brat during car rides, my grandparents would have me look for different shapes in rocks, like some people do with clouds."

Dez rolled her eyes and returned her full focus to her phone. Tegan was looking at the road ahead and couldn't actually see the eye rolling, but she practically felt the air in the car shift as if moved by the very force of it.

Tegan gave up her attempts at conversation and instead tuned the radio to a country station and turned up the volume despite the heavy static. She didn't particularly care for the music, but it had the desired—if childish—effect of making Dez fish some earbuds out of her pocket and glare at Tegan as she stuck them in her ears. Tegan just grinned and sang loudly along with the song even though she didn't know the words or any of the upcoming notes. She saw a hint of amusement as Dez's mouth quirked in a half smile.

Tegan subsided into humming quietly. She was going to have to give up the vision of an adoring intern trotting after her and jotting down every word that came out of her mouth, at least until Dez quit. Tegan certainly wasn't going to fire her, especially after struggling through Dez's three predecessors. At least Dez was usually on time, friendly enough with clients, and competent with all sorts of animals since she had grown up with a menagerie of chickens, dogs, and goats. Incessant snark was her least charming attribute, but Tegan could live with it.

It was disappointing that Dez didn't seem to share her interest in vet work, but few people did. Tegan's grandparents listened to her case histories, but more because they loved her than because they were interested in the details of her job. Her friends were the same way, indulging her need to talk about her passion for animals in the same way she politely listened to them talk about movie stars or soccer. And Tegan had quickly learned not to bring up anything work-related with her last girlfriend. Fay had been bored to death in Yakima, only coming here to work at a winery and make connections in the industry, and anything related to the city was off-limits in conversations. Since most of Tegan's life had been spent here, with only a few years in Pullman, Washington, for vet school, she had needed to carefully monitor everything she said, sticking to topics like books and travel and avoiding anything more personal.

Tegan turned onto the driveway leading to Chip's ranch. Fay was long gone now, and Tegan's life had returned to normal. If she felt a little stagnant at times, it was okay. Better than living with the uncertainty and impermanence that sort of relationship could bring.

She parked in front of the log building and opened the back end of her Jeep where she had stowed a tote full of predrawn syringes. She handed it to Dez, who had miraculously stuffed her phone in her back pocket, and picked up a box full of paste dewormers.

"Hey, Doc Evans. Good to see you," Chip said, bypassing the steps and jumping off the porch to shake her hand.

"Hi, Chip. How's construction coming?"

"Oh, you know…" he said, letting the sentence trail off, unfinished. "But you'll get to meet my new wrangler today. I mean, Activity Coordinator. She's awesome. She's smart, worked in some really fancy hotels. She's down at the barn now, waiting for you."

"That's great, Chip," Tegan said, forcing a smile even though his comments concerned her. Over the past few weeks, she had met two of his previous brilliant new trail guides, and she had been less than impressed by them. The third one hadn't even bothered to come to Yakima before quitting. Now he had hired someone from a fancy hotel? She must have some reason—and probably a shady one—for trading in that lifestyle for one on a nonfunctioning ranch in the country.

"Just vaccinations today?"

"Yes, and deworming. Plus I'll need to check Penny's teeth." Tegan noticed the tight lines around Chip's mouth, even though his smile never wavered. Feeding and caring for the horses was a constant drain on his resources, especially since absolutely no income was being generated by the ranch. He might have been able to keep the trail riding venture going even before he opened the guest rooms, but without someone qualified to lead the rides—or at least someone who stuck around for more than a week—the horses were left to while away their days in the corrals.

She gestured with the box she was holding. "Deworming's on the house this time, though. I found this box in one of my storage rooms, and it needs to be used right away. It'd just be going to waste otherwise."

"Wow, that's great. Although you know I'd pay for anything the horses need, of course."

"I know, Chip. Come on, Dez." Tegan didn't want to linger, since Dez looked like she was about to say something. She reached out and grabbed Dez's sleeve, tugging her along the path leading around the main lodge.

"We stopped on the way here and bought those tubes of dewormer," Dez said, luckily once they were out of earshot of Chip.

Tegan shook her head. Chip would never accept discounts or any other financial assistance from her, so she had to find creative ways to help him. She had spent four years trying to do something about the condition of the horses in this trail string, including offering her services for free and trying to get the local authorities involved, but she had been unsuccessful. She had been forced to stand by and watch the animals drop weight and suffer from dirty living conditions and poor treatment. Then Chip had come along with his dream of starting a ranch and had bought the horses along with the land. He'd been as appalled as Tegan at their situation, and now the animals were healthy and safe. Tegan would do whatever she could to help Chip keep them that way. If he couldn't get the ranch going soon, who knew what the next owner would be like.

"You said you didn't want to talk about work, remember? Besides, I forgot. I must have been thinking about another box I found."

"Old softie."

Tegan was about to deny it, but she caught sight of Chip's new employee and completely lost her train of thought. The woman was standing next to a hitching post, holding a purple halter upside down and staring at a phone propped on top of a pole. She was dressed casually in gray sneakers and a matching cardigan, with a pale blue shirt and dark-washed designer jeans. Her short hair was straight and blond, with long bangs she occasionally swiped out of her eyes.

Tegan absolutely believed the fancy hotel part from Chip's description of his new employee. She had a much harder time picturing her leading a trail ride on one of Yakima's dry and dusty trails. Beauty aside—and Tegan was trying desperately to ignore how lovely she was—this woman did not look like she was going to stick around long enough to help Chip's business.

She chided herself mentally for making snap judgments. Just because someone didn't look like a stereotypical ranch hand didn't mean they weren't qualified to do a good job. She needed to at least give the newcomer a chance to prove herself. She didn't want to see Chip go through another staff change, or—especially—see these horses get passed along to a new owner who might not care as much about them as she and Chip did. She pushed aside her misgivings and walked closer. "Hello. I'm Tegan Evans, the vet. Chip said you were going to help us vaccinate the horses today."

The woman whirled around to face her with a startled expression on her face. Her eyes were the same light blue as her shirt, a color that could have appeared superficial, but instead managed to have a surprising depth. She snatched her phone off the post and put it in her jeans pocket. "Yes, I am. He said you needed me to halter and hold the horses, but not give them shots, right?"

"Right."

"Good. I can do that. I'm Alana Brendt."

Tegan shook the hand Alana offered, marveling at the feel of it in her own. Soft skin, a firm grip. Short, neat nails. Nice for touching, but not indicative of someone who did any work outdoors. Tegan was aware of her own ragged nails and calloused palms, her hands chapped from constant washing and disinfecting. Alana didn't seem to have handled anything rougher than a ballpoint pen in her life.

She stepped away from the intoxicating scent of Alana's complex and spicy—and likely ridiculously costly—perfume and pulled a metal clipboard out of the tote Dez had put at her feet, gesturing toward the paddocks with it. "Let's start with Blaze and Trooper," she said. "Lead the way."

Alana started walking, then stopped and shook her head. "Blaze and Trooper? I'm not sure which ones they are. I just got here about an hour ago."

"I'll show you," said Dez, walking through the barn and stopping in front of a paddock to grab a halter. She handed the second one to Alana. "If we cach catch one, we can get out of here twice as fast."

"All right," Alana said, tossing the purple halter she had originally been holding onto the ground and taking the one Dez gave her. She followed her into the corral, leaving the gate standing wide open behind her. Tegan sighed in exasperation, closing the gate just in time to thwart Trooper who had spotted the open doorway and was heading toward it. Dez looped her lead rope over Trooper's neck and held him still while she slipped his halter on and buckled it in place. Alana attempted to do the same with Blaze, furtively watching Dez and clearly trying to mimic her actions.

Oh, this was not good.

Tegan marched over to Alana and tugged Blaze's rope out of her hands. "This is backward," she said, undoing the halter and flipping it around. "This short strap goes under his chin, not up the middle of his face."

"Right, I know," Alana snapped at her. "I'm sorry, but like I said, I just got here. I'm feeling jetlagged."

"Jetlagged enough to forget how to put on a halter? Did you fly in from Australia?"

"Philadelphia."

"That's five hours. Who gets seriously jetlagged from a five-hour flight?"

"I made a teeny mistake. What's the big deal? The horse survived. Look at him—I think he slept through the whole thing."

Tegan was furious. This damned woman was obviously conning Chip for some reason. He was a nice guy and didn't deserve it, but most importantly, these horses would suffer if he had to sell the place and they got another owner like their previous one. She needed to find out what was going on, and then decide what she should tell Chip. Could he survive another staff change? If he kept putting off his grand opening, he'd be bankrupt.

Dez was watching the heated exchange with curiosity, and Tegan wished she would go back to playing with her phone. She shook her head and stalked over to get a syringe from the tote. She'd get her work done first and deal with Alana later, after she'd had time to think things through. She stepped back to Blaze and quietly muttered instructions to Alana, trying to keep Dez from overhearing.

"Put your left hand here. Don't pull on the rope, just hold it taut. Watch your feet because he might step forward when he feels the needle prick."

She quickly gave injections and deworming paste to both horses before shouldering Alana out of the way and unbuckling Blaze's halter.

"Hang it up like this. Never just drop a halter on the ground like you did with this one because a horse can step on it and get tangled. And never, never forget to shut gates behind you."

After her initial outburst, Alana remained silent. Tegan's anger melted away a little more with each paddock because the expression on Alana's face confused her. She didn't seem like someone mean-spirited or conniving. She obviously barely knew one end of a horse from another, but she listened to every instruction and didn't need to be told anything twice. By the third corral, Tegan was able to do her job without speaking a word to Alana. The silence wasn't a comfortable one, but the three of them started working together efficiently enough to at least make the visit a short one.

Chip showed up just as they were about to enter Penny's paddock. "Everything going okay?" he asked, smiling so hopefully that Tegan didn't have the heart to voice her concerns. She'd have to sit down with him sometime this week and have a heart-to-heart, but not now. Maybe Alana would quit in the next day or two and save her the trouble.

"We're just about done," Tegan said, avoiding his question.

"Then maybe you won't mind if I steal Alana away from you? I wanted to get her opinion on some furnishings for the rooms."

"Not at all. Dez and I can take care of Penny. See you later."

Alana followed him away from the corrals, not bothering to look at Tegan or say good-bye to her. Looking at bedroom furnishings seemed like a more suitable job for her than being a caretaker for the horses, so why had she even bothered to take this job? Tegan knew exactly how much it paid. One of the main perks of the position was regular access to horses and trails, which would be a nice bonus for someone with a passion for riding and the outdoors, but not for a non-horseperson like Alana seemed to be.

"That was weird," Dez haltered Penny as she spoke and maneuvered her against the fence to keep her still during her exam. "At first she seemed to have forgotten how to put a halter on. She got better fast, though, so maybe she was just joking around."

"Maybe," Tegan said noncommittally. Unlikely. The only reason Alana seemed more competent as they had moved from one paddock to the next was because Tegan had told her what to do and she'd listened. Tegan took a deep breath, smelling the aromas of animals and a barnyard. Those were usually scents she liked because they were constant parts of her day, but she found herself strangely missing the unfamiliar fragrance of Alana. The citified smells of sophisticated perfume and expensive shampoo should make her run in the opposite direction, not tempt her to trot after the source like a hound after a fox.

"She's pretty, though," Dez said, as if sensing the detour Tegan's thoughts had taken.

Tegan avoided eye contact as she carefully slid her hand into Penny's mouth to check her teeth for rough edges. *Pretty* wasn't sufficient. Gorgeous, maybe. Jaw-droppingly beautiful, perhaps? She gave Dez what she hoped was a casual shrug. "Was she? I didn't notice."

"Mm-hmm." Dez's voice oozed skepticism. "I could see you not noticing. Especially the way you blushed when you shook her hand. Or the way you kept touching her, like when you put your hands on her hips to move her to the other side of Cookie."

"Ouch! Damn it." Tegan carelessly got her finger bitten by Penny as she was pulling her hand free. "Her teeth are fine, so go ahead and turn her loose. And the next time I complain about us not talking enough, please remind me of this conversation."

Dez gave Tegan one of her rare grins. "You're the boss."

CHAPTER THREE

A lana turned off the engine and sat in the cab of the truck, folding her arms over the steering wheel and resting her forehead on them. She hadn't had a moment to herself since Chip had called her away from the vet, and she needed to try to process what had happened today. She felt too mentally exhausted and confused to figure out what was going on, though.

She gave up and got out of the pickup, pulling her suitcase off the passenger seat and propping it next to her as she stared at her new home. In her previous jobs, she had been housed on-site, staying in the hotels where she worked and enjoying the privileges of laundry service and restaurant meals. Her rooms had been tiny, but low-maintenance and cheap. She had thought she'd have the same type of living arrangements here in Yakima, but apparently that was yet another erroneous assumption on her part.

Her accommodations were still included in her salary, but Chip had given her a key and directions to a rental home less than a mile from the lodge rather than a room in one of the wings. He had intended this as a perk for the position, because of the house's size, privacy, and distance from the noise and mess of construction, but Alana wasn't sure what she'd do with extra rooms and a large yard. Luckily, he had told her the place was furnished, because all her worldly belongings fit into the carry-on at her side. She was prepared to squish everything she owned into a small closet and a medicine chest over the bathroom sink, not to expand into a three-bedroom home.

Not that she'd need to worry. She doubted she'd have this job for long, once Tegan told Chip how incompetent she was. She had assumed she would be able to bluff her way through the simple task of holding horses, but she had failed within the first two minutes of meeting Tegan. If she had only had a few more minutes to watch videos and practice, she might have been able to pull it off…

Or, if she was being completely honest, if she hadn't been so disconcerted by Tegan herself, she might have been able to remember the footage she had seen.

Dusty tan-colored boots, a navy plaid Western shirt, and worn jeans came together to produce a sexier look than Alana could have imagined. And the woman wearing them…she had turned Alana's insides upside down, just like the halter she'd been holding. Tegan seemed to have been created for the purpose of making the world around her more beautiful. Her dark brown hair with its hints of red and her gold-flecked hazel eyes reflected the colors Alana had seen in Yakima's landscape and had judged as blah and monotonous. On Tegan, however, those same colors seemed infinitely varied and striking. Alana sighed. She had no intention of falling for anything in this town. Not the hills, not the sparkling rivers, and definitely not the lovely vet who noticed too much and saw past her masquerade far too easily.

Alana locked the truck out of habit even though she was too isolated to worry about vehicle prowlers. Besides, no one with any sense would want to steal the old white Ford with *High Ridge Ranch* stenciled on the side in bright red paint and a messy font that looked like a serial killer had scrawled it in blood. She had originally been excited by the idea of having her own car since she had spent most of her life in major cities where it made more sense to take a bus or subway than to deal with the hassles of parking and traffic. She was far from any sort of public transportation out here, though, so unless she wanted to walk at least five miles to a grocery store, she'd have to drive. Her first impressions of the truck had dimmed her enthusiasm slightly, but she'd make do. She had been counting on this truck to drive somewhere to take intensive riding lessons, so she'd be ready for the first guests, but she now had a better understanding of the chasm between her level of inexperience and what she needed to know for this job.

If she even wanted to accept the bother of trying, given the potentially hopeless battle to learn enough to function on the ranch. She had felt one brief second of pure elation when she saw the look on Tegan's face as she fixed Blaze's halter—Tegan was clearly aware of Alana's status as a complete beginner. The game was over, and her bluff had been called. Chip might be desperate for her to stay, but even he wouldn't let a total novice loose on the trails with his horses and guests. In that moment, Alana had felt relief course through her. She'd get her bag and go, letting Tegan deal with the smelly horses and Chip deal with another staff vacancy.

For some reason Alana still couldn't fathom, her relief had been rudely pushed aside by an avalanche of other emotions. Embarrassment. Frustration because she had made a mistake with the stupid halter, which should have been simple to use. And a stubborn desire to defend that mistake and prove she could adapt and learn. So she had shut her mouth and listened to every piece of advice Tegan had given her, even though she had wanted to yell or storm off to nurse her wounded pride while on a flight out of here. Or, in her less mature moments, kick Tegan in the shins.

And so she was still here. For now. No kicking, no running away, but waiting for Tegan to talk to Chip, and then for Chip to fire her. Alana walked onto the porch, with its warped wooden slats that might at one time have been beige but now were mostly gray and bare, with only small patches of chipped paint. She was concentrating on the question of what she would do if Tegan didn't tell on her and how she was going to learn to ride a goddamned horse in only a few weeks when a scratching noise startled her, and she dropped her keys. She looked around, half expecting to see Tegan leap out from behind one of the sparse bushes lining the porch, accusing her of being a fraud, but she was still alone.

She bent over to pick up her keys and jumped back again when she saw a flash of movement through the widely gapped slats. She hesitated, torn between fleeing to the safety of the house or running back to the truck and driving directly to the airport. She was close enough to the door for the house to win, and she jammed the key in the ancient lock and frantically struggled to turn it. The battered screen creaked and banged shut behind her as she ran inside and leaned back against the closed door, dropping her suitcase on the floor next to her feet.

She got out her phone and called the ranch. Chip answered with a breezy hello after about ten rings.

"Hey, Chip. It's Alana."

"Alana! Great to hear from you. Are you settling in okay? It's a wonderful old house, isn't it?"

"Yeah, wonderful," she said, glancing around at the living room's green shag carpet and the furniture upholstered in pastel florals. Either he was too delusional to listen, or Tegan hadn't talked to him about Alana yet. She'd worry about that later, though. "Look, there's something under the porch. I saw it running around."

"Oh, it's probably just rats. The place has been empty for a long time. Let me get the number of the exterminator I used when we had them in the barn."

Rats. Alana closed her eyes, willing herself to wake up from this nightmare in her rat-free room in Philadelphia. With her old, horse-free job. She opened her eyes to pastel and shag carpet.

"Here's the number. Do you have a pen?"

"Wait, I don't want them killed. But I don't want them here." Mostly she didn't want them lurking outside her door, waiting to pounce the next time she walked across the porch, but she hoped for some kind of compromise.

"That's kindhearted of you, but I should expect nothing less from an animal person like yourself. Don't worry. He'll probably be willing to set a live trap and release them somewhere else if you ask."

Alana fumbled in her bag for a pen and an old receipt for jotting the number down. Had she called herself an animal lover in her cover letter? Probably. She'd need to do some serious editing before she applied for another job.

❖

Either this was the way small towns worked or Alana's voice had been suitably desperate sounding, but for whatever reason, the exterminator said he would be right over to set some traps. Relieved she didn't need to have rats as housemates for long, she wandered through the rest of the house while she waited for him. Who knew what other sorts of vermin she would find, and she figured she might as well have him take care of everything in one go.

She needn't have worried about bugs or rats in the house, though. She saw signs of a recent cleaning in every room. The patchy carpets were dented with vacuum tracks, and there wasn't a speck of dust on any surface. Most of the appliances were brand new, still bearing their manufacturer's stickers and with instruction manuals taped inside. The glossy whiteness of them emphasized the age of the rest of the furnishings and wallpaper, which were an odd mix of florals, stripes, and other patterns.

Alana stood in the bathroom, where faded kittens gamboled across the walls around her, and peered into a plastic bag on the counter that was full of necessities like toilet paper, full-sized shampoo and body wash bottles, and toothpaste. She had found the kitchen just as well stocked, with some basic food in the fridge and dishes in the cupboard. She was touched by the effort Chip had put into the place, and drowning in guilt because she hadn't been completely honest with him. The guilt hit hardest, especially after she spent all of two minutes unpacking her suitcase, hanging her few clothes in the closet and putting a pile of books next to the bed. He had saved her the trouble of buying a load of housewares and linens that she wouldn't need once she left Yakima. More importantly, though, he had made her feel welcome and settled. She wasn't accustomed to filling such a spacious home, and she would have been depressed by how measly her belongings seemed in an otherwise empty house.

She went out the back door and down a short flight of cement steps, luckily free of any gaps where rats might make themselves at home. The grassy backyard was small and unfenced, surrounded by scrubby sages, dried grasses, and some large pine trees. She stood outside a garden shed for a full minute before flinging the door open, expecting a pack of furry bodies to pour out. Instead, she found the shed to be as clean as the interior of the house. She examined the lawn mower, which wasn't new and therefore wasn't accompanied by a manual. She was feeling a little foolish about her reaction to the rats, especially since she knew they were abundant in the cities in which she'd lived. At least there, though, she had plenty of people as backup in case of an uprising. Here, it was just her against the rats.

When she heard the rumble of a large truck coming up the drive, she closed the shed and walked around the side of the house. She would figure everything out, piece by piece. She would learn how to mow the lawn, ride a horse, and paddle a raft. Easy as could be, right?

"Hi, I'm Aaron." The exterminator came over and shook her hand as soon as she rounded the corner. He was about six inches shorter than her, wearing tan overalls and a green Henley. He had a flashlight and an electric drill tucked under his left arm. "You must be Chip's new trail guide."

"I seem to be," she said with a sigh. "I'm Alana. Thank you for coming out right away."

He waved off her thanks with a grin. "No problem. I'll just take a look under there and see how many traps I need to set."

She hovered near his truck while he unscrewed one of the latticework panels that skirted the porch and shimmied underneath. He was only gone for several seconds before his head popped out again.

"Empty out that cardboard box in the bed of the truck and bring it to me, would you?"

Alana stood on tiptoe and reached over the side of the truck, pulling some folded tarps and tangled bungee cords out of a large packing box and stacking them to one side. What was he going to do? Put a cardboard box and a piece of cheese under there? She had expected some sort of sophisticated rat traps, but she wasn't going to argue with the expert. Whatever got the job done.

As soon as she was near the porch, he held out a grubby hand and took the box from her. "Are there a lot of them?" she asked.

"Only six. Let me just double check to make sure, though."

Only six? One was bad enough. Two had her outnumbered. Six were enough to stake a claim on the house and make her move out. She was wondering whether Yakima had any decent hotels when she heard a rough snarling sound and jumped back a foot. Aaron scooted out feet first, tugging the box with him.

"Here you go," he said as he stood up and went to hand her the box full of rats.

She backed away several more steps. "I don't want them as pets," she said. "I thought you were going to set them free somewhere else."

"Look inside," he insisted, smiling and shoving the damned box closer to her. "They're adorable."

He must really love his job. He didn't seem ready to relent, so Alana decided to humor him and look. Then maybe he'd bundle the little cuties into his truck and take them far away. She cautiously peered into the box, reminding herself that they weren't going to launch themselves out of it and at her face. Then she frowned and came closer.

"They're puppies, not rats," she said, hearing an accusing tone in her own voice. Tiny, squirming puppies.

"Yep. Sweet little buggers, too. Well, here you go," he repeated, pushing the box into her arms. "Their mama is cowering under there, but she'll come out soon enough when she hears them crying."

"You have to take them with you," Alana said, hurrying after him with the bulky box in her arms. "I don't want puppies."

She didn't want to be here. She didn't want this unfamiliar job, or this nice but far too big house. She certainly didn't want puppies.

"I can't take them," Aaron said. "I already have two Dobermans. You can take them to the shelter, and they'll try to find homes for them. Or a local rescue group, although I know most of them are pretty full this time of year."

Alana didn't like the sound of his phrase *try to find homes for them*. "What if no one will adopt them from the shelter?"

"They'll be put to sleep. Don't worry, though. Puppies usually are easy to place." He tied a large slipknot in a length of cord and handed it to her. "Once she comes out, best to get this around her neck and take them all inside, or she'll try to drag them back under the porch. They'll be walking soon, and chances are the coyotes will get them."

He drove away, leaving Alana feeling stunned as she stood on the driveway holding the box, with the rope dangling over her wrist. She really hated this place. Coyotes. Puppies masquerading as rats. Sporadic cell service and far too much dirt. A job she wasn't qualified to do. Sexy vets whose hazel eyes saw past her pretenses. She set the box down and sat cross-legged next to it, resting her elbows on her knees and her head in her hands. She had made a simple mistake at her last job, and she had been prepared to accept exile as punishment, but this went beyond basic karma.

She heard a slight rustling sound and looked up to see a small face peeking at her from the gaping hole where the lattice had been. The dog watched her suspiciously with huge brown eyes, but she slowly crawled out from under the porch and slunk toward Alana and the box of puppies. She was small, and her matted fur was patchy with different colors. Alana couldn't tell which patches were dirt and which were her natural shades of brown. Her hipbones jutted out, and Alana could see the shadows of the dog's ribs as she moved steadily and bravely across the front yard. Alana blinked and wiped her hand across her eyes. She had been ready to cry for herself and the mess her life had become, but now she felt a surge of emotion pushing past her self-pity.

Puppies might be easy to place, but who was going to want this skeletal, dirty little adult dog?

Alana eased the rope into her lap and adjusted the loop until it seemed to be the right size for the dog, careful not to make any sudden moves that would send her back under the porch. She looked as fragile and delicate as the old lace curtains in Alana's new bedroom. The box next to Alana rocked a bit as the puppies moved inside it, whimpering as if they sensed their mother coming closer.

The dog stopped next to the box and raised onto her haunches, resting her front paws on the edge and looking inside. Alana was mentally rehearsing the best way to lasso the dog—hoping it would be easier than haltering a horse—when the dog gave a sudden heave and jumped in with her puppies. Alana caught the box before it tipped over and shut the flaps. She kept one hand on the top and stood up. Now what? She shivered, suddenly aware of the growing chill in the air as the sun dipped below the roof of the house, and picked up the box. It was wigglier and heavier with the addition of the agitated mother dog, and Alana staggered up the porch steps, with one arm under the box to keep the animals from falling out. She thought longingly of the time, a mere hour ago, when she had only been concerned about having a few rats under the porch. Ah, the good old days.

A distant howl of a coyote gave her the incentive she needed to sidle through the front door and carry the box into the empty downstairs bedroom. She set it on the floor and shut the door behind her as she went to the upstairs guest room and pulled the comforter off the bed. She stopped by the kitchen for a bowl and some water, then went back into the bedroom, where she put the blanket in the closet with the water bowl nearby. She opened the flaps and stepped back as the dog jumped out again, backing away from her with a quiet growl.

"None of that," Alana said, trying to sound more confident than she felt. She took the puppies out of the box one by one and set them on the comforter, stopping only two or three times to marvel at how soft the pups were. Each one had some variation of the mother's coloring, with tiny, fluffy earflaps and frowning mouths. She tried to force herself not to linger since they wouldn't be staying with her any longer than necessary, but she couldn't resist them and was soon lying on her stomach as the pups stumbled blindly around, raising their small heads to sniff the unfamiliar scents in the room and bumping into her as they haltingly explored their new home. *Temporary* new home, she reminded herself sternly, no matter how adorable the smallest puppy was as it chewed on a strand of her hair or how funny another pup looked when it tried to sit on its haunches and fell over instead. They could be as cute as they wanted, but Alana wasn't about to grant them permanent residency.

She sighed, melting inside as a pup licked her outstretched hand with a tiny, raspy pink tongue. She wasn't even sure why she was having to work so hard to convince herself that the puppies weren't going to be staying for long. That fact should be a given, not requiring any debate, but she felt the need to remind herself every few seconds that they would be leaving soon. And how had the simple process of taking the puppies out of the box turned into ten minutes of lying on the floor of the closet with them? She was both sad and relieved when a quiet whine from the mother dog gave her a reason to carefully push onto her hands and knees and crawl far enough away from the puppies for the mother to feel comfortable going to them.

She watched them nuzzle up to nurse for just a moment before leaving the room and going to the kitchen. She searched through the food Chip had conveniently left for her. Milk, eggs, coffee. Lettuce, of course. Some chicken. She made some hard-boiled eggs and poached chicken and chopped them up for the dog, leaving the plate near the water bowl. She made an egg salad sandwich for herself and sat at the wooden table in the kitchen to eat. Even though she had lived alone for years, she had always been surrounded by other people. Rooms above, below, and on all sides had been filled with coworkers or strangers. She felt the aching sense of empty space stretching in all directions. Worst of all was the stretch of time ahead of her before she could get back to the life she wanted.

She put her plate in the sink and looked through the phone book Chip had left on the counter. She found Tegan Evans, DVM, and dialed the number after only a slight hesitation.

"Dr. Evans." Tegan's voice was crisp and professional. The phone book ad showed the clinic was closed for the night, and Alana heard muted sounds of voices in the background, as if Tegan was at a party or restaurant.

"This is Alana. We met today at Chip's ranch." Alana paused, but was met only with silence. "I'm his new…um…Activity Coordinator."

"Yes, I remember," Tegan said in a sharp tone.

Alana sighed. What had she expected? A hearty hello and an invitation to come over for the party or out for dinner? "So, I found a dog and puppies under my porch, and the mother dog looks like she could use a vet. She's really thin."

"What kind of dogs?" Tegan switched gears immediately, resuming her professional voice.

"Oh, I don't know. Brown and white ones? What kinds of dogs are brown and white?"

Tegan's sigh was audible. "Never mind. Tell me about the mother dog. Has she eaten anything or had any water? Is she moving around, or lethargic?"

"She ate about a cup of plain poached chicken and hard-boiled egg. She drank a little water, too. She's not really lethargic, just wary. She jumped into the box with her puppies."

"All right. I'm not at the office now, but it sounds like they'll be fine until morning. Can you bring them in at eight?"

"Yes. That'll be fine."

"Good. If you think they need emergency care during the night, call Dr. Hannigan. Otherwise, I'll see you in the morning."

She ended the call before Alana could say thank you or good-bye. She sat at the table for a long time, fiddling with the paper with Dr. Hannigan's number on it and wondering over her mixed emotions about seeing Tegan again. She should be avoiding her, since Tegan knew about her lack of horse experience and could make her lose this job. Or maybe she should be glad to have a chance to see her, to convince her not to tell Chip about her misleading job application.

Or maybe she was just looking forward to being around Tegan again. She certainly made Alana feel alive, even though some of the emotions she incited weren't comfortable ones, like frustration and embarrassment. Some of them were pretty appealing, like attraction and intrigue. Alana had always prided herself on being in control at work and in her social life. She planned her career and her relationships carefully, aiming toward her goals with precision and forethought. Now, though, her future was blurry. She couldn't even predict what the next day would bring, whether she'd find herself holding another box of stray animals or discovering yet another disturbing requirement of her new job. Until now, she hadn't realized that she had been going through life while barely noticing it, since most of her thoughts and energy were focused on the next steps she needed to take. Suddenly, she found herself with nothing but the present. Where Tegan was, with her confidence and skills that made Alana feel incompetent at a job for the first time in years. And with her sexiness that made Alana aware of how many possibilities might open up when the predetermined route into the future took a detour.

Alana sighed and cleaned the kitchen until the counters and dishes were spotless again. She was just feeling a little lonely and exhausted after this mess of a day. She'd face tomorrow when it came.

The dog cried and scratched to get out of the bedroom, and Alana carefully opened the door to check on her. The dog squeezed through the opening and ran to the back door. Alana hesitated before letting her into the yard, but the grassy area was small and well lit. Hopefully she wouldn't run away and leave Alana alone with the pups. The dog seemed to have as little faith in her ability to take care of them as Alana did, though, and she went outside and came back in in only a matter of moments, disappearing like a skinny ghost into the guest room closet.

Alana refilled her water bowl and left the room. Maybe Tegan would be so distressed by her incompetence that she would confiscate the animals, and Alana would no longer be responsible for them. If not, she would get some real dog food, or maybe take the animals to a shelter if she could find a no-kill one. Then she'd be alone in this creaky old house. She lay awake for a long time, missing the sounds of hotel elevators and the footsteps of guests.

CHAPTER FOUR

Alana was up well before six, exhausted from spending most of the night hovering outside the puppy bedroom and occasionally peering inside to make sure all seven animals were still breathing. She hadn't been quite as convinced as Tegan had seemed to be that she would know intuitively what constituted an emergency that required a call to Dr. Hannigan.

They made it through the night without any emergency incidents, however. The mother dog scarfed down another bowl of chicken and egg while Alana sat cross-legged on the far side of the room and ate her own breakfast of a plain piece of toast and coffee. She originally meant to use the quiet time to bemoan her current predicament and figure out ways to get out of it, but she was distracted by the puppies. They were too young to do much besides squirm around, but every once in a while one would manage to wriggle on top of one of its brothers or sisters, and then tumble, nose first, down the other side onto the soft comforter. The mother dog glared reproachfully at Alana every time she laughed.

As soon as everyone's breakfast was finished, and the mother dog had bolted into the yard and back, Alana got the cardboard box out again. She used her pen to poke air holes in it until she worried she might have damaged the structural integrity of the box. It still seemed capable of holding its shape, though, so she put one of the fluffy new towels from the bathroom on the bottom of it and started piling puppies inside. The mother dog hopped in without needing to be encouraged, probably with the intention of getting her babies out again, but Alana quickly shut the flaps.

She paced back and forth in the bedroom for a few minutes, debating what to do next. She had expected the morning chores of feeding and puppy packing to eat up more time, but she still had more than an hour before her appointment. She was too nervous to wait, though, so she decided to get to the vet's office early. Even if no one was there, she figured she might as well be there and ready to go while she fretted about the day ahead instead of alone in this house.

She spent the ten-minute drive into Yakima mentally writing a to-do list for the day. She was accustomed to checking off work and social items, such as *Finalize menu for Saturday's bar mitzvah* and *Meet friends at Cardy's for happy hour* on a normal list. She longed to have those familiar tasks in place of her new ones of *Find home for six puppies and skinny mother dog* and *Learn to ride horses* and *Find out if sexy vet is going to tattle to new boss*.

She was not looking forward to the day ahead of her.

Alana arrived at Tegan's clinic a few minutes after seven. She pulled into the circular drive and let the truck idle while she checked out the property. The narrow two-story Victorian house was neatly painted white, with bright blue trim and fretwork. The windows were still dark and no other cars were visible, so she figured Tegan and her assistant hadn't gotten to work yet. The front lawn was surrounded by a colorful border of tulips and daffodils. Everything was tidy and perfectly in order, and the place didn't seem prepared for Alana and her newly messy life to descend upon it.

There were a few parking spots in front of the house, but Alana noticed another road branching off the main driveway and heading behind the clinic. She slowly drove around the house and discovered another larger parking lot in the back. An ancient silver Jeep Cherokee with a dent in the rear bumper was parked near a plain white metal barn. A gold-colored horse stood in one of the attached paddocks with her head over the board fence, watching Alana's truck drive by.

Alana parked next to the Jeep where she had a better view of the outdoor arena behind the barn. She turned off the engine and watched as Tegan rode into view on a brown horse with bold white markings on its face and legs. Alana exhaled softly, as if even too loud a breath would break the spell Tegan and her horse were weaving. They seemed to be in their own world out there, with only the thud of hoofbeats breaking the quiet of the morning. If Tegan had even heard Alana's truck, she gave no indication of it since she was clearly focused on her horse and the patterns they were making in the soft dirt.

For quite a while, Alana was only capable of seeing how gorgeous Tegan looked. Her slender legs were wrapped in snug leather chaps, and she wore a black long-sleeved T-shirt. She was covered from her neck to her toes, but every soft curve and muscular line was showcased by the simple fitted outfit. Alana had never really understood the whole sexy cowgirl mania before, but now she was a devoted fan.

Once she was able to claw her way out of the hazy fog of desire, she sighed again, this time with decidedly less enthusiasm. Even though she knew next to nothing—or absolutely nothing, if she was being honest—about riding, she understood that there was no way she'd be able to get anywhere near Tegan's level of skill in a month. Or a year. She barely moved in the saddle, and her hands were gently and loosely holding the reins, but the horse responded to every slight shift Tegan made. They galloped across the arena and slid to a halt with the horse nearly sitting on its rear. They spun in place rapidly enough for Alana to feel dizzy while watching. If she'd been actually on the animal, she'd have been flung into orbit. There was no way in hell she could ride like this.

Tegan slowed to a walk, and as she leaned forward to pat her horse on the neck she looked up and seemed to notice Alana's truck for the first time. Alana ignored the foolish urge to duck out of sight—it wasn't as if she could hide from Tegan for long that way. All she had to do was walk over and look through the window. Besides, Alana had an appointment. She was supposed to be here. She got out of her truck and waited for Tegan to dismount and walk through the gate and over to her.

"You're early," she said.

"I am." Obviously. "This is a truck," Alana said, pointing to it.

"This is a horse." Tegan laughed as she pointed toward the animal. "Although I might not be playing the game right since I'm not sure if that particular fact is glaringly obvious to you."

Alana realized she hadn't yet seen an expression on Tegan's face that didn't seem to fall somewhere in the range between mildly annoyed and highly annoyed, and she had to smile in response despite the smart-ass comment. Tegan's mouth was meant for laughing, with its slight upturn in the corners. And kissing, most likely, since her lips looked soft and mobile and expressive. Alana tried not to dwell too long on the thought of kissing her.

"I can recognize the species," Alana said with a haughty shrug. She was fairly confident in her statement, unless there were some strange horse types she hadn't yet seen. She'd been able to spot all the equines at Chip's ranch.

"Well, that's something, at least. Did you bring the puppies?"

Alana gestured toward the narrow back seat where she had carefully wedged the box to keep it from tipping over if the dogs moved too much. "Of course. I certainly didn't come here just for the witty conversation. Should I get them out now?"

Tegan peered through the window. "You have them in a cardboard box? That's not very sturdy for transporting animals."

"Yeah, sorry about that. I brought a couple dog crates on the plane with me yesterday, but I had already filled them with two other litters of puppies before this one came along."

"Right," Tegan said in a drawl, tapping her chin as if just now remembering Alana's recent arrival. "The plane. How's the jetlag coming along?"

Alana slapped playfully at Tegan's arm, and she dodged out of reach with another laugh. "It's cool enough outside," Tegan said. "Roll the windows down a bit, and they should be fine while I untack Rio. Then I can help you carry them inside."

Alana cracked the truck's windows a few inches and checked the dogs through one of the larger holes she had jabbed in the side of the box. Then she followed Tegan into the small barn, where she and her horse stood in the center of the aisle. She wasn't certain if Tegan's joking manner was a good sign or not. She didn't seem as irate as she had at Chip's ranch, which seemed positive, but she had also made it a point to bring up Alana's questionable equine knowledge within seconds of seeing her. After messing up with the halters yesterday and seeing Tegan's skills in action today, Alana had a feeling her only option was complete honesty. Tegan would see through anything less.

Still, she wasn't about to bring up the topic on her own.

"Are these both your horses, or are they patients?" she asked, petting the gold horse who had come inside her stall through the open door from her paddock. She watched Tegan unbuckle the bridle and remove the saddle, trying to memorize each step in the feeble hope that she could replicate the actions on her own.

"These are mine. This is Rio, and the palomino is Charm. I have two extra stalls for patients in this barn, and another one on the far side of the house that I use if I need to quarantine an animal."

Palomino. Alana filed away the term in her mind since she had heard the word before but had never connected it with anything concrete. One of Chip's horses had the same coloring as this one, although she couldn't remember its name.

Tegan quickly brushed the horse's already shiny coat and put him into one of the stalls. "We didn't work hard today, so he's okay to be put away now. I'll groom him later."

Alana nodded in agreement, as if Tegan's statement made perfect sense to her. They went back to the truck and she slid the box closer to the door.

"Be careful with the bottom because it isn't taped shut."

"Of course it isn't," Tegan said, shaking her head as if she was no longer surprised by any of Alana's foolishness.

Alana glared at her over the box as they lifted it from opposite sides. She supposed Tegan never traveled anywhere without a suitcase full of packing tape, leashes, and doggie treats in case of spur-of-the-moment rescues.

Tegan held the back door open with her foot, and they managed to squeeze inside without jarring the contents of the box too much. She led them through the back entrance of a white-tiled room with a metal table and handed Alana a frayed pink blanket out of a cupboard.

"Put this in the corner, and I can examine them on the floor. It'll be easier than trying to keep them on the table," she said as she draped a stethoscope around her neck and rummaged through some drawers. "Tell me again about how you found them."

Alana managed to turn away from the sight of Tegan—still wearing those damned ass-framing chaps—and focused instead on smoothing the blanket into place while she told the story of the rats and the exterminator. She had just about come to the part about making the dog some dinner when she heard a sort of gasping sound from behind her.

"Are you laughing?" Alana had thought her rescue story sounded quite dramatic in the retelling. She had expected some gasps of amazement, not hysteria.

Tegan was leaning against the metal table, wiping tears out of her eyes with one hand and pressing the other against her stomach. "No. Well, yes. I can just picture the expression on your face when he tried to hand you a box full of what you thought were rats. Oh, it hurts to laugh this much. Go on, finish your story."

She sat next to Alana on the blanket and opened the box, reaching inside to let the mother dog sniff at her hands before gently lifting her onto the blanket. Her demeanor changed abruptly as soon as she started handling the animal, and Alana let her irritation at the bout of laughter fade away. Tegan held the dog carefully, yet without any trace of hesitation in her movements. Her obvious kindness and care for the small creature made her even more attractive to Alana, showing the character of the woman underneath the beautiful skin and sexy body. At the same time, though, Tegan's competence and experience with animals threw Alana's tentative attempts to handle the horses yesterday into stark relief. There was no way Alana could pretend she possessed experience on a level with Tegan's. She continued talking about the night before, struggling to remember the details when all her mind wanted to think about was her calf, where Tegan's hip barely brushed against her, and the soft smells of hay and apples she noticed every time she inhaled.

She eventually stopped talking and watched Tegan examine the cowering dog. She slipped a collar around the dog's neck and handed the attached leash to Alana. "Come closer and hold her against you. I'm going to draw some blood for a heartworm test and I don't want her jerking away from the needle."

Alana scooted forward until her hip and thigh were flush against Tegan's. She reminded herself to breathe, to pretend the entire side of her body wasn't flaring to life because of the contact between them. Tegan already knew too many of her secrets. Alana wasn't about to let her in on this one.

She gathered the dog into her arms, shocked out of her arousal by the near weightlessness of her. Her furry coat had given her the appearance of having more substance than she actually had.

"She's so thin," Alana said, her voice barely above a whisper. She didn't want to give voice to the question in her mind of whether the dog was too ill to survive.

"She is," Tegan agreed. "But we'll help her get better."

We? Alana liked the sound of her and Tegan working together as a team, but only because she was sitting far too close to her. As soon as she put a little distance between them, she'd regain control over her senses. She wouldn't abandon the dogs but also wasn't going to be able to both care for them and find a way to keep her job.

Tegan finished poking and prodding the little dog and sat back on her heels, giving Alana the distance she had mistakenly thought she wanted. Tegan made a few notes on a clipboard, then set it to one side. "Okay. Time for the puppies."

She plucked them out of the box one at a time, weighing them on a small kitchen scale and inspecting them, which seemed to involve a lot of nuzzling and cooing.

"Are you examining them, or just playing?"

Tegan grinned at her, placing a pup next to its mother and diving into the box for the last one. "A little of both," she admitted. "They're irresistible. You have four girls and two boys."

"So, what breed are they?"

Tegan put the sixth puppy down on the blanket, decidedly not meeting Alana's eyes. "They're brown and whites," she said.

"Ha! I knew it. And you sounded so annoyed with me on the phone when I said that."

Tegan laughed. "Seriously, she looks like she has some spaniel in her. Maybe a little Cairn terrier. And likely a few other breeds, as well. What's her name?"

"Oh, I haven't named any of them," she said, reaching out and stroking one of the puppies with the tips of her fingers. "I can't keep them, you know. With work and everything. And I'm not really a dog person." Although she had probably said she was in her cover letter. Best not to bring *that* up. "But, I guess, in my head I've been thinking of her as Lace."

"Lace," Tegan repeated, writing the name on the clipboard. "Good. It suits her."

CHAPTER FIVE

Tegan left Alana and the dogs in the examination room while she went into her lab and ran the heartworm test. Once she had finished, she puttered around for a while longer, collecting brochures about puppy care and searching through the shed in her backyard for a suitable crate for transporting the puppies. She was stalling and she knew it, but she had to give herself time to think.

She should have talked to Chip yesterday about Alana or confronted her directly today. Instead, she had made teasing references to Alana's lack of experience, then had let the subject drop completely. She didn't mean to string Alana along with threats of disclosure. Rather, she was trying to figure out who she really was.

Tegan's first responsibility was to Chip's horses. If his ranch was a success, they'd have a good life with him. If he failed, they would have to be sold, and their future was less assured. Alana wasn't a qualified caretaker for them, but Tegan no longer had any doubts about her kindness. She had handled the horses gently the day before, even though she had clearly been frustrated with the situation. She freely admitted she wasn't a dog person, but she had taken the puppies into her home and brought them here to Tegan. She seemed moved by Lace's poor condition. And even though the story of Alana and her box of rats made Tegan chuckle every time she thought about it, the catalyst for the situation had been Alana's unexpected desire to livetrap the rats. Plenty of other people would have merely dumped a box of rat poison between the slats of the porch. Still, all the good intentions and kindness in the world couldn't magically give her the experience she needed to safely lead trail rides and handle a string of horses.

Tegan closed the door of the shed and lugged the large plastic crate across the back parking lot. She hated to admit the main reason she was equivocating about how to handle this situation. She was actually starting to like Alana. She was stunning, hindering Tegan's ability to swallow every time she touched her or came close. When Alana had her hands full, holding Lace or the box of puppies, she had the seemingly unconscious habit of blowing her long bangs out of her eyes, giving Tegan ideas about how it would feel to have Alana's breath puff against her ears and her neck. It made Tegan want to keep handing her things just to see her do it again.

Still, just like her kindness, all the sexy in the world wouldn't affect Tegan at all if it wasn't backed up by other, deeper attributes. And Alana seemed to have those, too. She seemed smart—okay, not about horses, but in general. She was funny and playful and strong enough not to back down from a fight. Unfortunately for Tegan, she also was out of her league in her new job, with her new canine charges, and in this new and unfamiliar town. Tegan had a habit of attracting women like Alana who needed saving. Damsels in distress who were using Yakima as a stepping stone, like Fay, or women with so much baggage they needed to rent a storage unit for it. Once the rescue was complete, the confidence restored, or the bigger and brighter opportunity available, then Tegan was discarded just like Lace had most likely been.

Tegan put the brochures on top of the crate and dragged the lot through the exam room door, moving slowly so she didn't startle Lace.

"This will work better than cardboard," she said, transferring the towel from the box to the new crate. "I keep a bunch of them around in case I find strays, or someone needs to borrow one, so you can keep this. And here's some information about what you should expect for the next few weeks in terms of vet care for these little guys."

Alana took the stack of brochures and stared at the top one— *Your New Puppies!!*—for a moment before looking at Tegan and shaking her head.

"I can't keep them, Tegan. I have too much to do at the ranch, especially if Chip...*when* Chip finally opens up for guests. Besides, they'd be better off with someone more experienced."

"Look, Chip won't have the place going for another month, and by then the pups will be about old enough to be adopted. It'll be easier to find a foster home for Lace once they're weaned and she's spayed. I can help you with a plan for feeding her, plus I'll give you my standard discount for rescues on exams, vaccinations, and worming."

Why was she arguing for Alana to keep these dogs, even as she was considering getting her fired and sent out of Yakima? Damn. She knew exactly why she was doing it, and she had to make sure Alana understood, too.

"We could try to find a rescue group to take them, but everyone's full right now. More than full in most cases. The only other option would be the city shelter, and even though it's a decent place, it's not no-kill. Lace might not—"

Alana held up her hand to stop Tegan. "I know. Aaron the rat guy told me. Puppies are easy to place, but not adults."

Tegan nodded. Alana clearly was aware of what might happen to a scruffy, skinny adult dog when there were always more animals than potential adopters. Otherwise, she probably would have driven the puppies directly to the shelter this morning instead of coming to Tegan.

"It's just a few weeks for you, but it could make all the difference in the world to her. We can start asking around right away and get some new homes lined up for when they're ready to go. If we weren't in the middle of kitten season, it might be different, but—"

"Kitten season? You hunt *kittens* in Yakima?" Alana had been perusing the brochures in a daze while Tegan talked, but now she snapped into alertness and stepped between the puppies and Tegan, as if she might declare open season on them.

"Jeez, no. We don't hunt kittens," Tegan assured her. She wanted to laugh at the outraged expression on Alana's face, but she carefully kept her face under control. "Kitten season is what rescue workers call the times of the year when most feral and unfixed cats have litters. Every shelter around here is in kittens up to their eyeballs."

"Well, good," Alana said. She was still frowning, though, as she knelt by Lace and her nursing puppies and rested a hand on the dog's head. The image of camouflaged hunters stalking tiny, mewing prey must have been enough to push her protective instincts in front of every other concern.

"Fine," she said. "I'll keep them. Just for a few weeks, though, and you have to promise to tell me if another home comes available."

Tegan smiled. One hurdle down. Now she had to broach the subject of Alana's job. She squatted next to the puppies so she was at eye level with Alana.

"Let's talk about your experience with horses. It appeared to be minimal to me, but Chip seems to think you have quite a lot. Any idea why?"

Alana turned her attention to one of the posters hanging on the exam room's walls, as if she was suddenly fascinated by pet dental care. "Oh, I suppose I mentioned loving horses and the outdoors in my cover letter. And maybe I said I had ridden before, in competitions. And I think I wrote something about liking to *fish*."

Her emphasis on the last word in the sentence, combined with her impish grin, made Tegan smile in response. She tried to cover it up by forcing her features into a suitable frown, but Alana seemed to see through it because her posture relaxed slightly and she stopped staring at the posters, looking directly at Tegan instead.

"Why did you lie to him?"

Alana held up her hand, palm out. "I didn't lie, I fudged. Everyone fudges on applications. It's expected."

"No, it's not," Tegan said. "Applications are meant to give an accurate assessment of your experience and skills so an employer can decide if you're a good match."

Alana laughed. "What dreamworld are you living in? Everyone does it. And in my defense—"

Tegan crossed her arms over her chest. "Oh, this ought to be good."

Alana ignored her and continued. "In my defense, I thought it was a desk job, planning activities and doing scheduling. I'm more than qualified to do that, especially at a small ranch like Chip's. It shouldn't have mattered if I said I recently won a Grammy or rode in the Kentucky Derby. I honestly thought I had the real skills I needed for the job. I sort of fudged so I'd be more suitable to the setting."

Tegan uncrossed her arms, not sure what to say next. Alana seemed to be forthright now, but it didn't change Chip's erroneous beliefs about her abilities.

"Like you said, it's a small ranch and it's in its first year. Or will be, once it opens. A place like this wouldn't have the need or the money to hire a full-time event planner."

"Yes, I know that *now*. But I didn't realize the mistake until I got here, just before I met you."

Tegan couldn't help but remember the moment when she first saw Alana. Beautiful, sophisticated, out-of-place Alana.

"And then I tried to explain it to Chip, but he didn't want to hear me," Alana continued when Tegan remained silent. Her cheeks flushed slightly. "I suppose I didn't try very hard, either. The whole hiring process was very fast since I really needed this job, and Chip seemed just as desperate to find someone for the position."

Tegan sighed. She had met the previous folks who had Alana's job, and her negative comments had been part of the reason they had left. One had been overly rough with the animals, and the other had been annoyingly blasé about schedules, wandering in to work whenever she felt like it and keeping Tegan waiting despite having made the appointments. Neither had been there longer than a week.

"I understand why Chip was in a rush to fill this position, but if you're really so overqualified for the job, and if you have as little actual interest in horses and hiking and everything as you seem to have, then why don't you just quit? Go find a more comfortable position back in Philadelphia or wherever?"

The poster suddenly became fascinating again. Alana stared at it, seeming to struggle internally about whether to confide in Tegan.

"I was fired from my last job," she finally said in a rush. "I made a mistake, or at least, didn't catch a mistake, and got canned. My ex-boss has been spreading rumors about me, and I couldn't find anyone who would give me a chance without a reference from her."

"You say the word *ex-boss* with the amount of venom usually reserved for *ex-girlfriend*." Tegan meant the comment to sound casual, and she was angry at herself for allowing a hint of inflection into the statement, as if she was asking a question and prying into Alana's romantic past. Which was none of her business and certainly none of her concern.

"She was just a boss and never a girlfriend," Alana said. She hesitated for a moment, tilting her head as if lost in thought. "I guess for me being betrayed by a boss was worse than by a girlfriend. I've always assumed I wouldn't get into a serious relationship until I had my career where I wanted it to be, so I've never been deeply involved enough to be at risk of getting hurt. But it was different with work because I cared about my future more than I've ever cared about another person. Does that sound sad?"

"Not really," Tegan said. She wasn't sure if her answer was unselfish, or if it was a response to the fleeting sense of relief she felt at Alana's admission. She had no business wanting to be the woman who could change Alana's mind about relationships, but she felt the desire wash through her anyway. "I guess it would be sad if you made the decision to put your career first forever, but I understand focusing on work as a priority over romance, for a while, at least. I did the same thing during school and while I was starting my practice."

Given her last relationship, Tegan would have been better off keeping her focus on work for at least a little bit longer. She decided to nudge the conversation away from the personal turn it had taken and back to the less emotionally charged—for her, if not for Alana—topic of careers. "What did you do to get fired?"

"There were four different events taking place in the hotel on the same day. The guest speakers for two of them sort of got flip-flopped. I might have been responsible since I was the one who initially called to schedule them, but my boss and I were both there on the day, running around and taking care of last-minute issues. I was willing to share the blame, but she put it all on me."

"That doesn't sound like a big deal," Tegan said. "Couldn't you just say you're sorry and get the speakers into the correct rooms?"

Alana stared at the ceiling now, apparently no longer interested in dental care. "The people involved were sort of high-profile. It might have had an impact on my boss's and the hotel's reputation, so she decided to ruin mine instead."

"This is getting more interesting by the second," Tegan said, still fighting a smile. "What were the two parties?"

"One was a dinner for a group of conservative politicians' wives. The other was a bachelorette party."

Tegan couldn't keep from laughing. "So the conservatives got an unexpected stripper? That must have been a shock. Still, I don't understand why they wouldn't just cover their eyes and forgive a mistake."

Alana ducked her head, but Tegan could see the quirk of her mouth. "They probably would have let it go once we got it sorted out. The bigger problem arose when their guest speaker showed up at the drunken bachelorette party, ready to give his inspiring speech."

"Who was it?" Tegan asked. When Alana didn't seem prepared to answer, she held up her phone, ready to play dirty to get the punch line of the story. "I have Chip on speed dial."

"So you'll criticize me for fudging, but you're willing to resort to blackmail. Fine. It was the Chief of Police." She continued, talking over Tegan's gleeful laughter. "In his dress uniform. We might have gotten it figured out sooner if he hadn't been wearing nearly the same outfit as our stripper, minus the Velcro."

Alana laughed, too, but it faded to silence again. She waved her hand at Tegan. "I don't blame you for laughing because it really is funny. But I lost my job because of it. And my home, since my hotel room was part of my salary. And my future plans, because the hospitality world really is quite small and connected, so everyone who might be hiring has heard about the fiasco."

"Everyone, except for a small-time rancher in an out-of-the-way city." Tegan sobered up when she realized the extent of Alana's predicament.

"Exactly," Alana said with a nod. "I was prepared to do my time here and wherever else I needed to go next, slowly making my way back to more prestigious hotels and resorts. Then Chip told me I'd be guiding tours, not just organizing them. I thought there might be some way to learn enough to get by during this first year, while there won't be many guests. But then you showed up, and I realized I didn't even have enough knowledge to pretend I knew what I was doing."

Tegan frowned. She felt she understood the situation better, and she believed Alana was telling the truth, but something was still bugging her. "I get it, why you need this job. But learning to ride and going rafting and hiking? It seems like an awful lot of trouble, especially if you don't enjoy any of it. There must be other people like Chip in other small towns who might be offering a more suitable position."

Alana shrugged. "Like I said, no one else would give me a chance, not even people I knew from school and other jobs. But Chip did. I felt I owed it to him to at least try."

Tegan hadn't expected that. She had thought all of Alana's lies were—understandably—meant to protect her and fool Chip.

"Oh," Alana said, suddenly looking at Tegan with a bright smile. "*You* can teach me to ride."

"Whoa," Tegan said, holding up her hands. "What are you talking about?"

"See? You know words like *whoa*, so you're qualified. Besides, you're the only one here who knows the whole story, and you have a personal interest in helping both me and Chip."

"I do? What reason do I have for helping you?" Tegan wasn't sure how she had gone from being the bystander vet to being involved in Alana's mess.

Alana seemed unperturbed by Tegan's suddenly snappish tone. "Well, I'm sure you want to keep him as a client, with all his horses and the care they need, so you want his ranch to be successful and make money. So he can pay you."

Tegan nodded. "Yes, I know my reasons for wanting Chip to do well. Why exactly do I want to help *you*?"

Alana gestured toward Lace and her puppies and grinned with the smug confidence of a player who had just drawn a royal flush. "Because if I leave Yakima, who's going to save these poor dogs?"

Chapter Six

Tegan sat alone at the reception desk, creating a file for Alana and her dogs. Last night, she had intentionally set Alana's appointment for the hour before the clinic officially opened partly to fit her into an already packed day, but mostly so the two of them could discuss what had happened at Chip's in private. Now, she was wondering if she would have been better off with Dez present. Her sarcastic, phone-obsessed presence would have ensured that the conversation stayed focused on vet business and not on the personal details about Alana's past. Then Tegan wouldn't have gotten herself into this mess.

She had agreed to go along with Alana's crazy plan because her logic had been impeccable, even though she had been wrong about the reasons why Tegan wanted Chip to succeed. Mainly, she cared about the horses. Second, Chip seemed like a nice guy who cared about his animals and his community. The income generated by him as a client was far down Tegan's list of reasons to help him.

And third—which happened to be first and foremost on Tegan's mind even though she tried to pretend it wasn't—she felt the thrill of anticipation at the thought of spending time in close quarters with Alana. Even though she had been irritated by Alana's incompetence the day before, she had looked for any excuse to touch her. To stand close and inhale the scent of her. If she could give in to those desires while helping Alana, the horses, and Chip, then why shouldn't she?

She wasn't going to resist her desire to help Alana, and not just because she had agreed to keep the puppies if she stayed in the area. She seemed to have gotten a raw deal at her old job, especially since she had been willing to share the blame, and she needed Tegan's assistance if she wanted to make this second chance work out. Alana was going about this career renewal plan in a convoluted way, though, and Tegan was certain she would eventually regret being pulled into the scheme. If Alana couldn't learn enough by the time the pups were weaned and Chip opened his ranch, Tegan herself would probably be running back and forth, taking care of her clients here and leading trail rides at Chip's until he found yet another replacement.

She was going to insist on being part of his hiring committee next time.

Alana had been determined to start as soon as possible, so Tegan had sent her out with a list of everything she would need for the puppies and for riding, including dog food, water bowls, and a safety helmet, promising to give her a riding lesson during her lunch hour. She figured the chances of Alana returning and not flying away while Tegan was in possession of the dogs were about fifty-fifty.

At ten to nine, Dez arrived, somehow managing to unlock the front door, wave at Tegan, take off her coat, and log into her computer without looking up from her phone a single time. For once, Tegan didn't feel her usual annoyance with Dez's preoccupation. She was exactly the person she claimed to be, without any falsehood or pretense. No *fudging*, as Alana euphemistically phrased it.

Tegan couldn't accept Alana's claim that everyone lied on applications. Her own case was admittedly unusual since she had never technically applied for a job. She had known she had a position waiting for her here with Dr. Peterson since she had been in middle school and had declared her intention to become a vet. And when he survived a minor episode with his heart five years ago, he said he was selling the practice to her and retiring before "the goddamned business" killed him. It hadn't been the most convincing sales pitch she had ever heard, but the price he offered was too good to pass up. Now she was the boss, not the one filling out applications.

"I have a question for you, Dez, just out of curiosity," she said. She paused until Dez looked in her direction. "Do you think most people lie on job applications?"

"Of course."

Tegan blinked in surprise. She had expected Dez to answer with some sort of sarcastic comment about being too wonderful to need to lie about it. She certainly hadn't thought she would agree with Alana.

"Did you lie on yours?" she asked, feeling much less confident with this question after Dez's breezy affirmation of the first one.

Dez sighed, as if Tegan's insistence on talking to her was exhausting. "Remember during my interview when you asked if I liked the nonglamorous side of animal care, and I said yes, I loved doing anything with them, no matter how menial?"

Tegan nodded, feeling a little sick to her stomach. "Yes. That's the main reason I hired you. Wait, you weren't lying, were you?"

"Yesterday I cleaned dog shit out of the kennels, held at least ten thousand horses in the glaring sun, wrestled with a muddy pig so you could clean its ears, and trimmed the nails of three irate cats. It was the worst day of my life."

The last sentence was delivered in a droll tone as Dez returned to her swiping.

Tegan huffed and turned back to her computer screen before swinging around again. "I can't believe you lied."

Dez shrugged. "You could fire me and hire one of the people lining up outside the door, trying to get my job." She leaned over and peered out the front window. "Oh, never mind."

Tegan laughed. They both knew she wasn't going to call Dez's bluff. If, in fact, she was actually bluffing and not hoping to be fired. Well, if so, she was going to be disappointed today. Tegan went back to typing, filling in the puppies' weights and genders.

"You know," Dez said, initiating an exchange for once, "I haven't seen the glamorous side of vet care yet. When is that going to happen?"

"Today," Tegan said, grinning over her shoulder at Dez. "There's a flea-ridden dog in kennel five who needs a bath and a nail trim. That's about as glamorous as it gets."

Dez got up with a long-suffering groan and went through the exam room and into the back of the clinic. Tegan smiled even wider when she heard Dez exclaim, "Ooh, puppies!" without even a hint of her usual world-weary sarcasm.

❖

Alana returned before noon, walking stiffly in her new boots and riding jeans and clutching a helmet under her arm.

"This shit's expensive," she said by way of greeting when she came through the clinic's back door. "I'm just leading trail rides, not training for the Olympics, so did I really need to buy all these things?"

Tegan looked up from the recently delivered box of vials she had been sorting. "Are you cranky, or nervous about riding?"

"Shut up," Alana said, but with a tight smile.

"Both, it seems." Tegan set the box on the counter and pointed at the boots. "You could wear the sneakers you had on earlier, but if you fall off, your foot might slip through the stirrup and get caught, meaning you'd be dragged along until the horse decides to stop."

She didn't mention that Charm's favorite activity was *stop*, so there wasn't likely to be any dragging, but instead gestured at the jeans. She paused for a moment, admiring how well they accentuated Alana's slender frame and long legs. What had she been saying? Oh, right. Jeans. "These jeans don't have seams in the crotch, so they'll be more comfortable for you."

She turned back to the table, fidgeting with the medications and hiding the flush she could feel spreading across her neck and cheeks. She really should steer clear of words like *crotch* around Alana. They made her thoughts spiral off topic and onto very unproductive tangents. She continued talking without looking at Alana.

"The helmet protects your brain in case you fall. Wear it every time you ride, no matter what, and make sure everyone on your trail rides does, too."

"You weren't wearing one this morning," Alana pointed out.

"I was hoping you hadn't noticed," Tegan said, turning back to face her with a guilty smile. "I promise I'll wear it from now on. Are you going to be this argumentative during the entire lesson?"

Alana paused, apparently giving Tegan's question some thought. "Yes. I need to know all the whys if I'm going to be explaining everything again to a group of beginners."

Tegan sighed. It was going to be a long month. "Fair enough. Let's get started."

They walked across to the barn and stopped outside Charm's stall. Tegan took her leather halter off a hook and handed it to Alana. "Remember how to put this on?"

"Since yesterday?" Alana asked with a snort of derision. "I think I can remember that far back in time."

Tegan rested her folded arms on top of the stall door, ducking slightly to hide her smile as Alana stood next to the patient palomino and flipped the halter upside down and then right side up a few times. It took her a couple tries to get it buckled on correctly, but Tegan was impressed that Alana worked it out on her own without asking for help at the first stumbling block.

"Good," Tegan said, coming into the stall with Alana. "Buckle it one hole tighter, though. See, now it's two fingers below her cheekbone. Too loose and it could get caught on something, and if it's too tight it will rub against the bone. Okay, come on."

Tegan led the way to the arena, with Alana following behind. Technically, she supposed it was Charm who was following her. Alana just happened to be holding on to her lead rope.

"Don't I need a saddle?" Alana called out to her. This time, her question sounded less like an interrogation and more like a plea. "I don't think I'm ready to ride bareback yet."

Tegan closed the arena gate behind them. "You're not ready to ride with a saddle yet, either. You need to learn how to lead your horse properly, then how to groom and tack her. Then you can start learning to ride."

"I only have a month, you know," Alana said, standing in front of Charm and stroking her forehead.

"I know, but you'll need to do all those things for your guests. That's why this whole idea is ridiculous," Tegan said, running her hands through her hair in frustration. Until she had started listing what Alana needed to learn, she had been focused solely on the riding aspect of their foolish quest. "We need to just tell Chip and forget about trying to—"

"Whoa," Alana said, putting her hand on Tegan's shoulder and switching gears until she was the calm and reassuring one and not the nervous student. "See? I'm already picking up the lingo. I'm a quick study, so just teach me the first step, and we'll go from there." She pulled a tiny notebook and a pen out of her back pocket. "I'll even take notes, and then I'll be able to remember what you've told me to do when I practice at the ranch."

Tegan nodded. "Okay, step one. Never ride with a pen in your pocket. It's a good way to stab yourself if you fall."

"No pens in pockets," Alana murmured as she wrote it down and set the pen and notebook on a fence post. "A lot of your tips so far have included the phrase *if you fall*. It's disconcerting."

"Noted," Tegan said, tapping her temple. She smiled, enjoying the way Alana—who was the one learning a difficult new skill in a stressful situation—had made an attempt to put Tegan at ease when she had started to freak out. "I'll be sure to find more soothing ways to phrase it, like when I teach you how to protect yourself if you and your horse mutually decide to part company during a ride."

"Yes, that's much better," Alana said, looking at Charm and shaking her head, as if they were commiserating together about Tegan's sense of humor.

"We only have forty-five minutes left before my next appointment, so let's try to do a little of everything today. Why don't you start by leading her around me in a big circle. Stay to one side, not directly in front of her. If a horse bolts or shies while you're leading it, you'll have a better chance of stopping it and not getting run over."

Alana changed positions quickly, with only a brief glare to let Tegan know her hypotheticals still needed some work. Tegan watched Alana's stiff walk in silence for a moment.

"You look like you're about to be judged in a halter class at a show," she said.

"Is that a bad thing?" Alana asked, keeping her gaze forward. "I watched some videos online while I was waiting for you yesterday, and this is how the people were walking."

"Well, it's not necessarily bad. Not if you really are about to be judged in a halter class in a show. But it's too stylized for a hot summer day on a casual ranch. Here, watch me."

She took Charm's rope from Alana and marched her around the ring. Alana laughed.

"I wasn't prancing," she said. "You're exaggerating."

Tegan smiled. "I was, a little. Now this is how I would lead her around. Of course, I'm still careful about how I hold the lead rope. You don't want to let it get looped around your hand in case she takes off and the loop tightens. That's a good way to lose a finger."

She asked Charm to halt next to Alana and handed her the rope again. Alana hesitated before taking it.

"This seems to be a dangerous activity, what with all the bolting and falling off and losing of fingers. Although, in Charm's case, it seems like you should be giving me instructions about what to do if she falls asleep or topples over."

Tegan patted the mare's shoulder fondly. She had been a gift from her grandparents, given to her for companionship and solace after Tegan's mother had made yet another unexpected and brief appearance in Tegan's life. Nothing could replace her parents or make Tegan less affected by their sporadic visits, but the horse really had made the loneliness a little easier to bear.

"She's earned the right to rest," Tegan said. "Someday, I'll show you the boxes full of championship trophies and ribbons she won."

Alana smiled at her with a kind of understanding in her expression, as if sensing the depth of Tegan's relationship with her animals. "I'd like that. And please don't interpret what I said as a complaint. If I had to list my ideal qualities in a horse, sleepy would be near the top."

Alana walked away from Tegan, doing a fair impression of her more casual posture. Tegan taught her how to stop and turn the horse before calling her over to the fence.

"We'll groom her out here, using the fence as your hitching post," Tegan said. She took the rope and tied Charm to the rail. "This is a quick-release knot. When I pull the loose end, like this, the whole thing comes undone. If one of your horses starts panicking while it's tied, you can release them and…This isn't funny. Why are you laughing?"

Alana was bent over, with her hands on her knees. She stood upright again and brushed the back of her hand over her eyes. "You're the gloomiest teacher I've ever had," she said. "I feel like I'm getting riding lessons from Eeyore."

Tegan laughed, too, swinging the end of the rope and swatting Alana on the leg. "I'm trying to save your sorry ass by preparing you for anything that might go wrong."

"And I appreciate it," Alana said, getting her notebook off the post. "Now, tie the knot again, but more slowly, and I'll make a diagram."

Tegan tied the knot again, then showed Alana how to groom and saddle the mare. She tried to keep her doom-and-gloom comments to a minimum, but she couldn't keep herself from giving advice about what to do if a horse tried to kick or bite or stomp on her. Even though Alana teased her relentlessly, she also paid attention to everything Tegan said, filling her notebook pages with diagrams, arrows, and sequential lists.

Once Tegan was satisfied with the way Alana had saddled Charm, she led them into the center of the arena.

"The last thing you do before mounting is check your cinch to make sure it's tight enough. Now, don't laugh." Tegan poked Alana in the arm even though Alana didn't seem to be amused anymore. The closer she got to riding, the quieter she seemed to get. "If your cinch isn't tight, your saddle will slip when you try to get on, and you'll end up underneath the horse. That's a bad place to be."

Alana simply nodded and scribbled.

"Okay, watch me," Tegan said, stepping next to Charm and swinging easily into the saddle. She sat for a moment, and then dismounted, handing the reins back to Alana. "Your turn."

"Are you sure?" Alana asked. "I'll be good and listen quietly if you have some more *if*s to share."

Tegan shook her head and patted the seat of the saddle. "Up."

Alana put her left foot in the stirrup and tried to hop into the saddle, but she lost her balance and swung back a step instead. Tegan was there immediately, catching Alana's waist and moving her back into position. Her hands slipped under the hem of Alana's T-shirt and rested on her warm, soft skin. She hesitated a heartbeat longer than she probably should have, but her hands seemed to melt into the contact, fusing her to Alana until she didn't want to let go.

Charm shifted slightly, and Tegan moved her hands lower. "Jump up, Alana," she said, bracing against Alana's rear and boosting her into the saddle.

Tegan stood in silence, fighting to catch her breath and regain her composure. Touching Alana's ass was right up there with talking about crotches on Tegan's new list of ill-advised activities. Alana was flushed and panting slightly, too, but Tegan didn't know if the cause was the nervous exertion of getting on Charm, or Tegan's touch. The mare was the only one who seemed calm.

"Well, you're on a horse," Tegan said, injecting a congratulatory tone into her voice and avoiding any mention of Alana falling off again. She pulled her phone out and checked the time. "We have... well, three minutes left."

"Three minutes?" Alana repeated, looking more relaxed now that she was on the horse. Or maybe she was merely relieved because the lesson was nearly over even though it had barely begun. "That ought to be enough time to teach me everything I need to know."

Chapter Seven

Alana unplugged the heating pad and removed the cord before she tucked it under the towel on the bottom of the dog crate. The added warmth would keep the puppies snuggly during her drive to the ranch. The route was short enough that the pad wouldn't have cooled completely by the time they arrived. Tegan had been cautious about having her transport the litter too much, but she had agreed they would be better off in Alana's office where she could check on them frequently when she worked full days.

Alana winced as she knelt on the floor and started to tuck pups into the crate. She had only had two lessons so far with Tegan and hadn't made it beyond a few minutes of walking while actually on the horse, compared to forty-five minutes of walking on the ground next to Charm. She had complained about the slow pace but was secretly relieved when Tegan ignored her nagging and concentrated more on horse handling than riding. Those brief stints in the saddle had left Alana aching more than she would ever admit to Tegan, even though she considered herself to be in reasonable shape. She was discovering the difference between doing reps in a hotel gym—which had been her preferred method of working out in the past—and doing real-world physical activity.

She paused when she got to the sixth and largest puppy, a mostly white male with dark brown ears and a lighter patch of brown surrounding his black nose. His eyes were open, and he was blinking at her, as if trying to get her into focus. Tegan had said they were about three weeks old. Only five more before they'd be ready to go to a new home. Alana was planning to start canvassing her neighborhood soon because she planned to have six new owners—seven if she included a foster or adopter for Lace—lined up well before then.

She kissed the little pup on the top of the head and put him in the crate. Lace followed, keeping her eyes on Alana as she moved. Alana stayed very still until she was inside the crate, and then she securely closed it. It made her sad to see how nervous Lace was around people, but she hoped the dog would become more trusting the longer she was inside and cared for.

She picked up the crate and carried it out to the truck, where she had already stowed supplies for the dogs and her riding helmet. She had been planning to ask Chip about bringing the dogs to work, but she had decided to just show up with them instead. Her old boss would probably have fainted at the sight of an animal crate in the hotel, let alone an actual animal. Not that Alana had ever considered getting a pet before, much less carting it around with her everywhere she went. She wasn't sure she would still recognize herself once she moved away from Yakima and got back to city life. Then again, maybe she would easily shed this new Alana, as if her time here had never happened.

Not likely. Horseback riding and dog fostering would no longer be part of her life when she left, but she had a feeling she wouldn't be able to push Tegan's memory away as quickly. The sensation of Tegan's hands on her waist during her first lesson, and then on her rear, pushing her into the saddle, was something Alana couldn't seem to get out of her mind. She felt like a memory foam mattress, and the marks of Tegan's fingers were imprinted on her skin. She had considered hopping around as if she couldn't mount again in her second lesson but had come to her senses and clawed her way into the saddle on her own. It hadn't been graceful—and hadn't felt as good as when Tegan helped her—but she couldn't expect Tegan to be here at the ranch every time she needed a boost.

Alana parked and got the shopping bag with dog food and her helmet in it, draping the straps over her forearm and hoisting the crate. It was less cumbersome than the cardboard box had been. She carried everything to the front door and managed to get herself, the dogs, and her bags through the door after several attempts. With some annoyance, she noticed a group of five construction workers sitting in the lodge's main room, watching her struggle with the door. Once she was inside, they turned their attention back to the flat screen television mounted on the wall above the fireplace.

Alana dropped her bags near the vacant reception desk and walked past it to Chip's office. He was sitting at his desk, staring into space and tapping a pencil against his knee, but he sat up and gave her his usual carefree grin when she knocked on the open door.

"Good morning," he said, standing up and noticing the crate. "Oh, are those the puppies Aaron found under your porch?"

Alana had carefully prepared a speech about why she had brought a litter of puppies to work, but she hadn't counted on the speed of a small-town grapevine. "Yes. I hope you don't mind if I..."

Her voice trailed off as Chip bounced over and knelt next to her, looking through the grate at the dogs.

"How cute! We used to have a cocker spaniel when I was a boy, and the mother reminds me of him a little. Are you planning to ride today? I'll keep them in here with me."

"Oh, are you sure? I was planning to set them up in my office, where they'd be out of the way. I know how busy you are," she said, trying to be polite even though Chip hadn't seemed to be busy either today or on her first day at the ranch. She wasn't quite sure what tasks were filling his days, but preparing for the grand opening didn't seem to be one of them.

"Oh, well, yes. Very busy. I had been hoping to take you out on the trails to show you around, but I need to stay in the office and supervise the work that's being done. I can easily puppy-sit at the same time." He sighed and glanced toward the door, through which Alana could hear the sound of the television and laughter.

"Actually, not much work seems to be getting done," she said, cautiously approaching the subject. "Or is it already break time for them?"

"Yes, I guess it is," he said. "Say, I have the perfect bed for the pups. Hang on."

He stopped by the thermostat and turned up the heat before disappearing out the door. Alana stood in place for a moment. It wasn't any of her business what went on inside the lodge. She had enough to do to prepare herself for her own job, let alone butting in on Chip's. And why did she care if he went bankrupt and the lodge never opened? She'd be off the hook, free to run away from Yakima and saddles and stray dogs.

She nodded to herself, appreciating the logic of her arguments, and then set the crate on the floor and went into the main room. She plucked the remote off the arm of a chair and stood in front of the workers, turning off the television over her shoulder.

"Who's in charge here?" she asked. The three men and two women looked at one another before one of the men hesitantly raised his hand.

"What's on your agenda for the day?"

"We're here to put up the drywall," he said, which she didn't think was really an answer to her question. "But the electrician isn't finished with all the rooms."

"Is he finished with some of the rooms?"

He looked at his crew again, and Alana wasn't sure if he was communicating telepathically with them or hoping someone else would take over and answer her.

"Yes?" he said, with the inflection of someone asking a question.

"Good. Then there's no reason for Chip to pay you to sit here and watch TV when you could be working on the rooms that are already wired. Right?"

She didn't wait for an answer but headed back to the office, taking the remote with her. Chip was standing in the doorway to the pool room, holding a child's plastic wading pool and staring at her. She heard the shuffling sounds of the crew getting up and leaving the room behind her, but she walked into the office without turning to check on them.

"Wow. You're amazing," he said, clutching the pool and staring at her as if she'd just dropped down from heaven. "I've had the hardest time getting people to do any work around here." He leaned forward slightly and lowered his voice, as if sharing a big secret. "I don't do well with confrontation."

No kidding. Alana was counting on that trait to guarantee she kept her job. She obviously wasn't the only person employed by him to realize that he could be a pushover. A kind one, of course, but kindness didn't always get the job done.

"I was raised in my family's hotel," she said with a shrug. "I was overseeing renovations and repairs before I was in my teens. You just need to expect people to do the work you're paying them to do. Don't accept less."

She felt a twinge of guilt as she spoke, since she wasn't exactly qualified to do the work he had hired her to do. Still, she was spending her free time and her own money trying to improve her skills. Or, rather, develop them in the first place.

"I know. I'll try," he said, putting the pool near the heater vent and lining it with a fleece blanket that had been tossed over the back of a chair.

Alana filled Lace's water bowl and set it near the pool before opening the crate and putting the pups into their new bedroom. She had been unsure about how Lace would handle the naturally exuberant Chip, but he stayed still, holding out his hand for her to sniff, and she seemed to accept her family's new location with her usual detachment. She didn't seem to have any expectations for herself, as long as her litter was safe.

"Tegan...Dr. Evans, I mean, said they're old enough to be handled a little bit, so you can hold them if you want. I'll come back in a while and give Lace her lunch."

"Okay," he said vaguely, his attention focused on the dogs. She sighed and stood up. She had been expecting to spend her day running back and forth between the corrals and her office to check on the puppies and Lace. Now it seemed they'd be all right, but she would have to come back here to check on the workers instead. It'd be a fair trade since she was better suited to hotel management than dog watching. She hesitated in the doorway, but as soon as she recognized the tiny hint of jealousy she felt when Chip picked up one of *her* puppies, she escaped to the barn.

She started by figuring out the names of all her charges. She used the process of elimination and the information about color and gender on their records to identify each one, and then she thumbtacked index cards with the occupants' names on them to each paddock. She wasn't sure if she'd mixed up two nearly identical chestnut geldings, but she didn't think the guests would know the difference if she was wrong. She only had to consult the books Tegan had given her to study once—to look at a picture of a dun horse. She wasn't about to let Tegan know the books had come in handy. They were obviously meant for a much younger reader, with their cartoon drawings and simple vocabulary. Tegan had told her she could be indignant about them if she wanted, but only after she had memorized all the material in them. Alana stuck out her tongue at the pile of books. Not only did she feel like she had returned to school, but she had gone all the way back to kindergarten.

Once she knew the horses' names, she went through an abbreviated version of her lesson with each one. She haltered them, led them to the hitching post, tied and groomed them. Each horse had a labeled hook with a bridle on it in the tack room, but the saddles seemed to be randomly shoved on racks and stacked on top of each other. She chose the one that was easiest to extract from the cluttered mess and used it as she rode each horse, merely walking in a circle or a figure eight before dismounting, putting the horse away, and moving on to the next.

Even those basic tasks were a stretch for her to perform. She spent two hours with the first horse—she chose Blaze because he seemed extra sleepy and patient—and half of it was wasted with her trying to untangle the bridle, which she accidentally dropped on her way from the barn to the corral. She was used to having Tegan hand it to her with all the tangly leather parts hanging neatly in place. She hadn't realized how much Tegan had been helping her along the way until she was left on her own without Tegan's words of advice and her dire warnings.

After four rounds of this, Alana was sweating and peeling off layers of clothes until she was left in a dirt-smudged tank top. Her legs were inexplicably sore, and she was ready to give up the charade and never go near another horse in her life.

Alana led horse five, Cookie, toward the corral, barely getting her out of the gate and closing it behind them before her paddock-mate had a chance to slip through. She stomped toward the corral, and the only positive thought she could muster was that Tegan couldn't criticize her for looking too stiff while she led this horse since she was too worn out to be bothered with good posture.

She flung the end of the lead rope over the wooden rail and tied a quick release knot before picking up a currycomb. She paused with her arm outstretched, ready to begin grooming, when she realized what she'd done. She released the knot to make sure it was correct, and then tied it again. With the previous horses, she'd needed to consult the diagram in her notebook and had made no fewer than three attempts each time before getting it right. This time, she hadn't even been conscious of the process.

She felt a renewed energy as she groomed Cookie. She was getting somewhere. Not very far, of course, but she'd take the inch of progress and be proud of it. She wanted to call Tegan and share her small victory, but she realized she really just wanted an excuse to hear Tegan's mellow voice, even if over the phone. Alana reacted the same way she had when she felt jealous about Chip and the puppies—she pushed those foolish thoughts out of her mind and focused on work instead.

After Cookie, she gave herself a break and went back to the lodge. Chip was sitting next to the wading pool, watching the puppies sleep. He tried to pretend he had just sat down again and hadn't been there the entire time she'd been at the barn, but she wasn't sure she believed him. She left him in there, watching Lace gobble her lunch, and went into her office to eat her sandwich alone. She checked on the progress of the drywall—which was moving along surprisingly quickly—and trudged back to the barn.

She had meant to work with all twenty-five horses, but ten seemed to be her limit for the time being. She'd put in a full day of work as it was, and she was too tired and achy to even lift her arms to halter one more horse. She felt a sense of accomplishment, though. The constant repetition had ingrained some of the horse-related actions, and she no longer had to think about every step before doing it.

Still, she was slowly learning how far she had to go. Moseying around an enclosed space for five minutes at a time was nothing like leading a trail ride with all its potential hazards, many of which were cartoonishly illustrated in one of the books Tegan had given her.

Her phone rang as she was walking back to the lodge, preparing herself for the upcoming task of prying the puppies away from Chip, and a jolt of excitement chased away all thoughts of stiff muscles from her mind.

"Hey," she said, pausing in the shade of a pine tree.

"Hey back," Tegan said, and Alana could almost hear her smile.

"So, I've been practicing, and you'll be pleased to know that I'm now an expert at quick-release knots."

"Good. I'm sure the ranch's guests will be just as happy watching you perform knot-tying demos as riding the horses." Tegan said. "Have you memorized the books I gave you yet?"

Alana pinched off a clump of long needles and pleated them with her fingers. "Just the chapter on the importance of finding a nice, non-smart-ass instructor."

Tegan laughed outright at that. "Well, if you're a desperate enough student, you take what you can get. How are the puppies?"

"Fine, except I'm concerned that Chip might give up ranch work and take a job as a puppy nanny instead."

"Uh-oh. I think you're joking, but I really can picture him spending his life walking dogs, running through parks with a big smile on his face. Anyway, I called because Dez asked for tomorrow morning off, and I'm scheduled to do a stable call at a breeding farm in Toppenish. If you want to come along, you'd get good experience handling horses that are more energetic than Charm and Chip's string. Plus, I'd buy you the best lunch you've ever had as a thank-you."

"I'd love to," Alana said, without even pausing to wonder what Tegan meant by *more energetic*. Fire-breathing? Was she about to experience the bolting Tegan had mentioned? She didn't care. She wasn't going to pass up the chance to spend time with Tegan, especially if she could justify it as work-related and nothing personal.

CHAPTER EIGHT

Tegan parked next to Alana's garish truck and let her engine idle while she waited. She had vacillated between looking forward to the morning with Alana and wishing she had just decided to go on this appointment on her own. Immediately after Dez had asked for some time off to attend a study session at school, Tegan had called Alana's number without giving it a second thought. Since then, she had worked through second and third and fourth thoughts. She was up to about forty now.

Some misgiving was because Alana wasn't ready to handle the hotly bred horses they would be seeing today. She could barely manage to lead Charm in a circle, and the mare's most disobedient action consisted of dozing off during their lessons. Mostly, however, she was concerned about her own reasons for calling Alana. They were all much more personal than she had insinuated on the phone. Alana wouldn't get much extra experience today, because Tegan planned to have the farm's grooms handle the horses for her. Tegan wanted to show Alana some of the more beautiful spots in Yakima. Introduce her to friends. Spend time with her. In her mind, she had justified this by telling herself Alana was new in town. She needed someone to help her adjust, help her appreciate the town and its people, help her escape feelings of loneliness and isolation. In truth, however, Tegan was the one who wanted and needed Alana's company. She wanted Alana to share everyday things with her, like work and spending time with her friends.

Things she should want to do with someone who lived here, who wanted to be here and was likely to stay for more than a year, or just a summer season.

Too late now. Tegan watched Alana as she walked off the porch and across the parking lot. She rubbed her palms against the rough fabric of her jeans, trying to wipe away the suddenly tingly feeling in her fingertips at the sight of Alana wearing a white T-shirt with an unbuttoned plaid shirt over it and tied at her waist. Her jeans and boots were already grubby and dusty after only a few days of wear. She *looked* like she belonged here, as long as Tegan didn't dwell too long on her trendy haircut and the fact that she had explicitly said she was only here temporarily.

Alana got into the passenger seat and shut the door. "I hope I didn't keep you waiting long," she said, smiling at Tegan and buckling her seat belt. "I had to make sure the contractors knew which rooms to finish today."

Tegan drove down the ranch's long driveway, avoiding some of the larger ruts. "Isn't that Chip's job?"

Alana gave her an exasperated look. "Apparently he's too busy tickling puppy bellies. I'm hoping he'll decide to adopt the lot. They'll keep him company on these long, lonely nights when there aren't any guests at the ranch."

Tegan glanced at Alana. "It's nice of you to help him. I'm sure he'll learn how to be more assertive the closer he gets to the grand opening."

"Maybe. Speaking of assertive, I want to talk to you about giving my horses expired medicine."

Tegan couldn't help but laugh at Alana's proprietary tone. One week ago, she barely knew what a horse was, and now she was claiming ownership of twenty-five of them. She had a feeling this was an important part of Alana's personality. When she took on a project, she immersed herself completely. "What are you talking about? And when did they become your horses?"

Alana paused, as if giving the question serious consideration. "Yesterday afternoon. And I'm talking about the dewormer you used the day we met."

She leaned forward and pulled a folded piece of paper out of her back pocket. Tegan paused before turning onto the main road and took it from her.

"See?" Alana said, pointing at Tegan's invoice.

Tegan pinched the bridge of her nose. She had itemized the farm call and the vaccinations, which she had included at cost, without her usual markup. In an empty space, Chip had written: *Plus old paste dewormer—free.*

"I asked him about it, and he said you found an old box of the stuff in storage and gave it to him."

Tegan sighed. "That wasn't exactly true. I had just bought those tubes. I just told him they were old so he wouldn't fuss about me not charging for them."

"You lied?"

"I prefer the term *fudged.*"

"Not so self-righteous now, are we?" Alana asked in a smug tone. "But it still doesn't make sense."

Tegan tossed the invoice back onto Alana's lap and pulled onto the road. "Did Chip tell you how the horses and corrals were part of the package he got when he bought the property?"

"Yes."

"What I'm sure he didn't tell you was how poor the living conditions had been for the horses. Alana, I had been trying to help them for years. You know how sick you felt when you were holding Lace and feeling how thin and scared she was at our appointment? Imagine if you didn't have the comfort of being able to help her, but just had to watch her suffer from a distance."

Tegan put on her blinker and merged onto Highway 82, heading east and skimming past the edge of Yakima. "Once Chip took charge, he called me out and we got to work getting the horses healthy again. He spent hours cleaning the paddocks and a lot of money on feed and vitamins and shoeing. I help out as much as I can, but he can be very stubborn about wanting to pay full cost."

"So do you magically discover old boxes of medicine every time you come out?"

Tegan grinned. "Sometimes other clients have already paid for bags of supplements but changed their minds about wanting them. Last time I dewormed them, I told him mice had chewed through the boxes the paste tubes came in. I said I couldn't put them on my shelves and sell them that way, so I might as well use them for his horses. Todd, the farrier, does the same thing. We just want to help because we appreciate what he's done."

"Well, from now on you're dealing with me," Alana said. "And I'm perfectly happy accepting help for the horses, like a multihorse discount or something, but only if it's reasonable for you, and you're not losing too much of your profit. Plus, once the ranch is making money, the discounts stop."

"Deal." Tegan reached out her hand, and Alana shook it, then gave it a squeeze and didn't let go right away.

"Thank you," she said. "For helping the horses and Lace. And me. You seem to collect a lot of strays."

Tegan rested her hand on her lap, still able to feel the pressure of Alana's fingers even after she had let go. Alana's statement was truer than she realized. She had been a stray herself as a child, in a way, and had naturally attracted them ever since.

Alana was quiet as they drove the rest of the way to Toppenish, a small town about twenty minutes from Yakima. They were surrounded by rounded hills, some sparsely dotted with sage and basalt boulders. Others were covered with densely planted wheat or hay that looked like a solid blanket from some angles but had perfectly ordered rows when viewed from another. The early morning sun draped the irregular hills in patches of shadow and light. Tegan never tired of the beauty she saw around her every day, but she was afraid to ask Alana what she thought. She didn't want to hear Alana say that she preferred views of skyscrapers and elegant hotels to this, even though she was certain it was true. Better not to ask, so Tegan let the silence stretch between them.

After exiting the freeway, Tegan drove down a rural road and into her client's driveway. It was as long as the one leading to Chip's ranch, but the similarity ended there. The fields on either side here were bare of trees, edged by perfect white board fences, and diagonally cut by large irrigation systems.

"Oh, horse babies," Alana said. She swatted Tegan's thigh before she could correct her. "I know, I know. Foals, colts, fillies."

"No tests today, I promise," Tegan said. She halted in the middle of the driveway and pointed to a group of leggy youngsters that were wandering over to inspect the intruders. "These are yearling colts, and the weanlings are in the pasture just beyond them. Fillies are on this side. This year's foals and the broodmares are closer to the house, just over the hill."

She started driving again, and the horses kept pace as long as they could, skidding to a halt when they reached the fence, and wheeling around to gallop away again.

"They're fast," Alana said, watching over her shoulder until they crested the hill.

"They're Thoroughbreds and bred for the track, although some will be jumpers or pleasure horses."

She parked next to a large gray barn with cupolas and bright white trim and waved at the woman coming out to meet them. "We're here to ultrasound one of the mares and find out if she's pregnant," she told Alana. "Plus, I'm sure we'll have two or three while-you're-heres."

Alana paused as she was reaching for the door handle. "Whats?"

"*While you're here, could you check this colt's leg?* That sort of thing. I always schedule extra time when I come to one of these larger farms because I know I'll be seeing more animals than expected. Once we're done, I'll take you to see the broodmares and foals."

"Hi, Mariah," Tegan said, getting out of the Jeep and shaking hands with the farm's owner. "How are you?"

"I need a cigarette. That's how I am."

Tegan ignored both the comment and her own desire to give Mariah a lecture about the dangers of smoking. She'd tried before and knew she'd be wasting her time. "This is Alana. She's helping me out today."

Mariah grunted in Alana's direction then turned back to Tegan. "C'mon. The mare's in here."

Tegan handed a box of supplies to Alana before reaching into the back seat and picking up her portable ultrasound machine.

Alana leaned close to her, nearly making Tegan drop the expensive tool. "Smoking is bad for you," she whispered.

"Yes, I know. I've mentioned it before, but if you want to bring it up to her again, you can."

She watched Alana glance over at Mariah, who was waiting near the barn entrance with an impatient expression. Her gray hair was tightly braided, and she was dressed head-to-toe in brown canvas. Tegan was sure she did all her clothes shopping in the Carhartt section of the local feed store. She carried a riding crop everywhere she went, and she was currently smacking it against her calf. She was unfailingly gentle with her animals and Tegan had never seen her use it on a horse, but she wouldn't be at all surprised if she heard that a too slow stable hand had felt its sting.

Alana looked at Tegan again. "I think I'll let it slide this time."

"Wise choice." Tegan bumped Alana with her shoulder and headed into the barn. Mariah went into the first stall and clipped a lead rope on the young mare, handing it to Alana. Alana led her into the aisleway, and Tegan let the mare inspect the machine before she set it down next to her.

She soon realized she needn't have worried about Alana's ability to act as her assistant. She seemed different around the horse, somehow. More confident. More like herself, Tegan decided, even though she was still new to horses. The mare cooperated by standing quietly during the procedure, merely flicking her tail at an occasional fly.

Mariah remained in the stall, refusing to look at the ultra-sound because she was afraid it would bring bad luck. The mare had fooled her twice before so far this year. Once Tegan had finished her exam, she turned the machine so Alana could see the screen.

"Embryonic vesicle," she said, pointing at the dark, roughly circular spot on the screen. "You can come out now, Mariah. She's pregnant."

"Good girl," Mariah said, taking the lead rope from Alana and giving the horse a pat. "While you're here, can you check the colt in the third stall? Looks like he bumped his eye in the pasture."

Tegan winked at Alana as soon as Mariah turned away from them to lead the mare into her stall. "Sure. I have a little extra time today."

The colt wasn't as easy to handle as the mare had been, but Tegan managed to examine him and help Alana figure out how to hold him still at the same time, mainly by standing close to Alana and using her own body to pin the three of them in the corner of the stall. She stepped back once she had put some drops in his eye, suddenly noticing the slight chill in the shady barn when her body no longer was being warmed from contact with Alana. Tegan was secretly hoping to be asked to see another horse while she was there, preferably one that was enough of a handful for Alana to need her help, but Mariah gave them a bunch of carrots and sent them out to the broodmare pasture.

Alana reached through the fence and scratched the foal behind her ears, marveling at the puffy softness of her baby fur that Tegan said she would shed soon. She nibbled on the sleeve of Alana's shirt while her mother chomped on the carrots Tegan was giving her.

The view from the top of the hill was expansive, with variegated fields spreading for miles on all sides, green pastures next to stubbly yellow fields of already cut grains. It was peaceful and quiet, but in a way that almost felt oppressive to Alana who wasn't used to being this exposed. Even as she appreciated the beauty around her, she found herself longing for her safe and familiar walls.

"I went to the races at Belmont once with a group of coworkers when I was living in New York," she said, gently pulling her sleeve out of the filly's mouth before she managed to eat a button. "It's all color and noise and crowds. Completely different from places like this where the horses come from."

"Some thrive on the energy and the competition," Tegan said, breaking a carrot into pieces and handing it to Alana to feed to the horse. "But I'm sure a lot of them would rather spend their lives in the country, if they had the chance."

"Just like people." Alana smiled as the horse's whiskery lips tickled her palm. She had always been certain she belonged close to the excitement of a big city, and she still didn't think this type of country living was for her, but she was beginning to understand the attraction of a small town. Well, she certainly felt an attraction to Tegan, who happened to live in a small town.

"New York, Philadelphia. Have you always moved around a lot?"

"Not much at all. My family ran a hotel in a suburb of Newark, and I lived there with my parents and grandparents until I went to college. We always had people coming to stay from other places, but we rarely traveled beyond the city. I promised myself I wouldn't ever fall into the same rut. I did an internship in New York right after college, and then moved to Philadelphia. I took my second job there because it was with an international chain, and I thought I'd have opportunities to move someplace new and exciting."

Yakima hadn't been on her list of desirable exotic locations. She hadn't even known what state it was in until she looked it up after seeing Chip's ad.

"You'll make it happen, even though you've had a small setback. If it's what you really want, that is."

"Absolutely," Alana said, resting her chin on the fence and watching the foal tear off across the pasture while her mother followed at a more sedate pace. "Although I'm not hating it here as much as I thought I would."

She surprised herself with the comment. She hadn't even realized it was true until she said it out loud.

"Really?" Tegan asked, sounding as surprised as Alana had been. She leaned her back against the fence and looked at Alana. "What's made you change your mind?"

You. Alana acknowledged it internally but didn't say it. Tegan's determination to rescue every person or animal who was feeling pain. The scent of apples and zing of arousal that Alana experienced every time she was near her. The way she looked at the scenery around her as if she could hardly bear how beautiful it was. And the way she made Alana begin to recognize that beauty herself, even though she hadn't allowed herself to see it at first.

"I like the challenge of this job, and the satisfaction I feel when I make even a little progress," she said instead. "And the puppies are fun, since I've never had pets before."

The set time limit was helping, too. She could allow herself to fully be part of this community, be a dog owner, and be a ranch hand because she knew none of it was forever. She would be able to walk away from all of it without regrets or sorrow because it was all part of her plan. She wondered about Tegan—would she be willing to move their relationship to somewhere more intimate, more involved, if only for a short time? Alana was definitely willing to explore the option.

"I've always had pets but didn't really make many friends until I was in high school," Tegan said. "Your childhood sounds like it was interesting because you were exposed to new people all the time."

Alana's mind had been moving forward, looking at possibilities for a friendship-with-benefits with Tegan, and she struggled to return to the past. "I guess," she said. "Everyone moved on, though. People would stay for one night, or two. Maybe a week. We had some regulars, but they were adults who came for meetings and conferences, not kids my age. I worked in the hotel, too, starting way before I was legally allowed to, so I never had time to get involved at school. It was boring, really."

Tegan reached over and brushed Alana's bangs to one side, her touch gentle against her forehead, relaxing the frown that had settled there.

"Was it really boring?" she asked. "Or was it very lonely?"

Alana opened her mouth to confirm her original assessment of *boring*, but she closed it again, caught unaware by a slight shift in her perspective. Tegan seemed to sense her need to process her thoughts, and instead of pressing with more questions, she suggested they head to lunch.

The ride from Toppenish to the even tinier town of Zillah was a short one, which suited Alana just fine since she didn't want to dwell on her past for much longer. She had spent her childhood—and most of her adult life—surrounded by people. Hemmed in on all sides by other rooms with other occupants. Sharing a small suite with two other generations of her family. Making small talk with guests and seeing to their needs at all hours. She had never thought of herself as lonely before, had never thought someone so completely lacking a truly private life could ever *be* lonely.

Yakima was the type of place where she should feel isolated and alone, with its wide-open spaces and ever-present nature. With long evenings in a big, empty house. But she didn't feel lonely here. Not at all. Chip was friendly at work, and only a phone call away if she happened to spot a rat. The puppies and Lace managed to make the house feel warmer, even though they took up very little space in it.

And Tegan. Well, Alana had plenty of ideas about how Tegan could keep loneliness at bay during her year in Yakima. She just had to find a way to convince her that a short-term relationship could have enticing advantages.

CHAPTER NINE

A lana pushed aside her maudlin thoughts of loneliness once they arrived in Zillah. She couldn't feel lonely when she was with Tegan, no matter whether they were riding quietly or talking, and the restaurant in front of her was festive and crowded enough to make heavy internal monologues impossible. Rosamund's Diner and Tortilleria was housed in a huge warehouse style building alongside the highway and was brightly decorated in the colors of the Mexican flag. Black arrows painted on the walls pointed the way to the public entrance in front and the tortilla factory in back.

"Half the town must work here," Alana said, noticing the number of cars and trucks parked in the back part of the lot. She opened the door and saw the line of people waiting to order at the counter and the crowded tables in the dining area. "Wow. And the other half eats here."

Tegan laughed. "You're right. This place has been here for decades, so it's a local favorite, but it's close enough to the freeway to draw lots of tourists, too. They sell the food they make wholesale to restaurants and grocery stores in Yakima, which gives them enough business to make them one of the largest employers in the area. Most of the people you'll see in the restaurant are part of the family that owns it, though, along with local teens from the high school who are employed as part of a work-scholarship program."

Alana stepped inside the restaurant, marveling at the way business owners around here seemed interconnected with each other and with their community. She had always thought of restaurants and stores as isolated and individual, unless they were part of a chain. She inhaled deeply, savoring the competing scents from sweet and yeasty baked goods and spicy meats. The interior was somewhat plain, with a large counter area where diners placed their orders in one half of the rectangular room and wooden tables and benches squashed into the other half. Decorations were scattered here and there, as if they were afterthoughts. A burro piñata dangled over the salsa bar, and some vividly painted vases topped the plastic garbage cans. All the attention seemed to have been focused on the huge glass display cases under the counter. Two of them held fresh tortillas, still warm enough from the oven to make their plastic wrappers damp and clingy, and stacks of homemade tamales labeled with the names of different fillings. On the other side were the baked goods, with piles of intricately braided sweet breads crammed next to dozens of kinds of cookies. Alana moved closer, drawn to some puffy cookies topped with a layer of oven-cracked sugar, some hot pink and others a deep golden yellow.

Tegan stepped next to her. "Those are conchas and they're my favorite. They're not overly sweet, so you don't feel guilty eating an entire bag full of them."

A woman's voice, rich with a thick accent, called Tegan's name, and she looked up with a smile.

"Hey, Rosie. This is my friend, Alana. You're doing good business today, as usual."

Rosie waved across the counter at Alana. She was wearing a flowing colorful dress, similar to the ones the other employees had on, with an off-the-shoulder top revealing smooth skin. Earrings with tiny red parrots dangled from her lobes, and her smile was bright. "Nice to meet you, Alana," she said.

Alana smiled. "Are you Rosie, as in Rosamund?"

Rosie shook her head. "She was my great-grandmother, but I'm named after her. Most of the recipes we use here were hers. Do you know what you want to order, or shall I surprise you?"

Alana and Tegan looked at each other and nodded at the same time. "Surprise us," Tegan said. Rosie waved off Tegan's attempts to pay for their food and told them to find a seat.

They scanned the room for an open place to sit and hurried over to a table by the front window as soon as it was vacated.

"How do you know Rosie?" Alana asked, making a determined effort to ask the question in a casual and not a probing way.

"She volunteers with a feral cat program. They catch stray cats, spay or neuter them, and release them again. I do surgeries for them as often as I can."

"So she gives you free food in exchange." She seemed to have traveled back in time when she came to Yakima, back to an era when people bartered for goods and services instead of selling items in a store, complete with nonnegotiable price tags. She was charmed by the connections this casual type of system created, especially when she saw the way Tegan tried to help Chip's horses and Rosie's cats without a concern for her own paycheck. Still, she didn't believe it was a practical alternative to cash and credit cards.

"Sometimes," Tegan said, staring up at the taco-shaped piñata hanging over their table. "I usually try to wait until she goes into the back, and then place my order with someone else, but I was distracted today...um, by the conchas. I'm really hungry. I mean... never mind."

Alana wasn't sure why Tegan was blushing and acting un-comfortable, but she assumed it was because she didn't want Alana thinking she took advantage of Rosie. "Well, I think it's nice," she said, hoping to reassure Tegan. She searched for a change in subject but couldn't come up with anything besides one that circled back to their earlier conversation. She reluctantly followed the thread.

"This reminds me of my parents' hotel. Not the décor or food or anything, but because it seems to be a family business.

I was kind of like Rosie, working side by side with my family. I remember thinking how strange my best friend's life was when I visited her house since she barely seemed to see her parents. They were all too busy with their separate lives to even eat dinner at the same time. For me, everything was lumped together, with no distinctions between work and home and family."

Alana looked up and saw Tegan watching her. She felt a momentary jolt of surprise because she had been lost in her thoughts and almost forgot she was speaking out loud, to another person. "Sometimes I envied her, of course, because she had more privacy than I ever did. I couldn't get away with anything because there was always a guest or a grandparent or someone who saw me sneaking cookies from the basket in the lobby or hanging out by the pool instead of doing homework."

Tegan smiled. "I'm sure you managed to find ways to get yourself into trouble, despite the constant surveillance."

Alana shrugged. "Sometimes. Mostly I was quite well behaved. It was a passive sort of life, I guess. I was always waiting for someone interesting to show up. Waiting to be old enough to make my own way in life."

"You must have grown out of your passivity, then, because that's not a word I would even consider if I was going to describe your personality."

Alana wanted to ask which words Tegan *would* choose, but Rosie arrived at the table bearing two platters full of food. She sat next to Tegan and sipped an iced tea, leaning back against the wall. "What a day," she said. "I cringe every time I see one of those tour buses pull into the lot. So, Alana, are you from Yakima, or are you new here?"

"I just...hey, wait. Where'd your accent go?"

She laughed. "It comes and goes, depending on how many tourists are standing in line. My great-grandmother Rosamund came to the United States when my grandma was a little girl, so I was born here. Sometimes I change accents just for fun."

Tegan swallowed a bite of her tamale and playfully elbowed Rosie. "When I was here last week, she sounded like she just got off a plane from Paris. Week before, it was Russia."

"I do community theater, so it's good practice for me, as long as my mother isn't close enough to hear. Now, back to you."

"I'm the new Activity Coordinator at High Ridge Ranch, out near Selah," she said, still hanging on to the questionable job title. "I haven't even been here a week." It felt as if she'd been here far longer, however. She'd packed more into the past few days than she had anticipated.

"Oh, right. Out where those horrible people used to give trail rides. How are the horses doing?"

Alana was relieved when Rosie asked Tegan the question, giving her a chance to taste her food. The heavenly smells had been hard to resist, even for the sake of polite conversation. She had three miniature corn tortillas on her plate, each with a different topping. She chose one that appeared to be covered with seasoned pulled pork and added a spoonful of pico de gallo from a little cup and a squeeze of fresh lime. She folded the tortilla in half and took a bite, enjoying all the flavors and textures clamoring for her attention. Heat and crunch from the pico de gallo, tender, cumin-scented pork, accented by the acid from the lime.

She looked up and saw Tegan and Rosie watching her, as if they'd said something and were waiting for her response. She shook her head. "Sorry, but I can't talk to you right now. This is the most delicious food I've had in a long time, and it deserves my full attention."

"Thank you," Rosie said with a pleased smile.

"Pause in between tacos," Tegan said. "I want Rosie to hear your box-of-rats story."

"You just want me to talk so you can eat," Alana said.

"Maybe." Tegan shrugged, but she didn't get much food since she and Rosie were soon laughing too hard to eat or drink.

When Alana had first told the story to Tegan, she'd thought it would sound wonderfully dramatic as Lace and the pups were pulled from the brink of death—or at least the threat of coyotes. Tegan had laughed then, too, so Alana had decided to embrace the humor in it. She could imagine the howls of disbelieving laughter she'd hear when she returned to a big-city hotel and shared the anecdote with coworkers.

As soon as she finished, she went back to her meal, selecting a chicken taco next.

"So how did the two of you go from meeting at the clinic with the puppies to working together today? Doesn't your work at the ranch keep you too busy to moonlight as a volunteer vet assistant?"

Rosie's voice and smile seemed friendly, but Alana wondered if she was interested in more than a friendship with Tegan and was trying to find out why Alana was here with her. Then again, Tegan hadn't said she and Rosie weren't already dating. Alana watched Tegan for a clue about how to respond, but Tegan seemed to be studying her for the same thing. Alana suddenly realized they were trying to protect each other. Tegan couldn't say anything about Alana's lessons or her need to get as much horse experience as possible without divulging her secret about how unqualified she was for her job. Alana was treading carefully because she didn't want to jeopardize whatever relationship Tegan had with Rosie— well, part of her brain didn't, while most of her body was voting to jeopardize the hell out of it.

Alana took a deep breath, taking a chance that Rosie was as kind as she seemed and wouldn't call Chip and tell on her. For Tegan's sake, she had to give Rosie some sort of explanation. "Tegan's been giving me riding lessons," she said. "She thought it would be a good experience for me to handle the Thoroughbreds today."

"You're giving her riding lessons."

"Yes," Tegan said, keeping her eyes on her plate as she finished her tamale.

Rosie turned to Alana again. "And you don't get enough time with horses even though you're in charge of, what, thirty of them at the ranch?"

"Only twenty-five," Alana said, which didn't sound helpful once it was out of her mouth. She had a feeling they were going to be at this for a long time, with Rosie slowly dissecting every suspicious element in the story, unless Alana came clean. Or sort of clean. "I didn't realize how hands-on this job would be when I applied. Tegan's helping me brush up on my skills, so I don't let Chip down."

"Well, she's an excellent rider, so you're in good hands."

Alana smiled, making some sort of vague noise of agreement. She didn't trust herself to say anything more in case Rosie was able to read on her face just how much of herself she wanted to put into Tegan's hands.

Rosie got up and stacked their empty plates. "I'll get us some dessert."

"Sorry about that," Tegan said as soon as they were alone again. "Your job and our riding lessons are your private business, and I didn't mean for you to have to talk about them. Rosie'd never tell Chip anything, though, so don't worry."

"I won't," Alana said with a shrug. She grinned at Tegan. "Besides, I've started to realize that Chip is fudging just as much as I am. He's as qualified to be a ranch manager as I am a trail guide."

Tegan laughed. "Well, at least you're both working hard to improve. And you're both stubborn enough to make it happen."

"We will." Alana stood up. "They're putting out another batch of tortillas, so I'm going to buy some to take home. Be right back."

Tegan watched Alana walk to the counter, feeling over-whelmed. She felt like a fumbling teenager around Alana at times, tripping over her own feet at the sight of her bending over to look in the pastry case, or nearly upending her Coke when Alana took a bite of her lunch and rolled her eyes in ecstasy. But moments later, she felt more at ease with Alana than she'd ever felt with a woman. It was like being on a seesaw, without any of the predictability.

She was thinking about how often Alana had made her laugh over the past few days, and she smiled happily at Rosie when she set down a plate of cookies and took a seat across from her.

"Oh, yum," Tegan said, taking a yellow concha and breaking off a piece.

"What the hell are you doing?" Rosie snapped.

Tegan paused with the bite of cookie halfway to her mouth. She lowered her hand, glancing toward the counter where Alana was still in line. "What? What's wrong?"

"What are you doing with her? Secret riding lessons? Really? And is this a date?"

Tegan stared at her. She'd never heard Rosie raise her voice, unless she was acting in a play, and she wasn't sure where the anger had come from. "What's going on, Rosie? Don't you like Alana?"

"Of course I do," Rosie said, sounding more like her normal self. She reached over and broke Tegan's cookie in half. "She's smart and nice to animals, plus she's got a great sense of humor. Not to mention her physical attributes. Very hot."

"Then why were you yelling at me?"

Rosie wiped her hands on a napkin. "You told me to."

Tegan rubbed her temple. "I doubt it."

"Remember when Fay left?"

"Yes."

"Remember coming to my house and moaning about it for hours? Well, maybe you don't remember that part. You drank all my Tecate. Anyway, you told me that if I ever saw you falling for another woman who wasn't born and bred and prepared to live forever in Yakima, I was supposed to slap you across the face and ask you what the hell you were doing. I can't slap you in front of customers, but feel free to come back after we close, and I'll do it then."

"It's not the same," Tegan said, squinting as she tried to clear up the fuzzy memory of going to see Rosie that night. "Alana and

I aren't dating. Plus, she's always been honest about her plans to leave once she's been here long enough to get a good reference and another job offer."

Rosie leaned across the table toward her. "So was Fay, hon. She never hid her ambition to move to Europe. Trouble was, you weren't honest with yourself. You always believed she'd decide to stay."

Tegan crossed her arms and sat back. She still wasn't sure why Rosie was bringing this up since she and Alana weren't romantically involved. She'd thought about it, yes. Fantasized about it? Yes. But they were nothing more than friends.

Rosie shook her head, as if reading Tegan's mind. "I've done my duty, like I promised you I would, and I won't say another word about it after this. Just make me a promise, too, that you'll keep your eyes open this time. Be friends, date, have a fling, whatever you want. Just be sure you don't lie to yourself about what it means."

Tegan stared out the window for a moment before giving Rosie a sharp nod. She was quiet while Alana returned to the table and chatted with Rosie, asking about the different cookies and sampling a taste of everything on the plate. Tegan watched her as she laughed at something Rosie said, their voices fading into the background as a realization came forward. She didn't have to fight against her attraction to Alana if she didn't want to. She could acknowledge it. Find out if Alana felt the same way. Maybe explore where it would lead them, as long as she didn't try to look too far ahead.

Maybe. Tegan leaned forward again, sliding back into the conversation.

CHAPTER TEN

Tegan listened to the healthy rhythms of the standard poodle's heart and respiration. Just as she moved her stethoscope away and was about to pull the tips out of her ears, he gave a loud woof.

"Ouch," she said, and he turned his head and gave her a sloppy lick across her nose.

"Oh, he's apologizing. How sweet," Amy, his owner said, ruffling his ears while Tegan got a paper towel and wiped her face. Her last patient had peed on her foot, so she wasn't going to complain about a little slobber.

"He seems healthy," she said, taking two syringes out of her lab coat pocket. "Do you have any concerns or questions, though?"

"No. He's been doing great."

The dog didn't even flinch as she gave him his injections and chatted with Amy about a local obedience trainer. She wished all her appointments were this easy.

"Those are cute puppies," Amy said, pointing to the photo Alana had tacked up at the beginning of the week. She helped Tegan lift her large fluffy dog off the table and walked over for a closer look.

"Aren't they? The mom seems to be a spaniel mix, and the pups will be ready for adoption in about four weeks." She gave Amy a brief explanation about how Alana had found the litter.

"We've been thinking about getting King a little brother or sister. Could we take the kids over to meet them sometime?"

"Of course," Tegan said, fishing one of the cards Alana had made on Chip's printer, with her number and a tiny picture of Lace on it. "If you're interested in adopting after you've met them, I'd suggest getting King and one of the puppies together for a supervised meeting, maybe in two or three weeks, when the pups are a little older. We could do it here, in a neutral place, and we can find out how well they get along."

Tegan said good-bye and gave the examination room a quick cleaning. After lunch at Rosamund's, when she'd scared the crap out of herself by even considering an affair with Alana, she had wondered whether she should avoid her altogether, running away from temptation and the guaranteed pain she would feel when Alana inevitably left. Her determination to protect herself hadn't lasted long, though. She had made a commitment to help Alana with her riding, so she continued giving her lessons during her lunch hour. She drew the line at invitations to lunch or to have Alana accompany her on calls.

But once Alana had come up with the idea to post the litter's photo in the clinic's waiting room and two exam rooms, Tegan had to live with a constant reminder of Alana. Every time she saw the picture or answered questions about the puppies, she had to think about Alana and the possibilities she presented. A possibility for pain, yes, but also for some wonderful months spent in her company and in her bed.

Tegan sighed, resting her hip against the table for a moment before moving on to her next patient, who was currently yowling in a cat carrier in the waiting room. She wasn't even sure if Alana would be open to the kind of relationship Tegan was sidling around, but never directly considering. She thought Alana seemed interested in her, too, given the small hints found in casual touches and playful teasing.

She sighed and looked at the photo again. She had to admit Alana had been smart to suggest putting the picture here, where clients had little else to do besides look at the walls while waiting for their appointment to start. Even without making them wait an extra few minutes—as Alana had suggested—the picture was working. Aside from Amy, Tegan had two other clients who had expressed interest in them. Once Lace's six were adopted, Tegan decided she'd continue to highlight animals from the local shelters. She wasn't sure why she hadn't thought of it before, especially since she would know exactly what kind of home her clients were offering. She had a bulletin board near the reception counter, but it was covered with flyers and too cluttered to negotiate in a short time. A single photo in here drew concentrated attention.

Tegan opened the door to the waiting room and called in the cat's owner. She cleaned and rebandaged the cut on her patient's leg, and then disinfected and bandaged the puncture wounds he left in her wrist. Yet another glamorous workday. She locked the front door after Dez left for lunch and went out to the barn to meet Alana.

Alana already had Charm tied to the fence and was grooming her when Tegan got outside. She'd come a long way in a little over a week, and she moved around the horses with a soft confidence in place of the stiff nervousness she had shown at first. Practicing with ten to twenty horses a day had given her an intensive introduction to the animals, practically squashing months of lessons into mere days. Still, she had an overwhelming amount to learn before she'd be ready to lead trail groups. Even though she hadn't brought it up yet, Tegan had been assuming she would accompany Alana with guests for a while. She hadn't taken a vacation for ages, so she could shuffle her clients around for a month or two and find the time. She'd pretend she was just along for the scenery—which wouldn't be a lie, since she'd be riding behind Alana. She'd let Alana be in charge, but she'd be there in case one of her dreaded *ifs* happened.

Alana looked up at her and gave her one of those smiles that left Tegan's common sense in tattered ruins.

She stayed on the other side of the fence from Alana, as if the narrow boards could protect her heart. "Hey, there. I have another client who might call you about coming to see the puppies. Her name is Amy, and she and her partner and their kids adopted a poodle last year. He's a lot bigger than they'll be, but he's a gentle giant."

Alana paused with her brush in midstroke. "Are they nice?"

"I wouldn't send them your way if they weren't."

"I know. It's just happening so fast, and Chip is going to be really disappointed when they're all adopted."

Tegan rested her chin on her arms and smiled. She had a feeling Alana was the one who was going to find it harder to let go of the little pups than she had anticipated. "Do you think he'll want one?"

"I wouldn't be surprised if he decided to take one, but I don't want to take any chances." Alana stepped closer and lowered her voice, as if she didn't want anyone to overhear her devious plan. "I'm trying to figure out which one he likes the most, and then I'll give it to him as a present. He can't say no to a puppy with a sweet little bow around its neck."

"Just in case you're going to try the same trick on other people, I should warn you that I'm not going to open any box from you, especially if it's perforated with air holes, until they're all adopted."

"Please," Alana said with a dismissive wave. "I know where you've stashed the spare key to the clinic. Don't be surprised if you show up one morning and more of your kennels are occupied than there were the night before."

Tegan laughed uneasily. She was sure Alana was joking, but she decided to move the key, just in case. As soon as Alana had saddled Charm, she came into the arena with her.

"I'd like to have you try to canter today, even though it's not a gait you'll use on your trail rides. You need to feel what the movement is like, so you won't panic if a horse you're riding breaks into a canter from a trot."

"A canter? Are you kidding?" Alana slumped in the saddle with an exaggerated sigh. "I can barely get Charm to trot."

"She thinks if she waits you out, you'll get tired of asking and give up. You just have to be more determined to move than she is to stand still."

"My mind is stubborn enough, but my body is on her side. I'm so sore I can barely get in and out of my truck."

"You need a massage," Tegan said without thinking, mesmerized by the way Alana was rubbing her thigh.

Alana's hand stilled, and she looked at Tegan with a slow smile curving her lips. "Are you offering?"

Tegan stalled, searching for something to say that would sound witty or suggestive, or even that would change the subject entirely, but her mind was empty of everything but the truth. "I'm thinking about it," she said.

Alana's smile opened into a laugh. "Good. Let me know what you decide."

Tegan tried to forget the conversation, at least until the lesson was over and she'd have time to consider every angle of it. While Alana was riding, however, she needed to be focused on keeping her safe and teaching her as much as possible. Still, Tegan spent a significant part of the hour contemplating which muscles she would most like to massage.

They managed to get through the lesson without incident. Charm's canter wasn't much faster or bouncier than her walk and jog, so Alana didn't have any trouble staying balanced in the saddle. Her face was flushed by the time she managed to convince Charm to move, though.

"She didn't even get sweaty," Alana complained as she removed the saddle pad and revealed Charm's pristine coat underneath. "To look at us, you'd think I was the one carrying her around."

"She'd probably prefer…"

Tegan didn't finish the sentence because she saw an ancient and bright blue Chrysler parking next to Alana's truck.

"Your next client?" Alana asked.

"No, my grandparents." Tegan watched them get out of the car with a familiar sense of foreboding. She usually saw them on the weekends, but they rarely came to the clinic during the week, unless Tegan's mother was somehow involved. Her suspicions were confirmed when her grandmother got some containers of food out of the back seat.

"Hello, Tegan dear," her grandmother said, giving her a one-armed but tight hug. "I brought you some food. Peach pie and tater tot casserole."

"Thanks, Gran," Tegan said, taking the containers from her and trying to smile. She glanced at Alana, hoping she would take Charm and go into the barn, leaving her to deal with this in private. Of course, she didn't but walked over to join them instead.

"Alana, these are my grandparents, Maisie and Howard. This is Alana. I was just giving her a riding lesson."

"You're teaching lessons now?" Maisie asked Tegan with a frown after they had all greeted each other.

"Just the one."

Her grandparents looked at her with nearly identical expressions of concern. "I didn't realize you were going through a rough patch. Howard, write her a check."

"Sure thing. How much do you need, pumpkin?"

Tegan winced, not making eye contact with Alana. Maybe she somehow had missed the pet name. A sound of quickly muffled laughter behind her let her know Alana had most definitely heard. Great.

"Gramps, please put your checkbook away. The clinic is doing well, so don't worry. Alana is a friend. She wanted to learn to ride, so I've been helping her."

Her grandfather finished writing and tore out the check, sliding it in between the two Tupperware containers. "Well, here's twenty for you, anyway. You can use it for groceries."

"Thank you," Tegan said, knowing from experience not to bother arguing. She was just going to redeposit the money into their account anyway. "So, is she staying with you again?" she asked, referring to her mother without identifying her as such.

Maisie put her arm through Howard's, probably seeking moral support because she hated talking to Tegan about her mom. "She's coming over on Saturday and she wants to see you. I told her I didn't think you'd want to, but I promised I'd try."

"We can have lunch. Roast chicken," Howard said.

"Yes." Maisie beamed at him as if he'd come up with the perfect way to make Tegan feel better. "And ice cream."

Tegan stood in silence, feeling the old anger washing through her yet again, the way it did every time her mother returned. She always wanted something from Tegan and her grandparents, whether it was their presence and attention, a place to stay until she felt like leaving, or cash. Usually all three. Tegan hated being manipulated, but she would go to lunch for her grandparents' sakes.

"Goodness, look at the time," Alana said, even though there wasn't a clock in sight. "I need to make an appointment with Dez for the pups' next visit before I get back to work. It was lovely meeting you both. Tegan, thank you for the lesson. Should I put those containers in the break room fridge for you?" She spoke in rapid-fire sentences, as if she'd just realized how uncomfortable Tegan was and wanted to get away as quickly as possible.

"Thank you," Tegan said, handing her the food and giving her hand a quick squeeze of gratitude. "I'll see you tomorrow."

"She's pretty," Maisie said before Alana had gotten very far away. "Are you dating her? Why don't you bring her over for dinner some weekend?"

Tegan groaned. She could only handle one uncomfortable conversation at a time. "I'll come Saturday, but let's not make it a special occasion. I can go through a drive-through on the way and bring burgers or something."

"It won't be any trouble. Besides, you know we'd want to make it nice for you, not because she'll be there."

"I know," Tegan said. "I appreciate it."

She walked them back to their car, thanking them for the food and promising again to be there on Saturday. Once they had driven away, she put Charm in her stall and went through the back door of the clinic and into the waiting room. There she found Dez and Alana standing on either side of the reception counter, eating her peach pie directly out of the tin with plastic forks.

"Hey, pumpkin," they said in unison when she walked in.

Tegan ignored what they said, concentrating instead on what they were doing. "I don't remember saying you could eat my food."

"You've seen my paychecks," Dez said, in between bites. "I think throwing in a dessert now and then is the least you can do."

"This is amazing," Alana added. "How does she make the peaches taste like this?"

"Taste like what?"

"I don't know. Extra peachy."

Tegan figured she was used to canned ones, or the supermarket produce that was picked well before it was ripe. Neither of which was anything like the real thing, fresh and warm and juicy, right from the tree. Tegan pictured feeding her one when they came in season, and she filed the image away for later. "She buys them when they're in season and cans them herself. Go ahead and take the rest home with you, if you want. I'll probably get another one this weekend."

"Hey!" Dez protested when Alana picked up the pie tin and headed for the door.

"Don't complain. There's casserole in the fridge," Alana told her. She turned to Tegan. "Walk me out?"

Tegan held the door for her, and they headed across the parking lot. Alana put the pie on the front seat but didn't get right in the truck.

"I told her about the pet name," she said, wiping her hand across the top of the dusty rearview mirror. "But I didn't mention anything else you talked about. I didn't want you to worry I did."

Tegan took Alana's hand and gently rubbed the smudge of dirt off her finger. "Thank you," she said. She hesitated, relieved because Alana wasn't asking prying questions, but rather allowing her to share if she chose to. "It's my mother. She's coming for lunch on Saturday, or maybe to stay with them longer. I never know."

Alana was quiet for a moment, turning her hand so it was loosely clasping Tegan's. "They seem to love you very much."

Tegan nodded. "They raised me. My dad…I remember how angry he would get. Smashing plates, screaming at my mom. When it got real bad, she'd take me and we'd show up at my grandparents' house in the middle of the night. She'd cry and say she was leaving him for good, and we'd spend a week or two at their farm."

Tegan laced her fingers through Alana's and rested against the truck so their shoulders and arms were pressed together. "It was such a peaceful place. So quiet. Gran would bake cakes and pies for me, and I'd spend hours wandering through the woods and playing with their animals. And then my father would come. Cry, apologize, say it would never happen again. You know the pattern. And Mom would pack our things and we'd go back."

Alana inhaled slowly, trying to calm her own anger while she listened to Tegan talk. She dropped her head to one side until it rested on Tegan's shoulder.

"It would happen again, of course. I was five the third time she was packing our bags after he'd come with flowers and tears. Gramps came into the room and picked me up. He told her she was an adult and she could make the decision to go back to an abusive man if she wanted, but he and Gran weren't letting me go."

"She left you?"

"She chose him."

Alana shook her head, her cheek brushing against Tegan's shirt, wishing she could deny what Tegan was saying. She couldn't imagine what conflicting emotions the little girl must have been feeling. Abandoned, as her mother walked away from her, but also relieved to stay on the farm.

"Have you seen her since?"

Tegan's laugh was harsh and humorless. "Plenty of times. The pattern didn't change just because my thread was pulled out of it. For the first few years, I'd try so hard to take care of her when she'd come running back to us. I thought if I could make her feel as happy with my grandparents as I was, then she'd want to stay forever. By the time I was twelve or so, I stopped making much of an effort. Now, I'd be happy not seeing her at all, but she knows I'll come over when she asks me to because I don't want my grandparents caught in the middle."

"I'm sorry," Alana said. The words were useless because they couldn't change the past or make the present any easier, but Alana hoped Tegan could sense how much she cared.

Tegan squeezed her hand and rested her head against Alana's for a moment before she straightened up and stepped away.

"I need something to look forward to on Sunday. How about a trail ride? We can take a couple of your horses and I'll show you some of the trails you'll be using."

"I'd love to," Alana said, feeling her mood brighten at the thought of an afternoon of solitude with Tegan and the horses. Maybe they could discuss the massage Tegan had so enticingly mentioned. "I've ridden every day, but I haven't been out of the corral yet."

"Great. I'll see you then."

Alana got in her truck and started the engine, lowering the window and calling out to Tegan who had just reached the porch. "Hey, Tegan. If your grandmother feels like baking a chocolate cake this weekend, bring it along."

Chapter Eleven

"Oh, Alana, I thought I heard you come in," Chip said, walking into the reception area with a jar of dog treats in his hands and craning his neck to look behind her into her office, as if she was hiding the puppies from him.

"They're at home today," she said, answering his unspoken question. "I only came in to make a few calls, but I'm heading back to the house to check on them. It's my day off, remember?"

"Of course," he said. "Why are you here, again? Isn't Marcus feeding the horses?"

Alana's first stop when she had arrived an hour ago was the corrals to make sure the barn chores had been done. She probably should make an appointment for a full body scan to find out what strange, horse-smelling, puppy-sitting alien had taken over her body. On a normal early morning in Philadelphia, her first stop would have been the hotel's spa for a free manicure.

"The horses are fine. I called the pool service this morning, and someone will be here Monday to check the pump and filter, and then fill the pool. I didn't realize I needed to give them the serial number from the pump, so I came in to get it."

"You're amazing, Alana. Thank you."

He said the exact same words to her at least once a day, usually after she had taken care of some aspect of his job he either had forgotten about or was trying to avoid. In this case, he had probably thought he could just stick a hose in the pool the morning the guests were due to arrive. "No problem," she said, before tackling the next item on her list. She tried a tactful approach first. "So the grand opening is getting closer. Exciting, isn't it?"

"Yeah. I mean, sure is!" He looked more concerned at the prospect of having guests than he ever had at the possibility of never actually opening the ranch.

"We have guests booked?"

He nodded. "Five rooms starting the Thursday before, and ten over the weekend."

"That's a good start. Have you decided what to do for the grand opening weekend? Any activities?"

He frowned, spinning the jar of treats. "Well, we'll have trail rides. I wanted to lead some nature hikes, and maybe some more challenging climbs for the more experienced guests. There are some great walking trails along the Naches. I might not be able to get away from the desk, though, since I'm sure problems will come up on our first weekend." He sighed, obviously already in dread about dealing with those inevitable issues. "And I was going to get a Grand Opening sign made and hang it over the door."

"All excellent ideas. Have you considered maybe doing something to involve the community? Some sort of party?"

"No."

Alana made a conscious effort to unclench her hands and relax her hold on the slim folder she was carrying. The circuitous approach was clearly not working, so she opted for a more direct one. She didn't want to stand here all day having this conversation.

"I was thinking of something casual, like a barbecue on Saturday. We could have some lawn games in the back and lead kids around the corral on some of the quieter horses."

He smiled. "That sounds like fun. Do you think it would be better to just invite the guests who are staying? That sounds like a cheaper option."

"Cheaper, but less visible. Look, catering only to tourists limits the potential of this ranch. You want local people to think of

High Ridge when they're planning anniversary weekend getaways or hosting friends from out of town. Locals might want to come for the trail rides, or to go white-water rafting with a group instead of going on their own. They'll generate income without the overhead that guests incur, like housekeeping, laundry, and staff hours." She handed him the folder. "I hope you don't mind, but I called around and got a few quotes for food, tables, and such. Look through this, and if it sounds like a good idea to you, I can finalize the arrangements."

He took the folder and flipped through the pages. "You've put a lot of effort into this. You really think it'll help the ranch?"

"I believe so. I wouldn't try to convince you to spend more money if I didn't think it would pay off in the long run."

"Okay. Let's go for it."

She nodded. "I'll make the bookings tomorrow. Remember they're coming to inspect the kitchen this afternoon. Everything seems to be in order, but call me if you have any questions."

"I don't know what I'd do without you," he said, but then he laughed. "Well, I know exactly what I'd do. Go bankrupt."

She smiled and waved off his joke, even though she thought he might be right. She had come here determined not to get involved, but that plan had gone out the window and she didn't care. He hated the tasks a manager had to perform, and she thrived on them. Not like her parents. She wasn't going to do Chip's job for him forever. It just was nice to feel competent and capable for parts of her day, as opposed to feeling overwhelmed and inept during the horse-related parts. Besides, she needed something to take her mind off Tegan and the annoyance of having to wait until Sunday for more than an hour with her.

"Speaking of going bankrupt," she said, holding up the personal check he had left sitting on top of her desk. "You need to open a business account. And incorporate, maybe. I don't know enough about that to help, but you have to separate your personal accounts from the ranch somehow."

"I'll look into it," he promised, which meant she'd be making more calls this week. He handed her a dog treat. "For Lace. And say hi to the puppies for me."

"Any one puppy in particular?"

"Nope. All of them."

"All of them it is." She was going to need six festive bows.

She drove back to the house and gave Lace her treat before letting her out the back door and in again. She went into the upstairs guest room she had been using as an office and picked up a stack of photos of the litter. Time to do some door-to-door puppy marketing.

She had gotten in the habit of leaving the dogs' bedroom door open to allow Lace freedom to go to the back door when she needed. The puppies had been furry little lumps until earlier this week, pulling themselves a few inches along the floor at a time before collapsing and taking a nap. With a surprising swiftness, they had become more mobile almost overnight and had been exploring every corner of their bedroom. Now they seemed ready to branch out, and when she came downstairs, she found them in the living room, making unsuccessful attempts to scale the sofa and reach their mother. Lace was curled in a tight ball in the far corner of the couch, watching Alana with wide eyes, as if in anticipation of getting in trouble.

Alana sat on the other end of the sofa and watched the puppies jump at the couch, missing the seat by about six inches and falling backward again and again, toppling harmlessly onto the thick shag. They stubbornly refused to give up, and Alana ruefully guessed they'd be clambering up like little monkeys before the week was out. She had been feeling quite smug about her puppy handling skills, thinking she had managed to produce the puppy equivalents of Charm. She'd read articles and blogs about people complaining that their puppies chewed on everything and got into everything, all the while thinking to herself: *You must be doing something wrong—mine sleep all day.*

She reached over and gave Lace a reassuring pat on her head. The pups had gotten quite demanding, jumping on her and biting her ears with their sharp new teeth, and she probably needed more alone time than she got during her quick forays into the yard. Alana slid off the couch and onto the floor, stretching her legs out in front of her. The pups immediately gave up on their mother and swarmed her instead.

Alana did her best to remain unaffected. She wasn't a dog person. She kept repeating that to herself, but it didn't help her remain aloof as the pups chewed on her shoelaces and got into little snarl fights with each other on her lap. She picked up the female runt of the litter—disentangling her from the bigger sister who had been sitting on her head—and cradled the puppy against her neck. This one was nearly identical to Lace, only in miniaturized version, and Alana had been calling her Chantilly.

Not out loud, of course. When she spoke about them to Tegan or Chip, she referred to them by generic group names. The puppies, the litter. At night, when no one else was around, Alana called them by the names she had given. They'd probably be changed once the dogs went to their new owners, of course, but Alana allowed herself this small indulgence since this was the one and only time she'd ever have a pet, unless she decided to have a cat or two around when she retired. Dogs couldn't travel with her and weren't allowed in hotel rooms. If she wanted puppies in her life, she'd either have to change careers or be satisfied going to pet stores now and again and looking at the dogs. Neither was likely to happen.

"Ouch," Alana said when Chantilly bit her earlobe, nearly giving her an ear piercing with her needle-like teeth. She set her back with her littermates and got up, calling for Lace to come with her. She jumped obediently off the couch and followed Alana into her room, with the pups trailing after her. Alana stepped out and closed the door. From now on, unless she was in the house and could monitor explorations, the dog bedroom door would need to be firmly shut.

"Time to find new homes for you," she said, with absolutely no pangs of sadness. Well, not really sharp ones.

She got in her truck and drove to the first house along the road from hers. She was accustomed to thinking of neighbors as the people who lived immediately beside, above, or under her. Close enough to hear through the thin walls. The other houses in Alana's new neighborhood might not even be in the same zip code for all she knew.

Alana knocked on the door. The house looked similar to hers but was slate blue and in need of a paint job. The front yard seemed nice enough, and a privacy fence hid the back from view. An older woman opened the door and peered out at her. Alana could see the chain firmly in place.

"Hi. I'm Alana, from next door." She waved in the general direction of her house. "I've come by to see if you're interested in adopting a puppy."

The woman shut the door, and then reopened it wider, without the chain. "You're living in the old Harrison place?"

"Sure," Alana said. She had no idea, but she wanted to sound agreeable.

"What did you say you're selling? Kittens?"

"Puppies. And they're free, complete with vaccinations and a coupon for getting them spayed or neutered." Thanks to Tegan.

"Oh, I don't want a puppy. Are you sure you don't have kittens?"

Alana was getting exasperated and she hadn't even been at the first house of several on her road for five minutes. She was about to say no and leave, but she hesitated. Who knew what might move into the recently vacated nursery under her porch? She might as well keep her options open. "Not right now. If I find any, would you like one?"

"No, I don't want a kitten. Would you like to come in for a cup of tea?"

She held the door open wider, and Alana got a glimpse of a living room laid out like hers, with similarly outdated furnishings.

"Maybe another time. I need to take flyers to a few more houses today. Would you like one, in case you change your mind?"

"All right."

Alana handed her the photo of the litter, while engaging in a swift internal debate. She really didn't have time for tea. Still, it wasn't as if the puppies needed to be adopted out today, since they couldn't leave Lace yet. The woman's crestfallen expression when Alana had declined her invitation was enough to sway her decision.

"Actually, a cup of tea would be nice. Are you sure you don't mind?"

"Not at all. Please, come in."

An hour later, Alana managed to extricate herself from the house. She had sipped a rather nice oolong and listened to Gladys talk about her family, admiring photos as they were brought to her from various surfaces around the room. A deceased husband whose face had been creased with smile lines—just like she imagined Chip's would be when he was in his eighties. A son in nearby Ellensburg and a daughter in the Tri-Cities area, both of whom seemed to need a stern lecture about visiting their mother more often. The house was big and lonely and filled with reminders of the past instead of signs of the present. It could use a kitten or two to help circulate the stale air of memories. Alana tried to imagine her vast house if the puppies hadn't joined her in it. It would have a completely different atmosphere, and Alana probably would have felt lonely enough to invite strangers in for tea. Her house wouldn't have been crammed with mementos but would have been bare of everything but the basic necessities of survival.

Alana drove away after promising to visit again. The next house on her route was an unadorned postwar ranch style home. It was painted an unobtrusive olive green, but the front door was a garish purple. A child's plastic tricycle was parked near the porch, and Alana wondered if its owner had been responsible for picking the door's color.

The girl who answered the door was the most likely suspect. Alana had little experience with children and had trouble guessing ages, but this one looked like she wasn't quite old enough for school yet.

"I don't know you," she stated, with a fierce expression on her face. She looked ready to yell *Stranger danger!* and whip out a can of pepper spray, so Alana hurried to identify herself.

"My name is Alana, and I live in the old Harrison place, just up the road." The Yakima version of street cred. "May I speak to an adult?"

The girl slammed the door, and Alana stood on the top step of the narrow porch wondering if she was going to return with a parent, or if she was dialing 911. She was about to slink back to her truck when the door was opened again by a woman about Alana's age with a blanket-wrapped baby in her arms.

"Can I help you?"

Alana struggled for a moment with a question of ethics. She could see the young girl making a poor attempt to hide behind her mother and still watching Alana with suspicion. If Alana whipped out the adorable puppy photo and said she was giving them away, then the girl might add her voice to Alana's in an attempt to get one. Two against one. Three, if the baby was old enough to know what a dog was. The mother looked as exhausted as Lace had today, though, and Alana didn't think she needed to add another responsibility to her list.

"I'm canvassing the neighborhood because I found some P-U-P-P-I-E-S under my porch and I'm looking for homes. You look like you have your hands full, though, so I won't bother you."

"I can spell," the little girl said, stepping out from behind her mother and glaring at Alana.

"Of course you can, Michelle," the woman said, shaking her head at Alana and mouthing *No, she can't.* "I'm Jennifer, by the way. Come on in and have a cup of coffee."

"Oh, well, okay." Alana was going to be too caffeinated to sleep. It would take her weeks to get the puppies adopted if she had to stop for hot beverages each time she knocked on a door.

She sat on a stool at the kitchen counter and looked around while Jennifer poured the coffee. The house was clean but cluttered with Michelle's toys and the baby's paraphernalia. The puppies would love this place. They'd destroy it, of course, but they would love it.

Jennifer put two mugs on the counter, along with a sugar bowl and a carton of whole milk. Alana added a little of both to her cup.

Jennifer had her coffee black, inhaling deeply before she took her first sip. "I stopped breastfeeding last week, so I can have coffee again. I missed it."

"Mommy drinks a lot of coffee," Michelle said, with heavy stress on *a lot*.

"No, I don't, Michelle," Jennifer said, before mouthing *Yes, I do* at Alana. Alana wondered if all conversations were the same in this house, with a combination of spelling and mime revealing the hidden meaning behind the spoken words.

Jennifer propped her chin on her palm. "Tell me some adult things," she said.

"Um…what kind of adult things?" Alana asked, confused by the demand.

"Anything. I decided to be a stay-at-home mom until Brandon and Michelle are both in school, but I got to work at a local tax firm last month." She sighed, as if reminiscing about a fabulous vacation to Fiji. "It was wonderful. People talking to me about 1089s and charitable donations. Interest rates and rollover IRAs. Adult things. I've been going through withdrawal since April fifteenth."

"Oh, those kinds of adult things. Okay, here goes." Alana took a deep breath, fortifying herself before she spoke. "I recently lost my job in Philadelphia because I sent the Chief of Police into a bachelorette party as the stripper. I got a job leading trail rides, but I've never been on a horse before coming here, so I'm taking lessons and trying to cram years' worth of practice into one month. When I got to my new house, I thought I had rats under the porch, but they turned out to be you-know-whats, so I'm trying to find homes for them." *And I'm wildly attracted to my riding teacher, and I think...I hope she feels the same way because I want to have sex with her this weekend.*

Alana kept the last part to herself. Adult fantasy, rather than adult reality.

Jennifer was laughing at Alana's recitation. "This is exactly what I need," she said. "I have a lot of questions, but the most pressing ones are about the bachelorette party. Just let me get Michelle occupied in her room with some crayons, and then I want to hear the unabridged version of the story."

By the time Alana left, it was getting late and she gave up the project for the day. She was tempted to try one more house because it was close to dinnertime, and the next residents might offer her a meal instead of coffee or tea, but she went home instead. Home to puppies and egg salad sandwiches, and to an entire evening spent contemplating the fantasy she'd concocted around Tegan and their trail ride.

Chapter Twelve

On Sunday, Alana arrived early, only to find Tegan waiting for her in the parking lot and talking to Chip. She got out of the truck and set Lace on the ground before hauling out the crate. It had been the perfect size for one quiet dog and six tiny, sleepy puppies, but now the boisterous youngsters took up all the space inside it. Alana had put a dog bed on the back seat for Lace, and she got some peace and quiet during her trips to and from the ranch. Lace ran over to Chip and Tegan, showing more enthusiasm for life than Alana had seen in her before.

"Hi, Alana," Tegan said, taking the crate from her. "I was just telling Chip that I was going to show you some of the trails today."

"I wish I could tag along," he said, taking the baby gate from Alana. He turned to Tegan. "I've been meaning to give her the grand tour of the ranch, but we haven't been able to find a time when both of us could spare an hour. I appreciate you taking up the slack for me."

Alana had made certain their schedules never worked out. She felt more confident in her riding, thanks to Tegan, but she doubted she would be able to pass herself off as an expert in front of Chip. Yet. She was getting better every day, and once she knew what to expect on the trails, she'd start putting in some serious mileage.

"I'm happy to do it," Tegan said, answering Chip but smiling at Alana as they made their way to the lodge's entrance. "I haven't ridden outside the arena for weeks now."

Once inside, Alana secured the baby gate to Chip's office door. She had bought it the day before, after coming out of the kitchen to find the puppies partway up the staircase, tumbling down two steps for every one they climbed. She had only been out of the room for a couple minutes, just long enough to slap together a peanut butter and jelly sandwich, but it had been plenty of time for them to get into trouble. Lace had sat in her corner of the couch, watching them with a serious lack of parental concern, so Alana had hurried to the store for something to contain the adventurous pups. She hadn't seen the need to buy two gates when she would only need them for another few weeks, so she had decided to haul this one back and forth, keeping it at the bottom of her staircase when it was in her house.

She set down her heavy tote bag that was full of binders for the ranch and the horses, as well as Tegan's riding books. She had managed to travel all the way across the country with nothing but a carry-on suitcase. Now she couldn't start the five-minute trip from her house to the ranch until she had made three trips out to the truck with armloads of stuff.

Tegan and Chip unloaded the puppies, taking far longer to do the task than necessary. They carefully placed them into the wading pool, which was a joke as far as Alana was concerned because the first ones were out of it and tearing across the office before the sixth one had been set down. Alana was still attempting to determine which puppy Chip liked best, but he didn't seem to have a clear favorite.

"Are you ready yet?" she finally asked, after watching them vie for the pups' attention without showing any signs of stopping. "It's going to be dark soon."

"It's ten in the morning, so we have plenty of time," Tegan said, but she got up and climbed over the gate. "I don't know how you can stay way over here and watch them without wanting to play."

"We played all morning," Alana said. "The pups played at tearing the liner off the bottom of the couch and pulling the stuffing out, wad by wad. I played at trying to repair the damage."

Tegan laughed, looking wholly unsympathetic. "Did you get it fixed?"

"No. I just took some of the extra linens out of the closet and stuffed them under the couch, filling the gap between it and the floor." She paused, thinking about how peaceful the morning had seemed in the moments before she realized what the puppies were doing. "I should have known they were up to something since I was able to read more than one paragraph in my book without being interrupted."

"They're toddlers. This is their way of learning about the world around them. By the way, Lace looks great. She's putting on a little weight."

Alana left her tote in her office and led them out the back door, toward the corrals. "She's eating well, but the little ones have fierce appetites, so I think it's hard for her to keep up."

"We're aiming for just above a break-even point right now, so she's gaining a little weight and not sacrificing her own nutrition for them. You seem to be keeping her where she needs to be. She'll make faster progress once the puppies are nursing less, and especially after they're weaned."

Alana shut the corral gate behind them and gestured toward the paddocks. "Pick a horse, any horse," she said. "I thought I'd ride Blaze."

Tegan shook her head. "You're the leader. You can't be the one riding the most bombproof horse you have. Try Fitz today, since I'll be here to help you with him."

Alana haltered the large bay gelding and brought him into the corral. He had been easy for her to handle and ride, but she hadn't ventured beyond the small fenced enclosure. Tegan had chosen Banjo. At least, Alana was pretty sure it was Banjo. He was one of the two geldings she couldn't tell apart.

They groomed the horses in silence, serenaded by chirping birds and the muffled hammering sounds coming from the part of the ranch that was still unfinished. Alana wanted to ask Tegan about yesterday's lunch, but she gave her space instead. Later, maybe, once a ride in the sunshine and open spaces of the ranch eased the worry lines from her forehead and put some color back in her pale cheeks.

Once they had saddled the horses, Alana led Fitz over to the mounting block.

"Hey," said Tegan. "What are you doing?"

It must be a trick question, since the answer seemed obvious. Alana double-checked her cinch and scanned the rest of her tack. The horse was clean, and everything was in place.

"I'm getting on the horse. Why, is there some weird pre-trail ride ritual I'm not aware of?"

"Don't use the block. Mount from the ground." As if to illustrate her point, Tegan vaulted effortlessly onto Banjo's back, which wasn't saying much since he was one of the shortest horses in the string.

"Why make it harder than it has to be?" Alana asked. She had been using the block every day since she figured out what it was for.

"If something happens on the trail, and you need to dismount, how are you going to get back on? Or are you planning to have one of the horses haul the block like a sleigh on every ride, just in case you need it?"

"I can get on from the ground, I just prefer not to." Alana thought her logic was sound, but Tegan didn't look impressed, so she hauled herself—with considerable effort—onto Fitz's back. Her graceless mount didn't help her case much.

"That was pretty," Tegan said.

Alana ignored her and headed toward the gate leading to the trails, which was closed. She sighed and started to dismount to open it.

"Uh-uh." Tegan stopped her. "Open it from his back. You'll come across gates during your rides, and you don't want to dismount each time. Especially when it takes you five minutes and three tries to get on again."

Tegan coached her through the frustrating process of shifting Fitz close enough to the gate for her to unlatch it, and then maneuvering him through it without letting go and having it swing shut again. She finally managed to open it, hold it for Tegan to walk through, and then close it again. Unfortunately, she was on the wrong side.

Tegan watched her with a grin, obviously finding the spectacle amusing. Alana finally got herself on the correct side of the latched gate and came up beside her.

"These rides can't be fun enough to make them worth all this trouble," she said. "We've been out here an hour, and we're only ten feet from the corral."

"You'll get more efficient," Tegan assured her. "Now, there are three main trails. The one to the right makes a short loop around the hill over there. It only takes about twenty minutes to walk and the terrain is flat, so it's a good one for beginners. The one we're taking is an hour ride. There's another that branches off a little way up this main trail. It's a beautiful ride and about the same length as this one, but it has some steep areas, and the footing is tricky in places. I can take you on it when you're feeling more comfortable with these ones, but it's not something I'd recommend for any but advanced riders."

Tegan started walking along the main trail. Alana looked longingly at the shorter version, before asking Fitz to follow Tegan. She wouldn't mind avoiding the steeper ride altogether, since she doubted Tegan had any useful advice to follow the phrase *If your horse falls off a cliff...*

"You should be in the lead," Tegan said, coming to a halt and letting Alana pass. "The ground is soft from here to the next curve, so we can trot if you want. Just don't let him get too fast. The horses will move out more in open spaces than in the corral."

Alana stepped into the lead for the first time. It was only Tegan behind her, of course, but she let herself feel proud in this moment. She had worked harder to prepare for this job than for anything else she had ever done, and she—

"Are we going to trot or not?" Tegan called out, interrupting Alana's celebratory internal monologue.

"Stop being a back seat driver," Alana said, giving Fitz a strong jab with her heels. He flung himself forward into a horrible, bouncing trot. She lurched forward, then smacked back into the saddle before she managed to pull him back to a walk.

"What the hell was that?" she asked, turning him around to face Tegan, who was, of course, slumped over in her saddle, laughing. "You seem to spend most of my lessons in hysterics. It's not good for my ego."

Tegan wiped her eyes with the back of her hand, still giggling sporadically. "Sorry. You looked like a kernel of popcorn."

Alana rolled her eyes. "Very nice. Seriously, is there something wrong with him?"

"He was trotting. I did warn you it'd be different out here than in the corral."

"I didn't realize *move out more* meant *rattle the brain right out of your skull*. I'm going to be sore tomorrow." Alana reached back and rubbed her seat, trying to ease the sting from hitting the saddle.

"Need help with that?" Tegan asked.

"I might take you up on that massage later," Alana said, noncommittally. She still hadn't figured out if Tegan's flirting meant as much as Alana wanted. She didn't think Tegan would be the type to tease without follow-through, though.

"I hope you do. Come on, let's finish the ride. I'll show you how to post to the trot to make it more comfortable. Try to mimic what I'm doing." Tegan set off down the trail at a slow trot. Alana gave Fitz a tentative squeeze with her legs and he followed. She would have been distracted by Tegan and the confident, rhythmic way she rode a horse, but most of Alana's energy was focused on not falling off. Once she got the hang of posting, she started to enjoy the excitement of Fitz's trot. He covered more ground with one step than Charm did with twenty.

By the time Tegan brought Banjo back to a walk, she felt like most of the residue from the day before had been washed out of her. She reached out and broke a small branch off a juniper growing alongside the trail, inhaling the sweet resin scent of it as she rode. A light breeze, growing stronger as they descended toward the river, balanced the heat from the sun. No sounds of civilization reached this far, where only the muted drone of the Naches and the occasional *scree* from a hawk broke the stillness. Add the horse moving cheerfully underneath her, and this would normally have been Tegan's idea of a perfect day.

Now it was even better, because Alana was here. She was a new element in Tegan's happy-place scenario, and she made everything else richer because she was here.

Their companionable silence was punctuated every once in a while by Tegan's comments about how to balance when riding down a hill or how to stop horses from sneaking bites of grass during a ride. As much as she could, however, she tried to give Alana enough time to simply enjoy the ride without it being a constant lesson. She didn't try to fool herself into thinking Alana would become a nature convert and would learn to love flaky red basalt and stunted sage as much as she did, but she was sure Alana was appreciating Yakima's unusual beauty more than she had when she first arrived.

Once they had descended into the ravine, she steered Banjo onto a narrow side trail that led to a clearing on the edge of the river. She dismounted, leading the gelding across the slippery oval rocks and to a place where the water gathered in a calm pool before tumbling over some large boulders and disappearing around a bend. She took off her helmet to let the wind cool her while Banjo took a long drink. Alana joined her there with Fitz.

"I wish I'd had more time to teach you about birds and plants so you could identify them for your riders, but we have too many more important topics to cover."

"It's all right," Alana said. "Every so often I'll point behind the group and say, Look, a red-tailed hawk! Oh, darn, you missed it."

Tegan laughed, but it dwindled into a sigh. "Thank you for coming on a ride with me today. It really did make yesterday easier since I was looking forward to being out here. To being with you."

"Me, too." Alana bumped Tegan with her shoulder and didn't move away, staying in contact with her. "Was everything okay yesterday?"

Tegan shrugged. "The usual. I was stiff and silent. My grand-parents pretended to be cheerful and normal, like we were a happy family that got together for lunch every week. Of course, if you're trying to act like everything's normal, it seems more abnormal than ever."

"What about your mother?"

"She thrives on these types of situations. She gets to be the center of attention, plus she's made all of us change our plans and sit through an uncomfortable meal just to accommodate her. The food was good, though."

"I'll bet," Alana said with a soft laugh. "I ate half of that pie for breakfast the next day."

Tegan was tempted to follow the subject of food, avoiding talking about her mother and focusing instead on the dishes her grandparents had served. She didn't, though. She needed to confront what she had gone through head-on.

"I've been thinking about the ways I've contributed to the situation between me and my mom," she started.

"It's not your—"

Tegan put her hand on Alana's arm to stop her, even though she liked the way Alana leaped to her defense. She turned so they were facing each other. "I know the choices she made and the situation I was in weren't my fault. I'm not blaming myself for that. But when I was little and my mom would come back, I'd make a fuss over her. I'd plan menus with all her favorite foods, make her presents, fawn over her. Hoping to make her stay, but never succeeding. It sort of became a warped family ritual."

They were silent again, and then Tegan said the sentence she had been chanting to herself like a mantra every time she thought about Alana and how much she wanted to be with her.

"You're going away, too."

"I am," Alana said, her gaze direct and her words honest. Tegan was glad she hadn't made an attempt to sugarcoat her plans by saying maybe she would stay, or who knew what the future would bring.

Tegan sifted her fingers through Alana's bangs, her whole body tingling at the feel of her soft hair, slightly damp from being tucked under her helmet. "I survived it, each time she left," she said. This mantra had replaced the other somewhere around midnight last night, when Tegan made her decision about Alana. "I can survive this, too."

"You're sure?" Alana breathed, barely above a whisper.

Tegan nodded, her hand on Alana's cheek, her thumb caressing the corner of her mouth, drawing her closer until nothing was between them anymore. In their kiss, Tegan tasted sunshine and trail dust. Truthfulness and the promise of something spectacular, no matter how short.

Alana moved closer, her free arm around Tegan's waist and her hand pressing on Tegan's lower back, until they were flush against each other. Tegan felt her breasts cushioned against

Alana's, her hips shifting against Alana's as desire built inside her. Their breathing grew more rapid, creating a friction between them with each rise and fall of their chests that pushed aside the last of Tegan's doubts until she could only wonder at her initial hesitation. How could she possibly have refused this?

Alana's tongue moved against hers, fleetingly there and then gone, and then Alana took a step back. She felt the gulf between them like an ache, even though Alana was still right there, looking as flushed as Tegan felt. Aroused, close, Alana's hand shifting to rest on her waist. Yet, Tegan noticed an emptiness in every inch of her body where Alana had been in contact with her. After only a kiss. How much would she miss Alana when she was no longer close enough to touch? No longer in the same state, or maybe even the same country? And after they'd shared more of themselves than lips and tongues?

More than she realized, most likely. How certain was she that she wanted Alana anyway, no matter the cost? More than she could say.

Fitz pawed at the river's edge, sprinkling them with drops of cold water and making them laugh and pull apart.

"We'd better start moving again before he decides to roll in the water," Tegan said, putting her helmet on again.

They mounted and made their way back to the trail, riding side by side as soon as they climbed away from the river and the trail widened again.

Tegan talked as they rode, pointing out stories of lava flows that were told through the shape of basalt, and telling Alana the names of plants and trees that were unique to the area, giving her information to share with her riders. She didn't have an agenda of wanting Alana to fall in love with Yakima and decide to stay. All she wanted was to share herself with Alana, as fully as she could, and no picture of her could be complete without including the details of this place.

"I have to go feed Charm and Rio," Tegan said once they were back at the lodge and the horses were put away. She reached for Alana's hand. "I don't suppose you'd mind some company tonight? I could come by the house once I get the horses settled."

Alana grinned. "I don't suppose I'd forgive you if you didn't."

Tegan kissed her again, ignoring the temptation to linger, and walked back to her car. She couldn't help but think about the last time she had been here with Alana. The first day they had met, when she'd come to the corral and had seen Alana standing there with her phone and a halter. Only a day later, Alana had come to her clinic and enlisted her help. Had they really only known each other a little over two weeks? And now their relationship was going to change again. In a normal situation, they might be moving too fast. But in this case, when their time together had an end point neither of them could predict, Tegan wasn't about to slow down.

CHAPTER THIRTEEN

Tegan parked in the driveway next to Alana's truck. They had only been apart for two hours, but she had missed her with an intensity she hadn't expected after just a kiss. This kind of pain would be exquisite if she could always assuage it by seeing Alana. It was going to be torture when she had to live without respite.

She got out of the Jeep, muttering to herself to stop dwelling on Alana's departure. She had made her decision not to let it stop them from exploring a relationship, so she didn't need to think about it again for a while. She'd have plenty of time to mope in the future, and she didn't want to waste her time with Alana by focusing on what the time without her would be like.

She raised her hand to knock on the door, but Alana opened it a crack before she had a chance to do so. She reached through the narrow gap and grabbed Tegan's arm.

"Quick. Before they escape."

Tegan was estimating whether she had enough room to fit through the door—and she was fairly sure she didn't—when Alana pulled her inside anyway. She pushed Tegan's back against the door, using her weight to push it shut again, and braced her hands on either side of Tegan's neck.

"Hi," Alana said, leaning into her.

Tegan put her hands on Alana's waist and held her close. "Hi back," she said. She kissed Alana, feeling the curve of her smile against her lips and feeling the touch of her tongue all the way to her core. She encircled Alana with her arms, hugging her close and kissing her neck, her collarbone, her shoulder. Alana shivered at the contact, tilting her head to give Tegan better access. Tegan had been expecting an awkward entrance, but instead she felt as if she had come home. Except for the part where she had been tugged through the door, which had probably scraped some skin off her back, Tegan felt an immense and overwhelming sense of comfort.

Alana slipped her hands into the back pockets of Tegan's jeans, cupping her ass in a way that would have felt wonderful if something else hadn't been trying to puncture the skin around her ankle at the same time.

"Your guard dogs are exceptionally vicious," she said. Alana took a step back, releasing her hold on Tegan, and looked down.

"They're obnoxious little shits," she said with the tone of an exasperated but indulgent mother. She bent down and detached the mostly white male from Tegan's ankle. "This one's the leader of the gang," she said, handing him to Tegan. "Your client Amy and her family have put dibs on him."

Tegan held the pup, keeping her fingers out of reach of his teeth. She ruffled his feathery brown ears. "He's a good choice. He'll be able to hold his own even though King is bigger."

Alana laughed. "They're worried King will be jealous when he's no longer an only dog, so they're calling this one Prince. They can name him whatever they want, but it won't stop him from usurping the throne."

The puppy squirmed vigorously, so Tegan put him down with the others. She looked around the room, seeing the space where Alana lived for the first time.

"I like what you've done with the place," she said, taking in the bare surfaces and walls, as well as the old-fashioned furniture that must have been here for decades.

"I've taken the minimalist approach," Alana said, then she shrugged. "Actually, I've never decorated a home of my own, so I didn't have any idea where to start. I was able to hang posters in my room, or whatever I wanted, when I was little, but as an adult I've lived in hotel rooms that already had color schemes and paintings on the walls. Even in college, I was on a tight budget and didn't put any money into my dorm room." She jabbed Tegan playfully in the ribs with her elbow. "What about you? I'm picturing a dresser covered with horse figurines, championship ribbons on the walls, and about a hundred stuffed animals on your bed."

Tegan laughed. "You just described my bedroom at my grandparents' farm to a tee, and it still looks exactly the same. My apartment at the clinic is much more mature."

"Mature? Meaning you only have twenty stuffed animals on the bed?"

"Give or take."

Alana smiled, and gestured at the couch. "Have a seat. Would you like a glass of wine?"

"Sure." Tegan sat on the couch and reached over to pet Lace, who was curled up on a soft blanket next to her.

"The fruit stands are finally open," Alana said from the kitchen. She came around the corner and back into the living room holding two juice glasses with red wine in them. "For a few hours a day, at least. I got this merlot, which is from a winery in Prosser, and some blueberries."

Tegan took the glass Alana offered, with stenciled oranges circling its middle. She loved Alana's lack of pretentiousness. She seemed to be someone who would be at home anywhere, whether in one of her elegant hotels or in an ancient house in Yakima. She might prefer the former, but she fit just as easily into the latter. "Fancy," she said, clinking her glass against Alana's.

"Consider yourself lucky to have glass and not plastic. If Chip hadn't supplied me with dishes and utensils when I moved in, you'd be drinking out of one of those red disposable cups." She took a sip of her wine. "Mm. This is really nice. So, speaking of Chip, did you notice him favoring any of the puppies today? I hope he's not wanting Prince."

Tegan shook her head, scooping up the tiniest puppy that was currently trying to climb her leg. She put the pup on her lap, and Alana reached over to pet her, her wrist occasionally brushing against Tegan's thigh. She tried to concentrate on the conversation and not on the way her leg felt like it was catching fire each time Alana touched it.

"He seemed to like them all. I think you should see how many my clients and your neighbors want, and then just give him all the extras. He has plenty of room."

"Until he goes bankrupt and loses the ranch, you mean," Alana said. She draped her arm across the back of the couch and touched Tegan. Just a single finger tracing her ear, the fall of her hair, the path from her temple to her jaw. A slim point of contact that created an exponential response in Tegan until she thought she might explode because of the tension building inside her.

"He won't. Not with you around," Tegan said, amazed at how even and normal her voice sounded, since her body was on a rampage. "He used to lead awesome hiking tours around the area. That's how I originally met him, when I took his rock-climbing class. His business was really successful but small, and I think he expected the ranch to be a bigger playground, not an endless mountain of work. From the sound of it, you're practically running the place."

Alana shrugged as her fingertip moved down to explore Tegan's neck. "I'm taking care of a few loose ends. Mostly because his work is more familiar to me from helping my parents with their hotel. Plus, it keeps me from having to face how poorly prepared I am for my own job." She laughed, but Tegan heard more stress than humor in it. "It's like he and I are playing chicken, with the grand opening racing toward us and neither one of us really qualified to handle it. Waiting to find out which one of us will swerve first."

"You're doing better than you realize," Tegan said. Alana's hand had come to rest on her shoulder, and Tegan reached for it, drawing it to her mouth and kissing her palm. She smiled at a memory. "The first time we shook hands, I noticed how sexy and soft yours were. It was my first clue that you maybe weren't the rugged and experienced trail guide I was expecting." She laced her fingers with Alana's. "Now I wouldn't have any reason to doubt you."

"Yay. So my hands are more believable, but less sexy?"

Tegan laughed. "Much sexier, actually. Stronger, and just a little rough. Perfect."

She pulled gently on Alana's hand, drawing her close for a kiss. She tasted like wine and spice and magic.

Alana pulled back a fraction of an inch, still near enough for Tegan to feel Alana's breath against her lips when she spoke. "Why don't we get the puppies settled in their room. Then we can talk about my hands some more, and all the things they're capable of doing."

She stood up and took the juice glass Tegan had been holding—and had nearly spilled after hearing Alana's suggestion. Tegan picked up the drowsy pup that was still on her lap and another two who were sleeping on her feet.

"In there," Alana said, coming out of the kitchen and pointing at an open door. "I'll take Lace out back."

Tegan took her three puppies into their room and placed them in one of the fleecy, puffy beds in the closet. She closed the door behind her in case they tried to follow, and found two more at the foot of the stairs, trying to break through the baby gate. She had to search for Prince but finally discovered him behind the living room chair, where he was chewing happily on an expensive-looking shoe. Yeah, she'd wait until later to tell Alana about that. Much later. She picked up Prince and left the shoe where it was, settling him in the room just as Alana and Lace returned from the yard.

Alana shut the door and leaned her back against it, watching Tegan with an unreadable expression on her face. Tegan had just been thinking about how homey the scene had been, with her and Alana putting the canine children to bed like parents. She wondered if the same idea had been on Alana's mind, too, and whether the domesticity of the situation scared her or not. It was nearly impossible to label the evening as a casual encounter when they shared chores first.

Maybe the question to ask herself was if the situation scared *her*, not Alana. Alana had talked about being here for the season, maybe a year. If they continued their relationship through Alana's stay, there would be other everyday activities they'd do together, even though taking care of the puppies was just a temporary one. Shopping, making meals, visiting friends. Tegan felt a wave of panic rising in her, threatening to overshadow desire. She knew herself too well to think she'd be unaffected by the intimacy of having Alana in her daily life.

She also knew she wasn't about to let fear stop her from moving forward. She'd deal with the consequences when they came, not before. She crossed the distance between them and put her hands on either side of Alana's face, holding her gently even though the kiss she gave her was anything but. Firm enough to push away her concerns. A brief clash of teeth and tongues before they settled into a rhythm with each other and broke away with mutual gasps. Their entire relationship—past, present, and future—captured in a single kiss.

It broke the spell, and Tegan smiled at Alana. "I wouldn't mind a tour of the rest of the house. I'm thinking of redecorating my apartment and I'm looking for some tips."

"I think the only tip you need if you want to imitate my style is to throw out everything you own except for the bare necessities," Alana said. She waved her hand in a circle. "This is downstairs. That's about as detailed as I want to get about this part of the house. We can spend a little more time touring upstairs."

Alana led the way to the staircase. The latch on the baby gate was tricky to use, but she hadn't had any trouble before now. Suddenly, she was clumsy and uncoordinated, and Tegan finally reached past her and opened it with a snap.

"Thanks," she said quietly, glancing back at Tegan and seeing the same cascade of expressions she had been cycling through since she had arrived. Alana thought she could read most of them. Tegan's desire for her was as obvious as if she had the words printed on her shirt. Equally clear, but maybe only because Alana knew Tegan well enough to guess at it, was the battle between the Yakima Tegan—who thrived on the security and community she had fostered in this small town—and logical vet Tegan—who understood that loss was inevitable, but that some relationships were worth the risk.

She hesitated on the landing, feeling the warmth of Tegan's presence behind her. They both knew what it meant for Tegan to take a chance on a temporary relationship, but Alana was supposed to be the worldly one. The fly-by-night who moved from city to city, high-end hotel to splashy resort, having casual flings and breaking hearts along the way. Of course, she had never actually been that person, but she had always imagined she would be.

Then why had the easy camaraderie she felt with Tegan made her so uneasy? They had sat on the couch, surrounded by puppies and chatting about Alana's job over a glass of wine. They had put the little babies to bed together, like a couple getting ready to end the day. She had stood on the back porch and watched Tegan hide her mangled shoe, like a lover who was confident there would be a tomorrow for tears and upset, so why bother letting it spoil the mood tonight.

She felt Tegan's arms around her waist, resting with a comforting weight. "Are you okay?" she asked, putting her chin on Alana's shoulder. "I can go…"

Alana covered Tegan's arms with hers, holding her firmly in place. If Tegan was brave enough to be standing here, on the edge of something scary, then Alana was going to be right alongside her. She stepped out of the circle of Tegan's arms but kept hold of her hand and took her into the bedroom.

She stopped near the bed and moved closer to kiss her, but Tegan put her hands on Alana's shoulders and held her at arm's length.

"Wait," she said, in a voice barely above a whisper. Alana nodded silently, unable to guarantee that her voice would sound unruffled if she spoke. Tegan stroked her thumb along Alana's jawline, and then along the open V of her shirt. She undid the buttons with an agonizing slowness, treating the flannel shirt with as much respect and gentleness as if she was handling a designer gown. Somewhere in Alana's mind, she realized that Tegan's reverence was directed at her, not her clothing, but Alana couldn't face that fact directly or she would freak out, run downstairs, and hide in the room with the puppies until Tegan left.

She took a deep breath, which had more of a shudder to it than she expected, and let Tegan slide the shirt over her shoulders and down her arms before tossing it on the chair behind her. The gentle chafe of flannel across her skin gave her goose bumps, but she kept still as Tegan walked behind her, never breaking contact with her hands, and trailed her fingers from Alana's neck down her spine until she reached the clasp of her bra. It was unhooked and off so quickly that Alana gave a little squeak of surprise, which sounded decidedly unsexy to her but made Tegan laugh in a quiet, self-satisfied way.

Tegan stayed behind her, reaching around with her arms on either side of her ribcage, and unfastened her jeans with excruciating slowness. Alana swayed slightly, her knees growing weak and threatening to stop supporting her altogether, but Tegan held her steady for a moment before slipping her hands between Alana's jeans and her skin and sliding them down her legs. And then—oh Lord—her underwear.

Tegan stood up, still close behind her, and brushed her knuckles along the side of Alana's neck.

"I believe I owe you a massage," she said, her breath warm against Alana's bare skin. "Lie down."

Alana considered simply collapsing onto the floor—Tegan hadn't said *where* to lie down—because she wasn't sure her legs could handle the three steps it would take her to get to the bed. She somehow managed it, though, and got on the bed, on top of the comforter, with her head turned to face Tegan and her cheek pillowed on her crossed arms.

Tegan removed her own clothes with much more impatience and less care than she had shown with Alana's, before she climbed on the bed and straddled Alana, sitting lightly on her ass. Alana's nerve endings were already on high alert, and the sensation of Tegan's wet heat against her skin was nearly too much to bear. She made a strangled sort of moan and buried her face in the pillow, and Tegan laughed.

"I like that sound," she said, running her hands gently down Alana's spine, then back up toward her neck with a little more pressure. "Let's see what other noises we can coax out of you."

Some of Alana's arousal eased   it didn't go away, it just ebbed for the time being—as Tegan worked on her tense muscles, giving her an actual massage and not, as Alana had first thought, using it as an excuse to pounce on her. Alana was all for pouncing and hoped Tegan would get to it eventually, but she felt herself relaxing into mush under Tegan's hands. She moved up and down Alana's spine, with her thumbs on either side, and squeezed out the stress hiding there. She used the heel of her hands on Alana's shoulder blades and forced her to release the stiffness she had been carrying there since she had gotten fired and had been trying to pretend she was handling it just fine. Tegan spent most of her time kneading the muscles on the sides of Alana's neck and over the tops of her shoulders, where she carried the weight of her responsibility to the ranch and her constant awareness of how short she was falling.

As the knots inside began to come undone, Tegan moved to Alana's lower back. Her desire reawakened, ravenous and aching for more of Tegan's touch. She stretched, arching her back slightly to press her hips into Tegan's, turning her head to the side again.

"A little lower would be nice," she suggested.

She felt Tegan's lips press against the back of her neck. "That sounds like an excellent idea," she said.

Tegan took her time, stroking every inch of Alana from her bottom, down the outside of her thighs, and back up the inside of them. After what felt like *hours*, she felt Tegan's fingers between her legs. She felt soaked and so ready for Tegan's touch she thought she'd climax at the first hint of pressure from her fingers, but Tegan had other plans. Her massage here was just as thorough, tortuously meandering around before moving inside her.

"Oh yes," Alana said, unable to speak beyond the two syllables, ending with a drawn-out hiss as she moved her hips in time to Tegan's insistent rhythm. She came hard, and Tegan held her as she trembled through her powerful orgasm.

She lay still, fighting to catch her breath and regain at least some control over her muscles. As soon as she felt capable of doing anything more strenuous than inhaling and exhaling, she shifted onto her back and saw Tegan staring at her with something resembling wonder in her eyes.

"Wow," Alana said, reaching up to cup her hand around Tegan's neck. She used the other to push against Tegan's hip until she was sitting on her again. "That's the most inadequate word, but...wow."

Tegan leaned down and kissed her, and Alana felt Tegan's control fade away until slow and sensuous became desperate and hungry. Alana returned the kiss fiercely, bending her leg slightly so Tegan was riding against her thigh, and taking charge of Tegan with her tongue and hands until she climaxed, calling Alana's name.

❖

Tegan lay on her back in the darkness with Alana against her right side, her head nestled in the hollow between Tegan's shoulder and breast, and her hand splayed on Tegan's stomach. Holy shit. Tegan was in more trouble than she had anticipated. All her internal whining about how much she would miss Alana when she was gone seemed naive and foolish to her now. She'd had no idea the extent to which Alana was about to burrow into her soul after only one night—hell, only a few hours. How many more of her cells would be permeated by Alana by the morning, let alone by wintertime, until they belonged to Alana more than her? She wasn't sure whether she was about to burst into tears something she hated doing—or hysterical laughter, which seemed wholly inappropriate at the moment.

Alana's breathing was quiet, but not regular, and Tegan sensed she was awake, too. Hopefully feeling the same immensity of emotion and not thinking something along the lines of *Now how can I get her to go home so I can get some sleep?*

Alana's hand moved on Tegan's stomach, the texture of her palm etching small circles deep into Tegan's belly and her fingers moving in a whisper along her trembling skin. Spiraling downward in a way that was clearly not indicative of someone who was wanting to get someone else out of her bed. This was someone who wanted her to stay.

She inhaled sharply when Alana's explorations continued down her thigh, skirting the area where all of her cells that hadn't yet succumbed to Alana were congregated and waiting to be claimed by her. Tegan shifted as Alana's hand generated an energy inside her far out of proportion to its small, fluttering movements. Where Alana's cheek rested against her, Tegan could feel Alana's smile. Just when she decided she couldn't remain still any longer and was about to pounce, flipping Alana onto her back and underneath her, Alana hooked her ankle around Tegan's right calf and pulled it toward her abruptly, spreading her legs and sliding her hand between them.

The switch from tantalizing to determined caught Tegan by surprise, and she cried out, moving her hips in response to Alana's relentless rhythm until she hovered on the edge of her climax, caught between needing to come and never wanting the moment to end.

Alana raised herself up on her elbow and kissed her softly, and it was the tipping point for Tegan who couldn't have delayed her orgasm any more than the ocean could stop the tides. She wrapped her arms around Alana and rolled them both over until she was on top, straddling Alana's hips.

She kissed Alana with the same tenderness that had been her undoing moments before. "I didn't think you were asleep," she said, tilting her head toward Alana's hand when she reached up and tucked Tegan's hair behind her ear. "Thank you for the proof that you were awake."

"Anytime," Alana said. She laughed. "Seriously, anytime. Sleep is overrated. Besides, I can always take a nap at work."

"Good," said Tegan as she inched lower. "Because now I'm wide awake and just looking for something to do..." She moved until the ends of her hair brushed against Alana's collarbones, then the tops of her breasts, then her stiffened nipples. She lowered her head and kissed Alana's breastbone, feeling the change in movement against her lips as Alana's breath became more rapid, shallower. And lower, until the scent of Alana washed over her and everything—doubt, fear, worry—disappeared until the only thing filling her mind and her senses was Alana.

CHAPTER FOURTEEN

Tegan woke with a start, jolting to a half-sitting position as she tried to figure out where she was and whether she was late for work. The night before came back in a rush when Alana mumbled something in a groggy voice and reached out to pull Tegan into her arms.

She settled down again, with Alana curled warmly against her back. She had just dozed off when Alana sat up.

"I hear Lace," Alana said, rubbing her eyes. She looked at Tegan and smiled. "Good morning."

She bent down to give her a kiss, and Tegan slid her fingers into Alana's hair for just a moment, holding her tight before letting her go. She watched her walk across the room naked and get a robe out of the closet, marveling at the memories of Alana that were now imprinted on her body and heart. She got up, too, twitching the rumpled comforter back into place and getting dressed.

She had been anticipating some morning-after awkwardness, but the puppy-induced chaos that greeted her when she came down the stairs was enough to drive away any thoughts of shyness or unease.

"Can you take them out back?" Alana asked, coming out of the puppy room on her way into the kitchen. "I'll make coffee."

"Of course," Tegan said, wading through the puppies and opening the back door. Lace trotted outside, and the puppies scampered after her. Tegan hurried to catch them before they tumbled down the stairs, scooping them into one huge armful and setting them on the grass. They raced around, already sturdy on their tiny legs, and Tegan settled on the top step to watch them.

Alana poked her head out the back door. "Cream or sugar?"

"Black, please," Tegan said. A moment later, Alana came outside with two steaming mugs. She handed one to Tegan and sat next to her, wrapping her hands around her mug.

"I was wondering if you were going to bring me coffee in a juice glass," Tegan said, turning the mug in her hand. The design on it was a pretend postcard with *Yakima* written across the top and a row of apple trees underneath.

Alana smiled and bumped her shoulder gently enough not to make her spill. "I actually bought these. I thought they'd be fun souvenirs."

Tegan gave herself a stern mini-lecture about not getting weepy every time she was reminded that Alana was a transient here, not a local. "You seem to be embracing the fruit theme wholeheartedly."

"You haven't seen the whole of it yet. My plates have clusters of grapes around the edges. I think Chip bought them from a winery." She yawned and leaned her head on Tegan's shoulder. "Do you have clients this morning?"

"Yes. It's going to be a busy day. What's going on at the ranch?"

"I have a staff meeting this morning."

"Sounds interesting." Tegan took a drink of coffee, and then considered the way Alana had phrased her appointment. "Wait, do you mean you have a staff meeting that Chip is leading and you have to attend? Or are you leading the meeting yourself?"

"What do you think?" Alana sat up and rolled her eyes. "The other day, I asked him if we were going to get everyone together, from housekeeping to reception, and talk about the grand opening, answer questions, get to know each other. All that. Chip said it sounded like a good idea. I didn't say anything, waiting for him to suggest a date, but he just stood there, looking like he was about to be sick, so I said, Do you want me to organize it? And he gave this big sigh and said I was amazing and what would he do without me."

Tegan was laughing by the time Alana was done talking. She had a deadpan way of delivering stories, barely pausing for breath in between sentences, and she didn't seem to realize just how funny she was.

They lingered on the porch together as long as they could, talking and watching Lace lie patiently in the yard while the pups chewed on her ears and wrestled with each other. She tidied up the dog's bedroom while Alana showered, and then helped her load the animals into the truck.

"I'll see you tonight?" Alana asked as they kissed good-bye in the driveway. She had her arms around Tegan's neck and her forehead pressed against Tegan's. "I'll miss our riding lesson, but I don't know how long this meeting will go. I haven't even met most of the staff yet, and I'm sure they'll have a ton of questions."

"I'll come by here after work," Tegan promised. She kissed Alana once more and got in her Jeep, trying to look serene and detached even though her sex-addled mind was encouraging her toward great feats of immaturity. Like hanging on to Alana and begging her not to go to work today. Or initiating some sort of *I'll miss you more—No, I'll miss you more* conversation.

Lace had been an efficient alarm clock, and Tegan got to the clinic with time to feed the horses and shower before her first appointment. She dragged through the day, growing more and more tired from lack of sleep as the morning progressed. She perked up a bit right before lunch when Rosie arrived with her most recently trapped feral cat and a box of puerquitos for her and Dez. Tegan hadn't had anything for breakfast except Alana's coffee and a handful of blueberries, and she sighed with pleasure as she bit the head off the pig-shaped cookie. It tasted like a soft gingerbread, with warm spices, molasses, and a strong hit of cinnamon.

She left Dez at the reception desk with two cookies—not the entire box, or she'd eat them all—and led Rosie into the examination room, closing the door behind them. She peered into the crate and saw an adult gray cat staring at her with wide, frightened eyes.

"I guess I don't need to ask how you're doing today," Rosie said, leaning her hip against the table and smirking at Tegan. "Should I just say congratulations?"

"What?"

"What?" Rosie said, mimicking her in an exaggerated way. "I'm assuming it was Alana?"

Tegan bit back the impulse to say *What?* again. "I have no idea what you're talking about."

"Please. You're obviously a person who has recently had sex. Really, really good sex. I hate you."

The last was delivered with a smile, so Tegan ignored it, concentrating instead on how Rosie had known. Her hand strayed to her neck, as if checking for bite marks, before she realized she was doing it. Rosie laughed harder.

"Well, I'm glad to see you happy."

Tegan decided her best option was to focus on the appointment. "How did you find this one?" she asked, turning her back on Rosie and getting a leather glove out of a drawer. She opened the crate and reached in cautiously, bringing the cat out by the scruff of his neck. He was skinny, and his coat was dull, but he was going to be a handsome cat when he was healthy, with his blue-gray coat, white paws, and small white moustache.

"He's been wandering around the apartment complex in Union Gap for a few months," Rosie said, accepting the change in subject with grace. "The manager has been feeding him every once in a while, but some of the tenants complained and the owner said he had to go. Can you believe some people?"

Unfortunately, Tegan could believe it. She took off the glove, since the cat seemed docile, and gently pulled back his lips to check his teeth and gums.

"I'd guess he's about seven, give or take. He's already neutered."

"Two tenants who'd had cats left about the time he showed up. Probably dumped by one of them, but the manager wasn't sure which one did it, if either, since she'd never seen their pets."

Tegan shook her head wordlessly. She and Rosie had seen the same thing happen too many times to count. Someone deciding their animal was too much bother to take with them. Or their new home didn't allow pets, so they just let them go. Union Gap was a busy area, with most of Yakima's big box stores and fast food restaurants clustered together. The cat was fortunate to have survived the traffic long enough for Rosie to get him.

"Well, he's a lucky fellow," she said. This wouldn't be Rosie's normal catch-and-release, like the wilder feral cats she brought to be fixed. She'd find this one a new home. "I'll probably have to pull a tooth or two, but I'll be able to see them better when he's sedated. I'll take care of his nails then, too."

She stroked the cat and was rewarded with a rumbling purr. "We'll get him scheduled for dental surgery in the morning, but tonight he can rest and eat."

She picked up the cat and carried him into the back room, settling him in one of the large cages. She stopped by the bathroom on her way back, just to find out what Rosie had noticed to tip her off about Alana, but she looked the same. No telltale marks, no fingernail scratches. Well, her smile looked a little goofy. She tried a frown, but her reflection just made her laugh.

She went back into the room where Rosie was closing the door of the empty crate and getting ready to leave.

"Are you sure you're going to be okay?" Rosie asked.

Tegan frowned for real this time. "Yes. Like you said, I'm going into this without trying to fool myself into thinking she's going to stay. I'll be fine."

"That's not what I meant, although it's part of it." She paused, as if choosing her words carefully. "You have a soft spot for needy women, Tegan, and sometimes they take advantage of you. Okay, all the time. They take from you and never give anything in return."

Tegan felt her cheeks flush as she thought back to the night before. Alana had been anything but selfish. She knew Rosie was thinking about more than sex, but so was she. Alana took care of the people around her.

"It's different with her, Rosie. I agree with you, I've gotten hurt in the past because of needy women, but Alana isn't needy. She needed help learning to ride, true, but she's worked harder than I have. I gave her a few lessons during my lunchtimes, but she's been out at the ranch practicing for hours every day. Plus, she's managing the damned place. And taking care of six stray puppies. She's not fragile, even though she was in a fragile place when she got here."

"Oh, Tegan," Rosie said, her voice sounding sad. "I was worried she was going to be selfish and hurt you, but this is worse. She's going to be wonderful and break your heart."

Tegan looked away, blinking to keep her eyes from tearing up. "I know. She won't stay."

Rosie paused. "But you might go with her?" she asked quietly.

Tegan shrugged. She and Alana had time to figure it out. Alana wasn't the only one in the relationship, so the burden wasn't solely on her to stay if they wanted to make things work out. "It won't happen for a while, Rosie. She's committed to staying at the ranch for the season at least. We'll see how it goes."

Rosie was about to speak again when Dez knocked on the door and opened it. "Tegan? You have a phone call."

Dez's voice, so abnormally polite and quiet, made Tegan's heart thud in her chest. She immediately pictured Alana out on the trails alone, lying broken and bleeding after falling off a horse.

She hurried out and picked up the receiver. "Hello?"

"Hi, pumpkin," her grandfather said. "I'm at the hospital, sweetheart. Your grandma's okay, but she had a small heart attack. She's going to be fine."

Tegan rested her hand on the counter, feeling her energy draining away and leaving her hollow. "I'll be right there, Gramps, okay?"

"Sure. I'll be here waiting for you."

She hung up and felt Rosie's hand on her shoulder. She turned and was pulled into a hug. "Gran had a heart attack."

"I'll cancel this afternoon's appointments," Dez said, still sounding un-Dez-like. "I'll come back later and feed the horses, too, in case you're there late."

"Come on," Rosie said. "I'll drive you to the hospital."

CHAPTER FIFTEEN

Alana came out of the staff meeting feeling better about
the grand opening weekend than she had since arriving
in Yakima. She might not have been as cheerful about the long
meeting if Tegan had been home waiting for her, but she'd be at
the office all day, so Alana could put her out of her mind. She
only got distracted a few times while working through her agenda,
feeling her neck and cheeks grow hot when she remembered
particular places where Tegan had kissed her the night before, or
the wholehearted way she had responded to Alana's touch. Each
time it happened she would drink some water and continue. She
had considered pretending she was coming down with the flu to
explain her fevered look, but she figured Chip would pass out if he
thought she'd be sick and miss the opening.

They went an hour over her allotted time since most of the
staff had questions and seemed happy to get more than Chip's
vague answers from her. Even though Chip might not be cut out
to manage a resort, he had excellent instincts when hiring people.
His emphasis on having staff members feel like family seemed to
work, and the general atmosphere in the cafeteria, where they were
meeting, was enthusiastic and positive.

Alana's benevolent feeling toward Chip waned slightly when
she saw him doling out personal checks to the employees. She
pulled him aside once the meeting was over.

"Chip, you've got to find an accountant. My parents ran a hotel for years, and they always had an independent accountant come in to help with taxes and take care of payroll. You can't keep doing this on your own."

"I know," he said, gazing longingly at his office where the puppies were probably gnawing the legs off his desk. She stepped between him and the door to block an escape into his sanctuary. "I've talked to a couple," he continued, "but I wasn't comfortable with them. I want anyone who works here to be like—"

"Family, yes, I know," Alana said. "That's fine for the main staff, but this is different."

He looked at her with stubborn determination, and she stopped arguing. Let him hire his mother if he wanted. It was his business to run into the ground, not hers.

"Oh," she said, as a solution popped into her head. He didn't need to hire his mother, but *a* mother, nonetheless. She paused, considering all sides of the possibility and liking it more and more. "I might know the perfect person."

"Really?"

"Yes. I'll need to talk to her first and make sure she'd be comfortable with the work. I'll let you know right away."

"Thanks, Alana. You're—"

She waved him off. "I know. I'm amazing. I'm going to go over procedures with the housekeeping staff now."

She had gotten in the habit of telling him what she was about to do, and then pausing so he had a chance to come up with a task or project to tell her about, too. Leading by example. It hadn't worked so far.

"I thought I'd go for a short hike," he said. "I'll make sure the trail leading down to the river is clear for guests."

She sighed. Well, it was sort of work related.

He disappeared into his office with the puppies, and she went down the hall and caught up with the small group of housekeepers. With so few guests booked, there hadn't been any reason to hire a full staff. They hadn't seen the rooms yet, and when she took them inside one to go over the daily cleaning checklist, she had to wait while they looked around and exclaimed over the décor.

Alana was surprised by how much they liked it. She had told Tegan she didn't have decorating experience, but she and Chip had worked together to come up with the color scheme and choose the furnishings, so part of this belonged to her.

The guest wings weren't built of logs, like the main lodge, and the walls were paneled with wood stained a warm, golden brown. Most of the furniture was similarly toned, and the comfortable chairs and headrests on the bed were covered with brown faux leather. Splashes of color kept the rooms from being too boring. The window frames were painted a bright teal, and thick rugs in a rich maroon covered a large portion of the hardwood floors. Chip had brought smaller versions of his metalwork animals from his workshop, and each room had its own mascot.

She looked at the silver-toned coyote trotting across the wall over the bed and added *Make sure the wall hangings are still there!* to the housekeeping checklist. They'd be easy to steal unless she could convince Chip to bolt them down securely.

She had just about finished going through her list when Chip came in the room.

"There's someone on the phone for you, Alana. It sounded important. Someone named Rosie."

"Rosie? Tegan's friend?" She walked back to reception with Chip, wondering why she was calling. Although Alana had originally thought Tegan and Rosie were an item, she had quickly dismissed the idea once Tegan started talking about massages. And after last night, she had no doubt about where Tegan's interests lay.

She went behind the desk and picked up the lodge's main phone. "Hello? Rosie?"

"Hi, Alana. I wanted to let you know I just dropped Tegan at the hospital—"

Alana's clipboard slipped out of her hands and clattered onto the desk. "What happened?"

"Not her," Rosie hastened to reassure her. "Her grandmother had a mild heart attack. Look, I couldn't go in with her because I have to get to work, but I thought you might want to stop by."

"I'm on my way." Alana thanked her quickly and hung up. Chip was standing in the doorway to his office, watching her with a concerned expression.

"I need to go. Tegan's grandmother is ill. Can you watch the puppies?" Alana struggled to think clearly, when every part of her wanted to run out the door without anything getting in her way. "I've got food for Lace in my office in case I'm back late. Nothing else is scheduled for the day, and Marcus is taking care of the horses."

"Go," said Chip. "We'll be fine. Call and let me know what's going on if you get a chance."

Alana nodded and grabbed her bag out of her office. She was halfway to the door when she stopped and jogged back to Chip. "Where's the hospital?"

Tegan sat in the room with her grandmother, holding her hand and wondering why it hadn't looked this frail when she had been dishing up ice cream at Saturday's lunch. Somehow hospital beds and flickering monitors managed to sap the vitality out of a person until they seemed like a shadow of themselves. Her grandmother was talking and alert, but the instruments surrounding her were like huge neon arrows, pointing at illness and fear.

She had been a vet long enough to understand the weirdly slow nature of emergencies. On television shows, the rush to care for a patient had to fit in between commercial breaks. In reality, the exhaustive testing, considering of options, and just plain waiting around seemed to stretch endlessly onward. She'd faced this herself in the clinic, when a fraught owner brought in a pet, expecting her to save it within seconds and getting frustrated when it often took much longer. Once basic survival was ensured, the process of determining cause, treatment, and prognosis slowed to a crawl.

Tegan understood this, yet it still made her want to scream.

She wanted to stay until the specialist arrived, but her grandmother was overly concerned about Tegan and her grandfather. She was expending so much energy trying to convince Tegan she would be okay—consoling and reassuring her like she had when Tegan was a child and her mother had left again—that she wasn't letting herself get the rest she needed. Tegan finally acknowledged that her presence, while welcome, was putting added strain on Maisie.

"I'm going to check on Gramps," she said, bending over to give her grandmother a kiss on the cheek.

"All right, dear. I'm sorry you had to cancel appointments just to come down here."

"Don't worry about it. I'll have him write me a check to cover the fees I'm losing," Tegan joked.

Her grandmother laughed and slapped her hand lightly. "Go on with you," she said, waving toward the door.

"I'll be back soon."

Tegan started down the hall, then changed her mind. Should she have stayed? She walked back into the room, but her grandmother was already asleep, or at least resting with her eyes closed. Tegan headed back to the waiting room again.

She needed to call Dez and make sure everything was set for her to take the afternoon off. And Rosie, to let her know what was going on and to thank her for the ride. The one person she really wanted to call was Alana, but she had been coming up with excuses not to. Alana was in her meeting. She was probably riding. She was busy at the ranch…

The truth was, Tegan wasn't sure how Alana would react to the call. She'd be compassionate, of course. Tegan didn't doubt that. But they were something new together, something undefined.

How would this kind of situation be handled in their relationship? As much as she had defended Alana to Rosie, insisting she wasn't like Fay and the other women in her past, a tiny part of her was afraid she'd call Alana and hear something that, although polite and sympathetic, would mean Tegan had to face this alone. *Oh, I'm sorry to hear about your grandmother. Give me a call later, if you get out of there early enough to come over.*

Tegan stopped by the nurses' station to check on the next doctor's arrival time—still unknown—and to find out if any test results were back—not yet. She sighed and pushed through the swinging doors into the waiting room.

Her grandfather was sitting near the windows reading a magazine, and Alana was next to him, looking over his shoulder and pointing at something on the page. She looked up when Tegan came in and was across the room and holding her tightly before Tegan took another step.

"You're here," Tegan said, pulling back enough to give Alana a kiss.

"Where else would I be? Waiting for you at home and hoping you would bring me some Jell-O?"

Tegan laughed. Alana had basically described the scenario she had been fearing, but in a dismissive tone.

"Well, something along those…wait. How'd you find out I was here? Dez or Rosie?"

"Both," Alana said. "Rosie caught me at the ranch, and I got Dez's call on my cell while I was driving. Were you going to call?"

Tegan put her hand on Alana's cheek, hating to see even a trace of hurt and confusion in her expression. "I was. I wanted to right away, before I even got here, but I was worried…"

"That I really would choose to sit at home and not come down here," Alana finished for her when she paused.

"Yes."

Alana shook her head with a sad expression and went back to Howard, sitting down next to him.

"How is she?" he asked. His concern and fear seemed to be carved into the lines of his face, but he had been doing his best to act optimistic and strong.

"She's sleeping," Tegan said. She filled Alana in on what had been happening, and then noticed the magazine her grandfather was holding. "Were the two of you reading an automotive magazine?"

He looked down at his hands, as if needing to confirm what he was holding. "We were looking at this article on SUV tires."

"Neither of you has an SUV."

Alana shrugged. "We didn't have many choices. It was this, or my notes about the grand opening at the ranch."

Howard stood up. "I'm going to the gift shop to buy a book of crossword puzzles. I'll be right back."

"If we hear anything new, we'll come get you."

Tegan leaned back in her chair, feeling more at peace with Alana's thigh against hers, and their fingers entwined, than she had all day. Still scared and worried, but less shaky.

"How was your meeting?" she asked, stretching out her legs and crossing them at the ankles.

"I think it went well. There were lots of questions, and everyone seems excited about the opening. I don't know why, since Chip is paying them to do nothing until then. With personal checks."

Tegan winced. "Not smart. Maybe you should suggest he hire an accountant. Oh, I guess you already have," she added when Alana gave her a *no shit* look.

"I kept getting distracted during my meeting," Alana said, nudging Tegan with her shoulder. "Scenes from last night popped into my head at unexpected moments."

Tegan smiled at her. "Same here. I was either dozing off from exhaustion or blushing all morning. Rosie had barely been there three minutes before she was making snide comments about it."

Alana met her gaze, and some detailed images from the night before flashed into Tegan's mind, apparently conjured up by the conversation. She looked at Alana's mouth, watching the sexy way she was nibbling her lip, wanting to kiss her again and do some biting of her own.

They turned away from each other at the same moment. Now was certainly not the time or place for making out, but somehow the connection she had just felt with Alana gave her a sense of strength.

"Did Rosie bring another feral cat?" Alana asked, thankfully jumping to a more appropriate topic.

"She did. This one obviously belonged to someone before he was abandoned, or maybe ran away. He'll be adoptable, but you know how it is with older animals."

"Like Lace?"

Tegan nodded. "Although she's only three or four. This cat is closer to seven, but he could have a long and wonderful life ahead if the right person adopts him." She raised their linked hands and kissed Alana's knuckles. "Speaking of my day, I had an interesting conversation with Amy when she called to ask about setting up a meet-and-greet with King and Prince."

"Interesting in what way?" Alana asked with what Tegan thought might be a carefully casual tone.

"Well, she talked about coming to your house and seeing the puppies. Then she mentioned how difficult it had been to choose just one."

"Mm-hmm," Alana said. "I happened to be there at the time. We need to talk about your definition of interesting."

"How about this. She said she had a hard time deciding which of the five puppies she wanted most."

"Five? One of them must have been hiding under a table or something."

"Could be, could be." Tegan stretched the words out, amused by the way Alana was beginning to shift around in her seat.

"Do you want coffee? I could go get us something from the cafeteria."

Tegan continued as if she hadn't heard her. "I was thinking, if you were trying to keep them from choosing a puppy because Chip or another of my clients wanted it, you'd simply tell them which ones weren't available. But if you happened to have your own preference, but didn't want to admit it—"

"Crossword puzzle time," Alana said. She moved one seat over and beckoned for Howard to sit between them.

Alana dug a pencil out of her bag and gave it to Howard. Tegan headed back to check on her grandmother, giving her a wink on the way out of the waiting room. Alana wasn't ready to admit she'd stashed Chantilly in her room the day Amy and her family had come over. And when Tegan's other clients visited, as well. She would never adopt a dog and then leave it behind when she left, and she couldn't take one to live a vagabond's life with her.

When she found the exact right owner for Chantilly, she'd bring her out with a flourish. Until then, she would stay in the bedroom.

Luckily, Tegan didn't bring up the subject again. Alana stayed in the waiting room, doing her best to occupy the fidgety mind of whichever one wasn't back in the hospital room. She did crossword puzzles with Howard and told Tegan stories from her previous job to make her laugh. When she found out neither one had eaten all day, except for Tegan's cookie and Howard's questionable breakfast of apple pie, she forced them to go to the cafeteria while she stood guard near the nurses' station.

It made her sad that Tegan hadn't called her immediately. Not because she was angry about Tegan not trusting her to come to the hospital—they hadn't been dating, or whatever they were doing, long enough to anticipate how the other would react in unexpected situations. She felt sad because she hated the thought of Tegan being with women in the past who wouldn't have been there for her. She deserved so much more.

Of course, right now she hated the thought of Tegan being with any other woman, no matter how kind or unselfish. She couldn't imagine dating anyone but Tegan, herself. Maybe the feeling of belonging to each other would fade once Alana was out of town and busy with the kind of work she really wanted to do.

Ugh. She wasn't going to think about moving or moving on right now. She took out her phone and called the hotel attached to the hospital, making a reservation for Howard since he didn't even want to be as far away as Alana's house or Tegan's clinic. As she was ending the call, he and Tegan came out to the waiting room once more.

"She's sleeping now, and they suggested we go home and do the same," Tegan said, reaching for Alana's hand and pulling her to her feet. "The news is about as good as we could have hoped for, given what happened. A minor heart attack, but no signs of serious damage. She might be released as early as tomorrow, depending on more tests."

"I'm so glad," Alana said, kissing Tegan on the cheek and hugging Howard. They walked him down the corridors to the hotel, and then headed out to Alana's truck.

After a brief stop at the ranch to get the puppies, they finally got back to Alana's house. Chip had wanted to keep the litter overnight—claiming it was because he wanted to help her, not because he just wanted them there. She told him they would be more comfortable sleeping in their own room, although she had to admit to herself that she selfishly wanted to hang on to every moment she and Lace and the puppies had together. He'd be keeping one, whether he knew it or not, but her time with them was limited.

Her time with Tegan was limited, too. She had been relieved when Tegan had wanted to stay with her tonight. Neither was expecting a repeat of the night before right now. This would be a night for holding and sleeping, and Alana realized she didn't care what they did together, as long as they weren't wasting time by being apart.

She locked the front door behind them and turned to Tegan, her normally tanned skin turned ashy and dark smudges under her hazel eyes.

"Lie down," she said, pointing at the living room floor. Tegan looked about to protest, so Alana took hold of her shoulders and aimed her toward the couch. "Lie on the floor."

Tegan did as she said, and Alana set the puppy crate on the floor. "This is for your own good," she said as she opened the crate's door and six puppies tumbled out in their eagerness to get to Tegan. Prince went for her exposed ankles, but the rest converged on her face.

As tired and stressed as Tegan was, she couldn't keep her composure while being licked by a bunch of puppies. Alana watched for a moment, relieved to hear Tegan's shrieks of laughter, but she couldn't remain aloof for long. She got down on the living room floor and joined her strange pack.

Alana lay down, and Tegan gathered her close until Alana's head was resting on her chest and their bodies were pressed against each other. One of the puppies climbed onto Tegan and batted at Alana's nose with a tiny, furry paw. Alana smiled, nuzzling closer to Tegan and reaching out to pet the small pup. She had originally intended to help Tegan relax with the puppy pile, but now she found herself unspooling softly into Tegan's embrace and into the soft pleasure of having puppies struggling to climb over her hip and shoulders. Strange how everything she claimed she didn't want forever—this house, this town, these animals, a meaningful relationship with Tegan—were the exact things that seemed to make her feel happier and more at ease than she had ever felt. Was it merely the novelty of all this that attracted her? Lying close to her lover, playing with pets, and working at a fun job that wasn't merely a rung on a stress-filled career ladder were unfamiliar and unusual activities for her. Did her current joy in them mean she wanted them for a lifetime, or was she merely experiencing the effects of a long overdue vacation away from her real life?

With the abruptness of babyhood, the puppies shifted from frenzied to sleepy in a heartbeat. Alana gently picked up the pup that had been bopping her nose and set him on the floor alongside Tegan, where some of his brothers and sisters were curling up together. He yawned widely, unfurling his pink tongue and dropping onto his stomach next to his siblings.

Alana shifted until she was on top of Tegan, nestled between her legs and with her elbows on the floor on either side of Tegan's face, bearing her weight so her hands were free to sift through Tegan's hair and to caress her cheeks and lips. She wasn't sure how to voice the questions she had been asking herself since she was worried that she might sound as if she thought their relationship was just a holiday fling. Whatever it was, and however long it might last, it was more meaningful than anything Alana had experienced before. Did meaningful have to mean forever? Or could it be wonderful and temporary?

Alana's head ached from the questions, so she decided to ignore them and concentrate on Tegan instead. On the way her mouth parted in a sigh when Alana's finger traced the curve of her earlobe, and on the heat Alana felt against her thigh when she pressed it against Tegan's crotch. On the way their lips fit together with the ease of familiarity and the thrill of desire when she kissed her. Alana was confused by the way Tegan managed to embody a blend of the comforts of home with the excitement of a passionate tryst—two concepts that Alana thought should be in conflict but were instead perfectly meshed. She turned away from that, too, and distracted herself thoroughly by falling deeper into Tegan's kiss.

Chapter Sixteen

Two days later, Alana was ready to canvass her neighborhood again. She still had two puppies who needed homes, since Tegan's three clients and Chip, with her as proxy, had spoken for the other four. The smartest choice might have been to go to houses she hadn't been to before, but she had her own plans for the day.

Tegan was back at work after missing yesterday to take her grandmother home, and Alana had stopped by there in a roundabout route to this house. If Tegan hadn't been with a client, Alana would have been tempted to linger, but she was trying to cram all her missed appointments into the next few days. Alana missed her already.

She got out of the truck, pulled the pet carrier off the passenger seat, and picked up a plastic sack from the local pet store. She balanced the load she was carrying and went onto the porch to ring the bell. Gladys opened the door with its chain attached.

"Good morning. It's Alana, from the old Harrison place."

"Hello, Alana," Gladys said. She shut the door to undo the chain and opened it wider. She pointed at the crate. "Do you have your puppies in there? I'm afraid I still can't take one."

"In here?" Alana looked at the carrier as if she'd forgotten she had it in her hand. "No. This is a cat I'm taking to its new foster home. I thought I'd come by and see you on the way. Maybe get a cup of tea, if it's no trouble?"

Alana felt horribly awkward inviting herself in, but she had other stops today and really needed to get inside the house.

"Of course. I'll put the kettle on. Come in."

Alana went inside and set the carrier on the floor next to the couch. "Do you mind terribly if I let him out to stretch his legs?" she asked once Gladys had returned to the living room. "He's been cooped up in here for ages."

Less than ten minutes, really, but oh, well.

"I don't see why not," Gladys said.

Alana opened the crate, but the gray cat remained huddled as far back as he could get. "He's frightened, but I'm sure he'll come out if we just leave him be," she said, sitting up again and taking the cup Gladys offered. "He's skin and bones. He's been living out of the trash bins at an apartment building in Union Gap, right on a really busy road." Maybe she was laying it on a bit thick. "He was abandoned by his owners."

She moved the conversation to other topics, pretending not to notice the way Gladys was leaning over, watching the wary cat.

"Here he comes," Gladys whispered. Alana looked down and saw a gray face with moss-green eyes, a thin white mustache, and white whiskers peering out of the crate. He took a few more steps, moving cautiously, and then raced behind a chair. "He's beautiful."

Welcome home, cat, Alana thought, happily drinking her tea.

"What's his name?"

"He doesn't have one," Alana said. "Do you have any suggestions?"

"How about Charlie? He looks like Charlie Chaplin."

"Oh, that's a good name for him. Charlie it is."

When Alana left a while later, the cat stayed behind, along with the food and bowls Alana had bought and a stack of coupons for vet care that Dez had created on the clinic's computer this morning. She was surprised by how much less lonely the house had felt merely with the addition of one tiny beating heart. Her phone rang as she was backing out of the driveway, and she pulled over to answer, hoping it was Tegan telepathically knowing she had good news about the cat.

"Alana? It's Jim Krantz."

Alana's heart jumped when she heard the voice of her ex-boss's boss. She forced herself to calm down. He couldn't fire her again, for God's sake, so why should she feel intimidated? He hadn't been directly involved in her firing and subsequent humiliation, though. Maybe he felt he had missed out and was calling to make up for it.

"Hello, Jim," she said.

"I'll get right to the point," he said, sounding brusque, as if she was the one interrupting his day. "I fired Tabby. One mistake after another since you left. Cost us a fortune."

Alana's heart did something funny again, but this time it was gleeful. Vindication was sweet.

"I've been going over her books, and it seems you'd been catching her mistakes for months. I don't know who was the main one to blame for treating the Chief of Police like a stripper..." He paused midsentence and gave a snort of laughter. "It's not funny," he said, raising his voice.

"I wasn't the one who laughed," she said. She was half listening, and half thinking about how much fun it was going to be to tell Tegan about this phone call. Maybe he'd write her a letter of recommendation, explaining everything. That, along with Chip's reference, would give her plenty of options when she decided to leave. She decided she'd omit the part about leaving when she told Tegan about this. It was a touchy subject between them, even though they both acknowledged it openly.

"Anyway, we know you weren't completely responsible, if at all. You were carrying the weight of the job while you were here, so I figured you should have it. We've hired an outside company to handle events until we replace her, so we need you here as soon as possible."

Whoa. "I have a new job. I can't just leave." Or could she? Chip would be better off with just about anyone else but her leading his trail rides. She'd helped him with some management projects, but he really needed to start doing them on his own. Tegan could take the puppies for a couple weeks until they were ready for their new homes...

Tegan. Alana had a wild thought of her coming along, but she dismissed it quickly. Even if Tegan might have been willing to leave her practice, she wouldn't go now, with her grandmother barely out of the hospital.

"Nonsense. Aren't you at some dude ranch or something? Somewhere in Alaska? Get a flight and come back to the city where you belong."

Alana shook her head, trying to clear it. The increase in pay was ridiculous. The satisfaction of coming back in triumph after leaving in shame was worth even more to her.

But...Tegan.

She had been planning to leave, anyway. They both knew it. Why not do it now, rather than later when she would be so deeply in love, she might not be able to break away?

She leaned forward, resting her forehead on the steering wheel. When she thought about being in love with Tegan, it didn't seem like some future emotion. It was how she felt right now. All the more reason to run while she still could.

"I need to think," she said, talking more about Tegan than the job offer. "It's too sudden. I don't know..."

"Call me tonight. We need you here."

She tossed her phone on the passenger seat and tried to pull herself together. This was a dream come true. And Tegan was a dream, too—one she'd never known she had. She had until tonight, though. She had to focus on her next task, get through the next hour. Step by step she'd make it through until she had to call him back.

She managed to drive the short distance to Jennifer's house without hitting any mailboxes or trees along the way, even though she was distracted. Her mind wasn't sure what to focus on, opting instead to frantically chase its tail like a dog. She couldn't be in love with Tegan. How could she be in love with her?

How could she not be?

She knocked on the door, and Jennifer opened it, looking as frazzled as she felt, which managed to calm Alana. "The socks are so tiny," Jennifer said without preamble. "How can I keep track of them in the wash when they're so small?"

Alana wondered if she should turn around and leave. At the moment, Jennifer didn't sound like someone who should be handling all the accounts for a business if she couldn't even manage socks. "Um, put them in a lingerie bag?"

"Brilliant. Come in." She pulled Alana inside and into the kitchen, gesturing for her to sit at the counter and giving her a juice box.

Alana shrugged and unwrapped the little straw.

"Sorry," said Jennifer, standing on the opposite side of the counter in front of a large pile of children's clothes. "It's laundry day. It always makes me crazy, with all these weensy little clothes."

Alana took a sip of her juice and set the box to one side, reaching over and taking a red and blue striped shirt off the pile. She smoothed it out on the counter and folded over the sleeves. "What do you know about business accounting?"

"Hmm. I took classes in college, and it was part of the CPA exam, but my specialty is public accounting. If you have a specific question, I can research it if I don't know the answer offhand."

"Nothing specific. I was actually going to talk to you about a possible job. The ranch where I work needs a part-time accountant." Alana set the unevenly folded shirt on top of Jennifer's stack and selected a pair of corduroy pants that were about a foot long. They looked easier to fold than anything with pencil-sized sleeves. "The owner won't be able to pay much, but you can do a lot of the work from home. When you need to be at the ranch, you can bring the kids with you."

She looked around, suddenly realizing how quiet it was in the house. "Where are they? You didn't accidentally stick them in the dryer, did you?"

"I don't think so," Jennifer said. "But come to think of it, I haven't seen them for over an hour."

Alana stared at her, trying to figure out if Jennifer was kidding, or if she needed to call the authorities.

Jennifer laughed. "I never get tired of the way people look when I tell that joke. The kids are with my mother this morning, so you don't need to worry. I saw you reaching for your phone."

"Was not," Alana said, moving her hands back to the counter.

"Seriously, the job sounds wonderful. I have some good books I can read, and friends who are in corporate accounting and could give me advice."

"You'll fit right in," said Alana. "We're all learning as we go."

She lowered her head, concentrating on the pants she was folding. When she had first arrived in Yakima, she had been determined to remain detached at the ranch. Go there, do her job, go home. Get out as soon as possible. Now, when she had the great opportunity she had been hoping for, she was talking about *we* and imagining how much fun it would be to work at the ranch with Jennifer and Chip.

"I'll have to rewrite my résumé and get an outfit dry-cleaned for the interview. Do you know how many other applicants there are?"

Alana laughed. "There's you, and let's see…you. You can come out sometime when I'm there, and I'll introduce you. It's a casual place, and I honestly think the owner will be happier if you show up in jeans. He wants to create a family atmosphere."

"It sounds too good to be true," Jennifer said, holding a half-folded onesie to her chest. "A chance to keep current without having to pay for childcare. Adult conversations. Thank you."

Alana acknowledged Jennifer's enthusiasm with a twinge of something like guilt. She was so appreciative of a chance to work at the ranch—something Alana had, if she was being honest with herself, thought was beneath her when she first arrived. After working with Tegan and the horses, she had nothing but respect and envious admiration for disciplined riders. Even the work she was doing in Chip's place was something she had dismissed as boring and simple, after having watched her parents handle the tasks with ease throughout her childhood. Now she understood better how much adaptability and innovative thinking the managerial job required. She had called her family more often in the past month than she had over a full year when she had been in Philadelphia, asking their advice and sharing stories.

Now Jennifer was treating this opportunity as something special, the same way Alana should have done from the start. She only hoped Chip stayed in business long enough for Jennifer to read even one of those books she had. "Thank me after you've seen his accounting system. This might be a mess you won't be able to solve."

❖

Jennifer had been too excited to wait, so Alana took her to meet Chip right away. She sat in her office with the door open, listening to them talking from across the foyer. When Jennifer wasn't being overwhelmed by laundry day, she was quite ferocious, and she had quickly gone from trying to impress Chip as a potential new boss to lecturing him about how he was running his business. He seemed more than happy to hand the accounting reins over to her.

Her phone rang, and she felt almost giddy when she saw Tegan's name pop up on the screen. Lord, she had it bad.

"Hey." She closed her door and settled into her desk chair.

"Hey back," Tegan said, and Alana grinned. "I'm going to be working late tonight, but I was hoping I could take you out to dinner after. There's a new place downtown, on Front Street, that's supposed to have great steaks and salmon. And wine."

For all the time they had spent together these past few weeks, they hadn't gone on an actual date. Alana felt a mixed rush of anticipation and nervousness, more to do with her epiphany about how much she cared about Tegan than at the thought of going out to eat with her. Everything seemed to have changed from her perspective, even though nothing was different on the surface.

"It sounds nice. Especially the wine."

"Good. I'll make reservations and call back once I know what time."

"Is it dressy, or casual?"

Tegan laughed. "Yakima dressy, not five-star hotel dressy. Somewhere in between sequins and pajama pants."

"You just described my entire wardrobe, so I'll be able to come up with something." Alana picked up a brochure from her desk. "Say, have you heard of the Fresh Hop Ale Festival? I was filling the case of brochures in the lobby and found out about it. It looks like something fun we could do."

"Oh…um…yes. I've heard of it."

"Your voice sounds funny," Alana said, dropping the brochure again. "What is it? Did you meet your ex at the festival or something?"

"No, nothing like that. It's just…well, the festival is in the fall…"

"And you're not sure you'll still want to go with me by then? I'm not asking for a committed response right now. I only—"

"Alana, stop," Tegan said, her voice gentle, but firm enough to cut through Alana's growing feeling of anger. She wasn't mad at Tegan, but at herself. Just because she had just recognized how deep her feelings for Tegan were didn't mean she should assume Tegan felt the same about her.

"Of course I'd want to go with you," Tegan continued. "I want to go anywhere with you, whether it's mundane like the grocery store or something more festive. It's just, this is the first time I've heard you make any sort of plans for the future here, besides the grand opening at the ranch or when you'll be able to leave. I want to do as much as I can with you while you're here. You just caught me by surprise because I wasn't sure you felt the same way."

"Well, I do."

"Well, okay," Tegan said. "Are we good?"

"We're good. I'll see you tonight."

Alana ended the call and brought up Jim's number on her screen. She wasn't sure what she was doing in Yakima, whether or not her sense of being part of this community—part of Tegan's life and Chip's ranch family—was something real. She would eventually leave, probably, and return to some version of her old life, but not right now.

CHAPTER SEVENTEEN

Tegan drove them into Yakima, only letting go of Alana's hand when she needed to parallel park a few blocks away from Front Street. The entire downtown area looked nothing like it had when Tegan was a child, when the buildings had been in various states of disrepair and the neighborhood had been questionable at best, unsafe at worst. Then, many of the ground level shops had been vacant and most of the higher floors had been used for decrepit apartments and shady businesses.

Now the central blocks of the city were thriving. During the summer, the sidewalks would be filled with tourists who were there to visit winery tasting rooms, upscale microbreweries and pubs, and boutique stores that offered a break from the cookie cutter mall in Union Gap. Once-dangerous alleyways had become venues for street fairs and seasonal concerts, and the cost of renting one of the overhauled apartments was extravagant when compared to the rest of the region.

Tegan understood that the city needed the tourist dollars, and she appreciated the pedestrian-friendly streets and unique restaurants, but she never felt like she was truly in Yakima when she was downtown. She could be in any one of the small towns in Washington that was making an effort to cater to artsy, wine-loving visitors. To her, Yakima was in the groves and hills and dust surrounding the town, not in the artificially enhanced downtown streets.

She led them toward a three-story building, with brick walls that were painted a deep red and warm brown wood surrounding the windows and doors. The downstairs section was separated into a Vietnamese restaurant and the steakhouse, and upstairs was devoted to several art galleries and studio spaces.

Alana paused and looked up at the building's facade. "I wonder if they all shop from the same catalog," she said, gesturing down the street behind them. She looked at Tegan and must have noticed her questioning expression. "Tourist-hungry small towns," she clarified. "Maybe they buy a kit that comes with a certain number of shutters, planter boxes, and iron lampposts, depending on how many blocks they need to redecorate."

Tegan laughed. "I was thinking the same thing. I could swear I've seen this exact same street in at least twenty other places in Eastern Washington."

Alana grinned and bumped Tegan with her elbow. "It's beautiful, don't get me wrong. And from the perspective of someone in the tourist industry, it's a smart move. There's just a sort of sameness to it."

"Downtown had much more character when I was younger," Tegan agreed. "You wouldn't have driven down this street without reaching over to lock your door, though, so I suppose some individuality is worth giving up in exchange for safety."

They went inside and were seated immediately. Far too many tables for Tegan's taste were crammed into the space to maximize occupancy. During the high season, they would all be full, but tonight the few patrons were spread around the room, and she and Alana had some sense of privacy.

After they ordered, Tegan reached for Alana's hand again. She was wearing khakis and a shimmery green shirt that had nearly made Tegan call to cancel their dinner reservations. If this had been the day before, she might have done so in her desperation to take full advantage of any opportunity she had to touch Alana and slide her silky top over her shoulders and onto the floor. Something in

Alana's voice on the phone had changed today, though. Something that made Tegan believe she might stick around for a while. Not forever—Tegan wasn't stupid enough to believe in forever—but maybe until fall. At least for a few weeks. For the first time, Tegan trusted that Alana would still be there after dinner.

"How's the riding going?" Tegan asked, rubbing Alana's palm with her thumb and trying to focus on making conversation rather than crawling over the table and kissing her.

Alana shrugged. "Okay, I think. I'm more comfortable with the horses every day, but I'm still surprised every time I find myself on top of one. I completely skipped the horse-crazy girl phase when I was young. I suppose you were toddling after horses right from the start. Did you always want to ride?"

Tegan shook her head. For the first decade of her life she had only wanted her family to be put back together. There hadn't been room inside her for any other desires. "Not really. I liked animals and would play with my grandparents' cats and dogs, but that's not why I started riding. I used to wander alone for miles around their ranch and wherever else the trails led. I think they bought Charm for me just to get me off the ground and out of reach of rattlesnakes and coyotes."

Alana squeezed her hand lightly. "Where were you trying to go?"

"Nowhere in particular," Tegan said. She took a sip of her wine as she tried to find the words to explain why she had needed to walk. "I guess I wanted to find something, not go someplace. Subconsciously, I knew I wasn't going to find it at home, so I went out searching. That probably doesn't make any sense."

Alana raised their joined hands and brushed her lips across Tegan's knuckles before letting her go to make room for their plates of food. "It makes perfect sense," she said as soon as the server had walked away. "I felt the same way, but between school and the hotel I didn't have time to go looking. I kept waiting for something to come to me. Until I graduated."

"And you're still searching," Tegan said quietly, before crunching through a bite of her peppercorn-crusted steak. She wondered what Alana was really looking for.

"Not here," Alana said, looking almost as surprised by the words as Tegan felt when hearing them. "I suppose it's because Yakima is a side trip in my career, I guess, so I feel more present here than I have before. And because of you. There's no need to search for anything except for more time with you."

"I feel the same about you." Tegan used her fork to toy with the pile of multicolored baby carrots on her plate. As usual, she was disarmed by Alana's honesty and directness. Alana was talking about right now—not tomorrow or next month or any time in the future—but she never seemed to hold back on what she was feeling. Tegan was struggling to stay present with her, not to search for hidden meanings where there were none and not to spoil this moment simply because she was greedy for more.

Alana playfully kicked her shin. "I'm glad. Now, stop looking morose and trade me some of your carrots for my spinach."

Tegan curled her arm around her plate, as if protecting her food from Alana's invasion. "Greens are good for you."

"Yes, but they don't taste as good as carrots."

Tegan grinned, heeding Alana's advice and pushing her maudlin thoughts away. "Throw in some of your potatoes, and we have a deal."

They stopped by the clinic on the way back to Alana's and checked on Charm and Rio. Tegan measured out their evening feed while Alana visited with Charm in her stall.

"Was she your first horse?" Alana asked when Tegan came over and poured a scoop of grain into Charm's bucket.

"Yes. And Rio's her son," Tegan said, moving across the aisle and smiling at the gelding's impatient nickers. "She has great bloodlines, but we only bred her once. She retired from competitions as soon as Rio was old enough for me to ride. He's more energetic and seems to thrive on competition, while she's, well…"

"More of a stop and smell the roses type?"

"Maybe more of a stand still and hope some roses wander by for you to sniff type," Tegan said with a fond smile. "She's talented and won almost every class I ever entered with her, but she'd rather chill than work hard."

Alana followed Tegan back into the feed room and sat on one of the unopened hay bales, watching her close the feed cans and tidy the already neat space. "She must have been perfect for you when you were in your wandering phase."

"You're right. She was a steady and quiet companion, never expecting anything from me. I eventually stopped feeling like I was searching and just enjoyed being with her. I started meeting other neighborhood kids with horses, and the feeling of something missing from my life slowly went away. I suppose that's what my grandparents had planned all along when they got her for me."

Alana thought of Gladys and Charlie, and of Jennifer and her new job. Of herself, too, with Tegan quietly and thoroughly filling a need that Alana had never known how to satisfy. "People always seem to be looking for something epic, don't they?" she asked. "Something huge that will change their lives and make everything better. But maybe even the smallest shift in perspective can make all the difference."

Tegan walked over and sat next to her, moving slowly as if she thought a sudden move might startle Alana out of the barn and possibly all the way out of Yakima. "I don't know," she said softly, cupping Alana's cheek. "You seem pretty epic to me."

Alana leaned into the contact, sighing as Tegan brushed her fingers through the hair at her temple. Tegan's touch was light, skimming over her cheekbones and tracing a path down the side of her neck, but the feeling resonated inside Alana until her body was humming in tune to the movement of Tegan's hand.

She was trying to hold herself together, to accept how much her feelings for Tegan had grown and to find a way to reconcile those emotions with the plans she'd had in place for as long as she could remember. She had already given up the chance to slip back into her old life—into a better version of it, with the promotion—and she didn't regret the decision to stay. Especially once Tegan scooted closer, until their thighs were flush against each other and Tegan was kissing her neck. But would she find it harder to leave as week after week went by? Would she eventually find herself stuck in this place simply because she had settled for the easier path of staying?

Tegan kissed Alana on the mouth, with her hand on Alana's hip drawing her closer. None of this felt like settling to Alana. No part of Tegan's body, no conversation with her, no quiet moments spent in her company spoke of boredom or regret. Tegan's kisses felt like possibility, not limits.

Alana stopped bothering to analyze her feelings and just kissed her back with the full extent of her desire, turning their gentle movements into something deeper and less patient. She had enough to worry about with the ranch's impending opening and her role in it. Her relationship with Tegan might have a foggy future, and she might be torn between wanting to find out how far they could go together and her original plan to forge ahead on her own, but for the moment, Tegan was the best part of her life. The one part where she felt as if she was on solid ground. She was going to enjoy every second, for as long as it lasted.

CHAPTER EIGHTEEN

A lana spent Saturday's drive from home to the ranch focused on her to-do list for the day. She had rental equipment to confirm, interviews to conduct for a last-minute housekeeping replacement, and horses to ride. Always horses to ride.

She got out of her truck and Chip bounded down the stairs and came over to help her get the puppies into the lodge.

"I have a surprise for you," he said, once the dogs were settled in the office. "I thought you might enjoy a break from all the prep work you've been doing, so I made arrangements for you and Tegan to go on a rafting trip today. You'll be joining a group from a hotel in Selah, and it will give you a chance to experience what it will be like when you accompany our guests. What do you think?"

What did she think? She had too much to do at the ranch to spend an entire day floating down a river. And the thought of getting sprayed with water and baked by the sun was unappealing. And she had been so consumed with learning how to ride that she had hoped the other aspects of her job would just go away. She sighed as she looked at Chip, with his enthusiastic expression and obvious delight in her good fortune. She knew he'd much rather be the one going rafting rather than being cooped up inside the ranch. She'd rather he was going, too.

"That's great," she said, trying to muster a smile since her tone of voice sounded flat and unconvincing. She had no choice but to graciously accept the change in plans since she had no reasonable excuse for getting out of doing her actual work instead of co-opting Chip's. At least rafting would be easier than riding since all she had to do was sit in the boat. The other people wouldn't be the ranch's guests, so they wouldn't care if she didn't look like she was having fun.

"You'll love it. Hey, there's Tegan. I told her to come over, but she has no idea why."

Alana watched him relay his news to Tegan. She was hoping for them to share a commiserating eye roll or for Tegan to miraculously come up with a plan for getting both of them out of the excursion, but Tegan looked almost as excited as Chip.

She came over and kissed Alana on the cheek, resting her hand on her lower back. "That's not a very convincing smile," Tegan said in a low voice. "Don't worry. It'll be a good day."

Alana felt her smile morph into one that felt more natural. She'd get to spend the day with Tegan, which was worth sodden sneakers and the postponement of her planned day's work. She left her list of tasks with Chip and reminded him that he would have to take over the interviews in her absence, and then got in Tegan's Jeep. The drive to the hotel was far too short. If she had to be on this outdoor adventure then she would have preferred to have Tegan all to herself, but before she knew it, she was crammed in a bare-bones white van with two other couples and a family with two teenaged boys and was on her way to the Tieton River.

Alana settled back in her seat and held Tegan close against her side. "So, have you been on this river a lot of times?"

"Only twice, and it's a blast. Nearly continuous rapids, and some are Class III." Tegan sighed with apparent anticipation. "I've mostly gone rafting and tubing on the Upper Yakima, where there's only one Class II."

Alana wasn't quite sure what the classifications meant, but she was fairly sure that the lower number sounded less death defying. "I've never done this, so shouldn't I stick to Class I or less?"

Tegan patted her knee. "You'll be fine. The guides will explain everything and tell you what to do if the raft flips over or you fall out."

"This sounds like our riding lessons all over again, with all your scary hypotheticals." Alana groaned. "Will they cover what I should do if I'm attacked by a giant river squid?"

"Whack it with your paddle," Tegan suggested.

Alana pushed at her playfully, but her thoughts were moving too far ahead—surging along the rapids—to let her relax very much.

She didn't feel much better even after she had listened to the guide's instructions about paddling and aiming her feet downriver if she got dumped out of the boat. She strapped on her plastic helmet and gingerly sat on the edge of the raft next to Tegan.

"Since they seem so concerned about keeping us from falling into the river, you'd think they'd have us sit in the boat rather than perching precariously on the rim," she said, bouncing lightly on the inflated edge of the raft and nearly toppling backward.

Tegan tapped the bottom of the raft with her foot. "It needs to be flexible enough to skim over big rocks, so there's nothing to protect you down here. You'd have a painful ride."

"I think I'd rather have a sore rear end than a bashed-in head," Alana said. "At least I'll have you at home tonight to massage me back to health."

Tegan nodded. "You're right. You really should sit in the bottom of the boat."

The guide pushed them toward the middle of the river, and the swiftly moving water caught hold of the raft. After a few minutes of drops and eddies, Alana decided she had been overly intimidated by this Class III business. She eventually relaxed her death grip on the side of the raft and let herself look around at the scenery, paddling when the guide told them to.

Tegan poked her in the back. "Look," she said, speaking loudly enough for the others on the raft to hear and pointing to the cliff face bordering one side of the river. "An eagle."

The bird's pristine white head and tail stood out starkly against the coppery red backdrop. "Wow," Alana said, carefully shifting her position to watch the raptor as long as possible. "I've never seen one in the wild before."

Tegan pointed out some magpies and other birds, and Alana filed them away for use on future trail rides and rafting trips. She was facing backward and looking at a red-tailed hawk when she realized that the river sounded louder than it had before.

"Turn around, Alana," Tegan said, pressing her hand on Alana's shoulder. "There are some bigger rapids just around this turn."

"Bigger?" Alana asked. She thought the previous ones had been plenty big. She was even more convinced of that fact after they rounded the bend and ricocheted off a huge boulder, spinning a few disorienting times before flying down the river.

They approached another rounded boulder, much larger than the raft itself, and the guide yelled for Alana's side of the raft to paddle as hard as they could. Tegan did her part, of course. Alana and their two other seatmates froze for a brief moment before joining in, but they rammed into the rock, anyway. Alana struggled to keep herself on the raft. Was the guide really surprised that their attempts to steer had been ineffective? They seemed to be assuming a ridiculously high level of competence from a group of amateurs.

The raft careened around another bend and the man next to Alana leaned back too far and fell into the river. She felt his hand pull at her sleeve as he went, but luckily, he didn't get a firm grasp of it since he would have been more likely to pull her in with him rather than saving himself. If he had managed to drag her off the raft, she would have put him in the category of giant river squid and used her paddle accordingly. She felt the comforting presence of Tegan's arm around her, anchoring her in place.

The man seemed destined not to be the only person overboard. When the raft got caught in a whirlpool just below the boulder, one of the women on the other side from Alana held out her paddle for him to grab and ended up tipping over the edge.

"We seem to be losing people at an alarming rate," Alana called to Tegan over the roaring water.

"Just be sure that *you* stay on the raft," Tegan said. "You're all that matters."

As soon as the rapids decreased somewhat, the guides pulled the raft into the shallows and fished the two out of the river. Aside from a couple of scrapes and bruises, they seemed fine. Alana leaned against Tegan's shoulder.

"Well, we got through it," she said, with relief in her voice.

"We got through that one," Tegan said, kissing the top of Alana's head where it rested on her shoulder. "There are more up ahead."

"More," Alana repeated. "Are they just as bad?"

"Hmm," Tegan said noncommittally.

Alana sat up and rolled her eyes. "You might as well say it, then. They're going to be worse."

"Not worse, necessarily. Just...faster."

The river widened and the jutting rocks and frothy water gave way to gentle movement and murky depths. The grassy shore was dotted with picnic tables and cookout areas, and a few people were hanging out near the edge of the river. Alana could see around the bend ahead, where the rapids began again, but she assumed they had reached their destination since the rafting company's van was in the parking lot. She rested her paddle over her knees as she caught her breath, feeling water dripping off it and down her already wet calves.

She had actually enjoyed the second half of the trip, since no one else had fallen out and she'd figured out how to balance comfortably while the raft tilted and spun. Now that she knew what to expect, she would have been looking forward to coming back for another try if she wasn't so concerned about the responsibility she was going to have for her guests. Yes, the guides would be the ones in charge, but the burden of caring about her people and hoping to keep them safe rested ultimately with her.

Her worried thoughts were interrupted by one of the guides shrieking about the raft being about to capsize. Since they were merely floating along, Alana ignored him, until he and the other guide jumped out and flipped the raft over.

Alana submerged and sank several feet before rising up again and crossing to the raft with two long strokes. She clutched one of the nylon cords that wrapped around the raft and held herself above the water while she coughed to clear her throat. Judging by the shouts of laughter around her, the other rafters were far more delighted by the unexpected dunking than she was.

Tegan surfaced next to her with a big grin on her face. She hooked one elbow over the raft and used her other hand to push soaked hair out of her eyes and off her forehead. Tiny droplets of water stuck to her eyelashes, glinting in the sunlight and brightening her face. Alana wrapped her legs around Tegan's and tucked their hips together. She leaned forward and kissed Tegan, immediately aroused by the slippery, frictionless feel of the skin between them.

"Well?" Tegan asked. "What did you think?"

"You were right. I had a great time."

And she had. She loved spending time with Tegan in the nature she loved so much. She had liked the speed and stomach-dropping sensation when the raft plummeted down the rapids. She couldn't shake her concerns about leading these tours, though. She had planned numerous events before, but none of them had posed a real physical risk to the people involved, discounting fluke accidents. She wasn't afraid of trying new and potentially dangerous activities herself, but leading others through them was an entirely different matter. She wasn't sure she had the confidence to handle it.

CHAPTER NINETEEN

The week before the grand opening, Alana sat at her desk surrounded by checked off lists. Every room was clean and ready for guests, both the ones who had booked and extras in case of last-minute arrivals. The barbecue had been marketed and planned to the last detail. She tossed another list onto the pile and stood up. Everything was ready, except for her. She could squeeze in a few more lessons and plenty more rides this week, but she knew they wouldn't have a significant impact on her skills. She was either good enough to do her job right now, or she wasn't.

The past week had been nerve-racking for the entire staff as they went through the endless details necessary to get the ranch ready. Pre-opening jitters were evident everywhere, and Alana was getting accustomed to hearing the housekeeping staff dropping things and Chip muttering to himself whenever she roamed through the lodge.

Her week with Tegan had been exhausting, too. In the best way possible. They had spent an evening cooking a heart-healthy meal in her grandparents' farmhouse kitchen, and they had explored the city, with Tegan acting as tour guide to show her the unique shops and thriving farms in and around Yakima. Her favorite times, though, were always the nights spent with Tegan. The sex, yes. Alana had never connected with a lover as thoroughly and profoundly as with Tegan. But she also loved sitting in the living room with a glass of wine, discussing their days while the puppies destroyed their footwear and Lace dozed on the couch next to them.

She shook her head. How had she fallen under the spell of domesticity? Tegan had cast it, but Alana wasn't even struggling a little to come back to her senses. She got up, feeling suddenly edgy and like she needed to move. She went over to Chip's crowded office and stood next to the baby gate, looking at the unprofessional but appealing scene in front of her. Jennifer was the only one working. She was sitting at Chip's desk and going through some paperwork while gently rocking Brandon's bassinet with her stockinged foot. Chip and Michelle were on the floor, playing with the puppies. Lace was curled in a ball in the bed Chip had put in the corner of the room for her, where she could watch her litter and still feel protected by the walls behind her.

"I'm going to exercise some of the horses," she said. She usually referred to it with those words, even though her main objective had much more to do with her own riding practice than the horses' training.

Chip looked up at the sound of her voice. "Hey, you should take Michelle on the short loop. It'd be a mini-rehearsal for you before the weekend."

"I can ride," Michelle offered in a hopeful voice.

Jennifer turned around, and Alana expected her to mouth something along the lines of *No, she can't.*

"Actually, she can," Jennifer said, as if reading her mind. "Well, I mean she's been on horses. My sister-in-law has a farm, and Michelle rides with her when we visit."

"On her own?" Alana asked. She didn't like this idea at all. How could she be responsible for this tiny person? She sighed. She'd better figure out how, and fast, since she had families with young children coming this weekend.

"She knows the basics of steering and stopping. I walked the trail on foot the other day with her, and I think she'd be fine. If you don't mind, of course."

"It'll be fun," she lied. Her heart was already racing, and her palms felt sweaty. She rubbed them on her jeans. Hopefully Michelle was a good enough rider to race for help when Alana fainted due to stress and toppled off her own horse. "Let's go, then."

Michelle put down the puppy she had been holding, and it ran to the baby gate with her. Alana helped her through, and the puppy sat on the other side of the gate and whined. Alana felt like doing a little crying herself, but she forced a smile on her face as she and Michelle walked to the corral.

She picked Cotton for her. The Appaloosa mare was small and narrow, plus she had the smoothest trot of all the horses. Alana wasn't about to let Michelle do more than the slowest walk possible, but if the worst happened—she was beginning to sound like Tegan!—and Cotton broke from her walk, Michelle ought to be able to balance long enough to stop her.

Alana relaxed somewhat as they groomed the horses, because Michelle seemed to have been taught well. She couldn't reach to brush the upper part of Cotton's body, but she stayed in the safe zones while she worked on her lower half and legs. Alana finished the higher parts and took care of tacking both horses. She got Michelle mounted in one of the children's saddles and adjusted her stirrups before having her walk in circles around the corral until she was satisfied that Michelle could manage the basics of controlling her horse. Cotton had done this often enough to be sufficiently bored and slow, so Alana took a deep breath, mounted Fitz, and led them out of the gate.

She was actually doing it. Leading a trail ride. She only had one person behind her, and they weren't even a dozen yards from the main corral yet, but Alana felt the vastness of the open space around her, the enormity of what she was doing even more than when she had been out here with Tegan. She had been worried enough when it had been a vague future endeavor—one she had, honestly, never fully believed would come to pass—and now she realized what this weekend would bring. She wished more than anything that Tegan was riding with them today, talking her down from her spiraling anxiety.

She spent more time turned in her saddle to check on Michelle than was probably safe, but she couldn't help herself. She tried to make conversation, pointing out birds and bushes to put her charge at ease. It worked, although not in the way Alana had planned, since Michelle was soon giggling as she corrected Alana's mistakes. She knew a lot more about the local flora and fauna than Alana, and she seemed comfortable on her horse. If only she could reach the top of the horse's back, she'd probably be better at this job than Alana.

They turned onto the loop. It was one of Alana's favorites since it was short enough for her to ride quite a few times during a typical workday, on multiple horses. There were smooth spots with decent footing for trotting, and she knew she was close enough to the lodge for Chip to find her quickly if she fell off. She was even close enough to hear some sort of machinery at the lodge, probably the construction of the gazebo in the backyard.

Her muscles were slowly starting to unwind when she heard the buzzing sound getting louder instead of quieter as they moved farther from the main ranch site. She frowned, turning back again, but Michelle merely smiled and gave her a little wave as Cotton marched solemnly along.

They went around a sharp curve, and Alana halted, convinced something was wrong. The shrill whine was getting worse, and Fitz's ears were flicking back and forth. He didn't seem able to pinpoint the direction of the noise either, since the high walls of the canyon made sounds echo and magnify. It could be nothing more than a motorcycle on a nearby road, although Alana had never heard one this loud.

She was just trying to figure out whether to keep going or turn back when she looked back at Michelle and saw a small motorbike roar around the corner, directly toward Cotton. Fitz spun to face it, snorting and with his ears pricked tensely forward. The bike's rider skidded to a halt, nearly spinning in a full circle, and idled loudly.

Alana's relief that he had stopped was short-lived as she watched Cotton's reaction with growing panic. The mare half reared, terrified by the sudden attack by the loud, metal predator. Michelle managed to stay on, but she dropped her reins. Alana was trying desperately to think of something to say, some advice to shout to her, but nothing could stop the scene unfolding in front of her.

Cotton flipped her head, the whites of her eyes showing, and the loop of the reins slid to just behind her ears. One side was hanging low, and Alana knew what was going to happen before it did, but she was powerless to stop the mare from stepping on the dangling reins, then pulling back against the resistance her own hoof was causing and the painful jab of the bit against her jaw, the reins snapping and hanging down. Nothing to keep the mare, with her rolling eyes and panicked snorts, from running to the safety of her corral.

Alana snapped alert, turning Fitz sideways so he blocked the trail, although Cotton wouldn't have any trouble going around him through the sparse brush. She eased him sideways, talking quietly to Michelle and Cotton even though she doubted they could hear her over the still running bike.

"Shut it off," she said, not wanting to risk a yell. He either heard her or read her expression correctly, because he turned off the engine.

Alana inched toward Cotton, reading the signs of panic and indecision in the mare's stiff posture and the fear in Michelle's frozen body. *It's just like going through a gate,* she chanted to herself, sidling up to Cotton, moving Fitz a little to the right and a step backward. She saw Cotton get ready to spring about a second before she did, giving her just enough time to make a grab for the dangling reins at the same time as the mare barged into Fitz.

Alana jumped off her horse and held both sets of reins in one hand while she grabbed Michelle out of the saddle with the other. "Go over by that rock," she said, indicating a boulder far enough along the trail for Michelle to be safe if the horses kept dancing around her.

She looked up and realized Chip had arrived. He must have run from the lodge because his face was bright red and he was gasping for breath.

"Sorry," said the kid on the bike. Alana recognized him now as one of the new evening reception desk clerks. "I didn't realize anyone was out here."

"What the he—" Chip glanced over at Michelle, and then back at the boy. "What are you doing with a bike on the horse trails?"

"I didn't know. They weren't marked."

"Yes, they are. Walk that damned thing back to the lodge and get out of here. Don't bother coming back."

Chip stalked over to her. She had seen him in various stages of emotion, from good-natured to nervous, but this was the first time she had seen rage in his expression. He took Cotton's reins from her and gently stroked the mare's neck. She could see his hand trembling as much as her own.

"Good job, Alana," he said. "I'm very sorry this happened, but it could have been much worse if not for your quick thinking."

Alana stared at him, quite certain her face resembled a startled goldfish. She had been expecting him to turn on her next, and rightly so, for not being an experienced enough guide to have figured out what was happening far sooner than she had.

"I heard the bike, and when I looked out the window, I saw him heading out to the trails," Chip continued. "I couldn't stop him, so I ran. But you're both all right. It's okay."

It definitely wasn't okay. "I heard the noise but didn't know where it was coming from. I should have..." She stopped. She had no idea what she should have done, which made it even worse.

"Sound travels in confusing ways around here," Chip said, seemingly back to his normal self. He called over to Michelle. "Let's get back to the ranch. Why don't I lead Cotton, and you can ride the big horse. Alana can lead you."

"No way," Alana said at the same time as Michelle jumped up eagerly.

Chip put his hand on her upper arm and lowered his voice. "She had a bad experience just now. If we let this end with something frightening, the negative feelings might stick with her for a lifetime. Don't do that to her." For all his appearance of being lost and bewildered within the lodge, once he was out here, he seemed full of confidence and determination.

"I can hear you," Michelle said. "I wanna ride the big horse."

"Kids," Chip said loudly, rolling his eyes and shaking his head in mock exasperation. "Come on, then. Up you go."

Alana reluctantly lifted Michelle onto Fitz. The stirrups on her adult saddle wouldn't go short enough for her, so she was going to have to ride without them. Her legs stuck out nearly perpendicular to the ground because of Fitz's wide barrel. She held onto the saddle horn and smiled at Alana.

The horses had calmed down quickly, too, once the danger had passed, but Alana couldn't let it go as easily. Her mind raced through a series of alternate outcomes, none of them pleasant, and all of them her fault. Her inner turmoil was completely at odds with the rest of the group. Chip and Michelle chatted and laughed, as relaxed as they had been in the office while playing with the puppies. The horses reverted to being experienced trail mounts and walked docilely along the trail, swishing their tails at flies now and again.

Alana wasn't sure how she made it through the next half hour. Jennifer met them at the barn, and Alana had to listen to a rehash of the trail mishap from two perspectives. Now that the frightening immediacy of danger had passed, Michelle seemed to think it had been a grand adventure. Chip had been correct about getting her back on Fitz, and Alana was glad she didn't seem scarred by the experience. Chip's version was much more circumspect than Michelle's, and awkwardly complimentary toward Alana.

She got both horses untacked and in their corrals during all this, and she held Chip back when Jennifer and Michelle started toward the lodge.

"I quit," she said bluntly. She had been rehearsing a dramatic speech in her mind, but she captured the essence of it in two words.

"Don't be hasty, Alana," he said, holding both palms toward her and speaking in the same tone of voice she had used to try to keep Cotton from bolting. "You had quite a shock out there. Give yourself some time to process it. Maybe take one of the other horses out for a nice walk."

She shook her head. She wasn't going out there again. "You don't understand, Chip. Before I got here, I hadn't been on a horse before, aside from ponies at a fair, or wooden horses on a carousel. I lied on my application because I needed this job. I don't like fishing, either. I don't even like to buy them at the grocery store."

The last sentence ended on a higher note, and Alana took a deep breath to cleanse the hysteria from her voice. "I won't put any other people in danger because of my stupid belief that I could learn fast enough."

He followed her into the tack room. "I saw how you handled the situation, Alana. If I thought for one second that you'd done it poorly, I'd be driving you to the airport myself. You kept your head, you made good choices, and you didn't let the situation escalate. There are risks involved with riding, even if there aren't motorbikes around. You've worked so hard to get ready for our opening, so please don't run away now."

She pushed past him and hesitated in the doorway, unable to meet his eyes. "I'm sorry I lied and wasted the time you could have spent looking for a replacement. Everything is in place for the grand opening, so you don't need me for it. You'll be better off leading the trail rides yourself, until you can find someone else. And I'll return the money you've paid me."

She turned and jogged back to the lodge, hurrying in to get her bag so she didn't run into Jennifer or Michelle. When she got to the truck, with its slashes of writing on the side, she realized this wasn't hers either. Nothing here was. She had no choice but to take it, though. Chip could pick it up at the house later.

❖

Tegan parked behind the truck, nearly sick with relief to see it, until she realized Alana would probably leave it there and take a cab to the airport. She ran inside, afraid the house would be empty already, but she heard sounds of movement coming from upstairs.

She went up the stairs and stood in the hallway outside the main bedroom, unable to keep herself from remembering the first time she and Alana had been here together. Now Alana was standing beside the bed and tossing clothes into her suitcase. She didn't have much to pack.

Alana hadn't seemed to have noticed her presence, and when Tegan took a step into the room and the floorboards creaked, she whipped around to face her.

"You startled me," Alana said, with one hand pressed to her heart. "Why aren't you...? How did you...?"

Tegan answered her half-formed questions. "Chip called. He told me what happened, Alana. He's worried about you."

"Worried? He should hate me. I lied to him."

"I thought it was fudging," Tegan said, hoping to bring out Alana's playful side. The pale, shaken woman in front of her was almost unrecognizable.

"Lying."

"And now you're leaving, right before his grand opening. Don't you think that's selfish?" Tegan heard an edge of anger in her voice. She was concentrating on the subject of Alana leaving the ranch, unable to face Alana leaving her, too.

"It would be more selfish to stay. I don't belong here, especially not out on those trails. I thought I could make myself fit, and I really wanted to, but I was wrong to try."

"I'm sorry, Alana," Tegan said, crossing the room and putting her arms around her. Alana held herself stiffly at first but slowly melted in Tegan's arms. Not completely, but a little. "I wish I'd been there, but Chip told me how you handled it. I wouldn't have been able to do better."

Alana pulled away at this. "Of course you would have. You'd have done something better than I did, or faster, or sooner." She sat on the bed. "What would have happened if I hadn't caught her reins in time?"

Tegan cautiously sat next to her. "Well, Cotton probably would have run back to the barn. Michelle might have been able to hang on, or she might have fallen off."

Alana made a noise somewhere between a sob and a squeak and covered her face with her hands.

"This is a positive thing, Alana. Not the motorbike part," Tegan hastily assured her when Alana gave her a disbelieving look. "I know this hit you hard, but it's important for you to really care about the people you're leading on trails. That will make you conscientious about preparing for your rides. I'm sure you considered Michelle's safety and did your best to make the ride a safe one from the start. And you took care of her during and after the incident. Chip said you admirably waited to have your meltdown until Michelle was out of earshot."

Tegan smiled, trying to encourage Alana to laugh, but she didn't. She stood up and looked at Tegan with an expression of resolve that chilled Tegan from her core out to her extremities. She had seen the same fierce determination in Alana as she worked on bettering her riding, not giving up for anything. Now her single-minded tenacity had a new target: leaving.

"I don't belong here, Tegan. We all know it. I got..." She hesitated, sniffing as if holding back tears. "I got a call from the hotel where I used to work. They fired my boss and want me to take her place. The pay is great, and the bad reputation I got there will go away. It's a job I can do without killing myself trying to prepare for it or killing anyone else while performing it."

Tegan stood up, as well. She had thought she was entering this relationship with Alana without any expectations, but she suddenly realized there was a traitorous, masochistic part of her heart that had thought maybe Alana would stay. She was never going to learn, was she? The strangest part of all this, though, was how genuinely happy she felt about Alana's job offer. She couldn't reconcile how much she wanted Alana to stay, how hurt she was by this sudden departure, and how much she wanted to celebrate Alana's triumphant return to the hotel after being unfairly fired.

"I was coming by the clinic, Tegan. I was going to say good-bye."

"It's okay, Alana," Tegan said, although it was anything but. "Congratulations on the new job."

She started to leave, but Alana called her back. "Wait. That's all?"

Tegan leaned against the door frame and crossed her arms. "You know I want you to stay, so telling you wouldn't change your mind. If I thought there was a chance you'd have eventually decided to stay here with me for good, not just for the time being, then I'd fight for us. I'd help you work through what happened today." Tegan paused, biting her lip hard to keep her eyes dry. "But you're leaving sooner or later, and it will only be harder to face the longer we're together, so it might as well be sooner."

"The puppies. You and Chip will take care of them?"

Alana was crying now, but Tegan wouldn't let herself. Later she would. Not now. She was tempted to tell Alana she wouldn't take care of them. Pretend she would take them to the pound, just to make her stay. Instead she simply nodded and turned away.

Chapter Twenty

Tegan walked through the front door of the ranch three days later, trying desperately not to turn and look at Alana's empty office as she walked toward Chip's. She found him sitting at his desk, staring toward Alana's office.

"We're quite a pair, aren't we?" Tegan gestured across the foyer with her head, and then sat in an empty chair.

He sighed and shook his head. "Yes, although I'll bet it's harder for you. I miss her because I enjoyed her company and she made my life easier. I'm assuming you have other, more profound reasons to want her here."

Tegan nodded, not trusting herself to speak. She cleared her throat and tried to sound unaffected. "Maybe we were fools then, to care about her when it obviously wasn't returned."

He laughed without humor and looked away from the door and at her. "You know as well as I do that she cared too much. About you, especially. Me and the ranch, too. The puppies. Michelle and Jennifer. Otherwise she wouldn't have left once she realized how much she stood to lose if she made a mistake."

Tegan frowned. "She didn't mess up, though. Even if she had, she wouldn't have lost any of us."

"Maybe what happened at her last job kept her from believing it. She lost everything because of a mistake."

Tegan nodded. Alana had said as much to her. Her reputation, her home, her career. She had lost all of them in one instant, and…
"Wait. How did you know about her getting fired? She said she took this position because you didn't check references."

"Of course I checked them," Chip said in an indignant tone. "I called her last employer and heard about the snafu at the hotel." He tried unsuccessfully to hide a snicker behind his hand. "It's the greatest story."

"You should hear Alana give her version. She has the most hilarious way of telling it." Tegan's voice faded toward the end. Talking about Alana with Chip made her feel close, which only made it hurt worse when Tegan remembered she was far away. Philadelphia. With no dirt under her nails or dust in her hair from riding. No horses to groom or housekeeping staff to manage. No puppies biting her ankles and licking her face.

Tegan would have bet all her savings that Alana missed the puppy part. The rest of it? Probably not. Whether she missed Tegan didn't seem to be a factor. It hadn't been enough to keep her here.

She turned her attention back to the conversation at hand. "So why did you hire her after hearing about it?"

Chip shrugged. "Like we said, it was a mistake. And a funny one. Something about it felt off to me, too. Her boss almost seemed to enjoy making Alana sound horrible. I thought she might thrive in a place where people cared about her."

Tegan looked at him with new respect. His plan had backfired a bit, though. Alana had been prepared to come here, do her time, and get away unscathed. Forming connections seemed to have been harder for her to handle than being an unappreciated and maligned employee. "To be honest, we both thought you hired her because you were desperate. I didn't realize you had other reasons."

Chip rubbed the back of his neck with a rueful expression on his face. "I was getting low on options, wasn't I? My desperation might have played a role in hiring her, but it wasn't the only reason. And my instincts were right about her, for the most part."

Tegan had to laugh. It was probably the first time she had since Alana had left, and it sounded rusty to her. "Did your instincts also tell you she was an experienced equestrian?"

He laughed, too. "No. Her cover letter told me that. I reread it yesterday, and it's a quality work of fiction."

Tegan shook her head, smiling. Neither of them was trying to be mean about Alana's deception. There was something too gutsy and brave about it to criticize. "When did you know?" she asked. Chip had called her right after Alana told him about her absolute lack of prior experience and quit. If the information had been news to him, she assumed he wouldn't have been on the phone to her within minutes, telling her to bring Alana back.

"When did I know she was a complete beginner?" he asked, and Tegan nodded. "The first day she was out with the horses alone. I thought I'd keep an eye on her to make sure she didn't need help with anything." He rolled his eyes. "She needed help with *everything*."

"But you didn't fire her. Or help her, either." This must have been the day after their first lesson. She remembered how hard it had been for Alana to manage the simplest things with Charm, but also how hard she had worked.

"No, I was going to confront her, but I...well, confrontation's not my thing. So I watched, and she brought out horse after horse. Stayed out there all day, with books and notes and videos on her phone. By the end of the day, I could see how much she had improved, so I decided to let it go for the moment. I thought she deserved a second chance when I hired her, and I wanted to find out what she was going to do with it."

Tegan knew exactly what Alana had done with her opportunity. She had gone back to the horses day after day, getting better each time. Tegan sighed and put her palm against her stomach. Getting over a broken heart would be much easier if she could hate Alana. Instead, she and Chip were apparently forming an Alana fan club.

Chip leaned toward her. "I hope you don't think I wasn't considering the safety of my guests and my horses. I just wanted to give her time, see what happened. I always figured I'd go along on the rides, just in case I was needed."

Tegan grinned. "I was planning to do the same thing, since I had gone behind your back to teach her. I wouldn't have let her out there alone with a group if I didn't think she could handle it."

Chip waggled his finger at her. "Ah, I thought it was you. I assumed she was taking lessons somewhere, but I didn't know where."

"She would have been mortified if we'd both shown up for her first ride, intending to go along as chaperones."

"I'm sure we'd have paid somehow. She'd probably make me ride in one of the children's saddles." He shifted in his chair as if imagining how uncomfortable it would be. "She wouldn't have needed us, though. I saw her with Michelle and Cotton. You and I both know being a good trail guide requires skills beyond being able to sit on a horse. Clear thinking, the ability to read a situation, grace under pressure. She came here with those already in place."

Tegan nodded, thinking of how hard she had tried to keep Alana safe in the arena with Charm and on their trail ride. "Her riding skills are catching up quickly, too, but what she doesn't have are the difficult experiences longtime horse people have, like getting bucked off a bunch of times. They teach a person to accept that unexpected things happen with horses."

"And to pick yourself up and get back on. Not run away."

"Damn," said Tegan, propping her elbows on her knees and leaning against them. "If we'd had this conversation weeks ago, do you think we could have kept her here somehow?"

He sat back in his chair, seeming to consider her question. "No, I don't think so. What it might have done is made us try even harder to protect her. Inevitably, she was going to have to face an accident or mishap on a trail ride. I think she would have reacted the same way, no matter if it happened now or weeks from now."

Tegan sighed. "I didn't come by just to talk about her, although it did help a little. What I'm here about are the puppies."

"The puppies," Chip said, looking as longingly at the blanket filled wading pool as he had at Alana's empty office. "I miss them. How are they?"

"Good. Energetic. Anyway, I have two that aren't spoken for yet. Dez wants one, which shocked me, but I haven't let her know which yet. Alana had been trying to figure out which one you liked most, but she couldn't tell. If you're interested in adopting one, I wanted to give you the choice of the two."

"No, no. She can have either. I had actually planned to talk to Alana about adopting Lace. She's such a sweet dog, and I thought she'd like going on hikes with me and hanging around the ranch, If it's okay with you, of course."

"Oh." Tegan was happy for the dog, yes, but what nearly brought her to tears was the thought of how excited Alana would have been to find out that Lace was Chip's mystery preference. "I think you'd be perfect for her. Absolutely. The guests will love having her here, too."

"Cool," he said, sounding as excited as a young boy getting his first dog. He reached over the desk and pulled out one of his flat metal sculptures that had been tucked behind it. "Look what I made for the wall outside my office."

Tegan laughed with delight when he held up the life-size image of Lace. He had captured Lace's expression flawlessly.

"I love it. I'm going to spay her after the puppies are weaned, and then she'll be yours." She stood up, relieved by the good news, but weary after talking about Alana. "I'll be here this weekend, of course. Do you need me to lead any of the rides?"

"I'll cover those. We might need a hand with the children in the corral, though, just leading them around a few times. Jennifer's sister-in-law will be here to help, too."

"Of course." Alana had been excited about her plan to offer rides for the kids. Tegan could surely get through the afternoon in the corral without dwelling on Alana. Yeah, right.

She was almost to the door when he stopped her. "If you contact her, would you—"

"I won't," she said firmly. She had good practice at this since she had to yell it to herself a few times every night, when she'd reach for her phone.

"Okay. But if you do decide to—"

"I won't."

He held up a hand. "Let her know I want her back here. Right before all this happened, I was talking to Jennifer about how much of a raise I could offer Alana if she'd switch jobs with me. She could manage the place, and I'd be the outdoor guide. Of course, I'd still like her to do some of the trail rides, but I wouldn't mention them right away if I were you. Get her back here first."

Tegan exhaled, backing out the door. "Fine. But I'm not going to call her. Besides, she has her new job in Philadelphia. Or her old one with a promotion. Either way, she won't be coming back here."

"Oh, she's not in Philadelphia."

Tegan took three steps, and then turned around and went back to the office. "What? Yes, she is."

He shook his head. "She might be in the city, but she didn't take the job. I called there because I wanted her address for sending her last paycheck. Some Krantz guy said he offered her the position last week, but she called him back the same day and turned it down."

"Huh." Tegan sketched a quick wave good-bye and left the lodge. She sat in her Jeep at the fork in the road, idling without knowing which direction to take. She had understood, in some way, Alana's desire to go back to Philadelphia as a winner. It had made sense. It was like Alana had gone *to* a different place, a better opportunity. Now it just seemed as if she'd gone away from this one. Away from her. The difference was subtle, but it hurt like hell.

She started driving and then slammed on the brakes, stopping in the middle of the empty road. *Last week?* Tegan remembered their phone conversation, when Alana had brought up the hops festival, finally bringing up an activity more than twenty-four hours in the future. Was her decision not to take the job part of the reason why she was looking ahead with their relationship in mind? Tegan started driving again. She wasn't about to give in and call Alana, no matter what Chip thought, so she'd never know.

Chapter Twenty-one

A lana didn't make it past Ellensburg. Instead of waiting for the next flight to Seattle, she had rented a car with the intention of driving there. Then she would call Jim back and hope he hadn't hired someone else for her job. Get on a plane and fly to Philadelphia.

Her plan seemed reasonable. Then she got to Ellensburg.

The part of town she saw didn't have much to recommend it. Winds funneling through the mountain passes to the west threatened to bowl her over whenever she stepped outside, and what smelled like a million cows must have been pastured just outside the city limits. She only stopped because she could barely keep her eyes open or her attention focused on the road. Saying good-bye to Tegan in such a stiff, horrible way had left her exhausted. The imagined memory of Michelle being hurt on the trail—having superseded the true version of the event in her mind—haunted her.

She stopped in a hotel, deciding to brave the gusting winds, along with all the odors and dust they carried along with them, for just a brief rest. A night to sleep and cry before she picked herself up and moved on with her life. She accomplished at least one of her goals, weeping through the night into a pillow covered with a scratchy pillowcase, sobbing about all the hours she had wasted learning to ride and how foolish she'd been to turn down the job.

Eventually, she got past her self-pity and cried for Tegan and the puppies, Chip and Jennifer. Fitz with his bounding trot and Charm, who would prefer not to.

Around three in the morning, she was worn out. The emotions she'd experienced in the past month had been more intense and more capricious than anything she'd felt before. She'd studied hard in school, but a few late-night cram sessions were nothing compared to the physical and mental effort she had put into her riding. She had taken care of guests and cleaned their rooms, but those tasks had never brought her as much joy and heartwarming laughter as she had found while tending to Lace and her puppies.

She'd had girlfriends along the way, too, although nothing serious enough to interfere with her career plans. Her relationship with Tegan went so far beyond what she'd had before that she needed an entirely new vocabulary to describe and define it. A thousand synonyms for pain since Tegan was no longer in her life.

Alana turned on the television, letting the boring reruns and constant sound finally lull her into a restless sleep.

Her next day was spent much the same way, in a constant cycle of tears and loneliness. She snapped out of it on the third morning, after managing to walk from her hotel to McDonald's for breakfast and back without being blown to Oz. She had to make a decision, any decision.

She spent hours searching for an answer. Which job, what city. Her old career dreams didn't seem as enticing to her now, and the thought of endless travel and owning nothing more permanent than a few changes of clothes wasn't appealing. She realized she wanted to decorate a house and own some real wineglasses. Hang a painting on a wall and put a dog bed in the living room.

She wanted Tegan in her bedroom. Her mug next to Tegan's in the kitchen cupboard, and both their clothes hanging in the closet. She knew without a doubt that Tegan wanted her, too. What she wasn't as confident in was Tegan's ability to forgive her. She had made the choice to leave her behind, just like her mother had, time and time again. She wasn't sure she could make Tegan believe she would stay.

❖

She tried the clinic first, but the lights were out, and Tegan's Jeep wasn't in the lot. She sat in her rental car and drummed her fingers on the steering wheel, considering her options. She didn't have many—she didn't know where Rosie lived, and she didn't know any of Tegan's other friends. She didn't want to barge in on Tegan's grandparents at night. She decided she would have to wait. She'd find a hotel and come back to the clinic early in the morning.

She wasn't sure why she decided to drive by her rental house. She had a vague idea about trying to climb through a window and sleep in her familiar bed for one more night, but they were probably all locked. She drove down the street anyway and jerked to a halt when she saw Tegan's car in her driveway.

She walked slowly up to the porch, having weird and nostalgic thoughts like *Oh, this is where I first saw what I thought was a rat.* She was delaying the inevitable confrontation, not because she didn't think Tegan deserved to be angry, but because she wasn't sure of the outcome. An argument with a partner, when both expected to get through the rough patch and still be together the next day, was one thing. This was something else entirely. It could already be over for the two of them, if Tegan had shut Alana completely out of her heart after she left, or it could be finished before the night was over.

She felt strange knocking on what she still considered to be her own door. She heard scuffling noises, which seemed to go on for a long time, and then Tegan was standing in front of her, looking slightly disheveled.

"Hey," Tegan said in a voice Alana couldn't read. If she was surprised to see Alana, she didn't show it.

"Hey back," Alana said. She didn't get any response to her use of Tegan's normal greeting. Whenever she had heard Tegan say it to her, she'd found herself smiling. She sighed. She shouldn't expect this to be easy. "Can I come in and talk?"

Tegan left the door open and walked into the living room, leaving Alana to come inside and close it behind her. She walked over and sat on one end of the couch, facing Tegan who had taken a chair.

"I'm not sure how to begin," Alana said, after struggling to come up with a way to open a conversation between them.

"You seemed to know how to end it, when you left."

Alana sighed. This wasn't a good start. "The accident with Michelle scared me," she said, haltingly, struggling with each word. "I needed time to think..."

"Which you could have done here. Where did you go? Not Philadelphia, I'm assuming."

"A hotel in Ellensburg."

Tegan laughed. It was a harsh sound when it didn't have any humor in it. "Not exactly a step up in the hospitality world."

"No kidding. What is with the smell in that town?" Alana hesitated, then continued when she still couldn't get a laugh out of Tegan. "I know I could have stayed here to think things through. You would have helped me, and Chip, too. In the future—if there is a future—I won't run away. But this time, I needed to go, so I could come back."

Tegan rubbed a hand over her forehead. "This isn't making any sense. Maybe we should talk about it another time."

"No. We have to talk about it now. Please, Tegan."

Tegan had started to get out of her chair, but she sat down again. "Fine. Why don't you start by explaining why you had to go."

Alana rubbed her palms on her thighs. Her revelations had seemed to make sense when she had come up with them, but now they were muddled in her head.

"When I first came here, I felt like I didn't have any choices," she said. "I had to be here, had to stay long enough to build my references. Even when I started to enjoy the work and the people I was meeting, or when I turned down Jim's offer and decided to stay here longer, I never got past the thought of this as a temporary place. And when we...when we decided to be with each other, my eventual move was built into our relationship."

Tegan shook her head. "It had nothing to do with me wanting you. I chose to be with you despite your move, not because of it."

"Yes, but *when* we got together and how we got together were driven by it."

"Maybe."

Alana sighed. "Do you need to make this so difficult?" she asked in exasperation.

Her irritated comment got a slight reaction, at least, but Tegan quickly hid her flash of a smile. "Yes, I do."

"Great. Thank you." Alana paused, then continued. "I guess the motorbike incident broke me, in a way. In some bad ways, like my confidence and my connection to you and the ranch. But also in a good way. I got my chance to leave, and when I did, I had options and roads I could take. Seattle, Philadelphia, Ellensburg. But I chose here because this place has become my home. I chose you, because you're my life. I came back to stay, not to stay for a while."

Tegan heard the catch in Alana's voice as she spoke. She desperately wanted to believe her, but too many memories of being left behind in the past were crowding into her mind. She'd either need to tell Alana to get out and never contact her again, or she'd have to take a risk and trust her. Her heart and body were yelling at her to give Alana another chance. Her mind was cautious, but even when she tried to ignore her more emotional responses and look at the situation logically, she came to the same conclusion. Alana had never lied to her about wanting to leave. Why would she start lying now, by saying she wanted to stay?

"I want to believe you, Alana…"

"Then do. I love you, Tegan. You're the reason I turned down the job in Philadelphia. You're the reason I came back here. Not for my career, or my ambitions, or for anyone else. Just you."

"I love you, too, Alana. I can try to—"

She didn't have a chance to finish her sentence because Alana was across the room and kneeling in front of her chair, leaning forward to kiss her until Tegan couldn't even remember the words she had been about to say. None of them mattered anymore, anyway, except for the first three.

Alana pulled back slightly, running her fingers along Tegan's cheekbone and kissing her softly. "Can I see the puppies?" she whispered.

Tegan laughed. "Wow. The most romantic thing anyone has ever said to me during a make out session. Yes, let's go see the puppies."

Tegan watched Alana open the bedroom door and sit down in the midst of the yipping, tail-wagging litter of pups. She had been joking just now, but she suddenly realized her words had been truer than she thought. Puppies didn't belong in the life of a nomadic event planner or in exotic island resorts. They belonged in homes, with families. They were part of the life Alana was choosing to share with her.

"I got them all adopted," she said, squatting down and petting Lace, who was on the outskirts of the chaos.

"Already? I was only gone two days." Alana sighed. "Who else is taking them?"

"Dez is taking the female with the black ears. Her family has a lot of space and other animals, so she'll have a great life there. And then there's Chip." Tegan paused, drawing out the suspense. "He wants to adopt Lace."

Alana's expression lit up. "Really? No wonder I couldn't figure out his favorite puppy. This is even better."

"I have a message from him for you," Tegan said, scooting closer and picking up a puppy. "He wants to trade jobs with you, in a way. Hire you as manager, and he'll be in charge of most of the outdoor activities. On one condition."

"Yes," Alana said. "Whatever it is. Well, unless it entails taking crash courses in fishing."

Tegan laughed. "No. He wants you to help with the trail rides sometimes. He's not much of a rider."

Alana had seemed excited about Chip's offer, but now she looked hesitant. "Maybe. I'll try."

Tegan nodded. She needed to get Alana back on a horse tomorrow, before every last nerve disappeared. She dropped the subject for now. "Do you think you'll be happy in this job, Alana? I remember you telling me how you didn't want to manage a hotel like your parents. You wanted to travel and plan events."

"I still want to travel, but with you." Alana shook her head, cradling Prince against her chest. "I never understood why my parents liked their work until I started taking over parts of Chip's responsibilities. It's been challenging and fun, and I'm excited to see if we can make the ranch a success. Besides, I'll still be able to plan events. We need all the income we can get."

Alana put Prince down and hugged her knees to her chest. "You still haven't told me who's adopting Chantilly."

"Ah, I was wondering what you'd named her. She's the one you were hiding away when people came to see the puppies, isn't she?"

Alana nodded, looking bereft, and Tegan put her out of her misery.

"I was planning to keep her," she said. "I felt I wasn't heartbroken enough, so I thought I'd invite a constant reminder of you into my home."

"She's ours?" Alana asked, wading over to Tegan and wrapping her arms around her neck.

"Yes," Tegan said. "Ours."

Theirs. Tegan felt her heart slowly starting to trust that they could be a family, with the two of them and Chantilly. Charm and Rio and Alana's ranch horses. Her grandparents, and Chip and Dez, and all the people she and Alana had gathered around them. But for right now, Tegan wanted time for just the two of them.

She led them out of the room, carefully shutting the pups inside for the night, before pulling Alana to her again. She put her palms on Alana's cheeks and kissed her, moving her mouth slowly across Alana's even as her tongue pressed deeper, bringing them closer together until there wasn't a whisper of space between them.

Tegan groaned in protest when Alana moved away from her. "Upstairs," Alana said, her breathy voice and flushed neck proving she was as aroused by their kiss as Tegan was. "I want to be in our bed."

Tegan wasn't about to argue with that. She hurried up the stairs after Alana, catching her by the belt loops of her jeans once they reached the landing and giving her another kiss. Slowness gave way to haste as they unbuttoned and unzipped and flung their clothes onto the bedroom floor.

Alana pushed on Tegan's shoulders until she got on the bed and reached out for Alana to join her. Alana knelt on the bed at her feet, spreading Tegan's thighs and moving between them. She had a lifetime ahead of her for slow and leisurely love, but right now she needed to make up for the days of loneliness and questioning of the time they had spent apart. She leaned forward and put her mouth on Tegan, sliding her tongue through wetness and heat and binding them together more surely than mere words had been able to do. Tegan moved with her, one hand loosely wrapped in Alana's hair.

"I…love you," Tegan said, even her simple sentence broken into fragments by a gasp.

"I love you, too," Alana said, lifting her head for a brief moment to meet Tegan's passion-hazed eyes before her tongue renewed its attack on Tegan's defenses, breaking through them with ease and driving Tegan's hips against her mouth as Tegan's body shuddered through its climax.

Alana smiled with satisfaction and scooted up the bed until she was lying side by side with Tegan, who had one arm flung over her eyes. She lowered her arm and gathered Alana even closer.

"Wow," Tegan said, brushing Alana's hair behind her ear and kissing her gently. "Welcome home."

"Home," whispered Alana, making a sound halfway between a sigh and a moan as Tegan began kissing along her jawline and down the side of her neck. "It's the best place to be."

EPILOGUE

Alana twisted around in the saddle to look behind her for the twentieth time in the past five minutes. She saw the same sight that had greeted her each of the previous times—three horses sedately following Fitz along the flat, simple beginner trail. Penny swished her tail lazily at a fly, but otherwise the horses seemed lulled into quietness by the hot afternoon sun and the familiar path.

She faced forward again, allowing herself a moment to appreciate the tranquil beauty of the scrubland around her before her next frantic check on her preteen charges. The brush had softened to a silvery-sage shade of green, set against a background of rust-colored rocks and soil. Tall pines offered welcome shade and a lacy view of the cloudless blue sky. As pretty as the landscape was, it only managed to distract a small fraction of her mind. Most of her attention was fixated on the horses and riders behind her.

The younger children were being led around the paddock near the barn by Dez and Marcus, and Alana had reluctantly agreed to take the older ones on the easy trail. She had tried to get out of it by claiming she needed to run the grand opening, but she had prepared too well, and the event was moving along smoothly without her. If she had known Tegan and Chip were going to gang up on her in some sort of get-her-back-on-the-horse confidence boosting exercise, she would have planned for a couple of false emergencies to occur that would have required her presence on the grounds and not on a horse.

She halted Fitz and the line of horses to point out a small woodpecker tapping away on a dead trunk. She wasn't about to admit it to either Tegan or Chip, but they had been correct about getting her back on the trails. She was still nervous about getting everyone back to the barn safely, but she was growing a little more relaxed with each ride. With the first set of riders, she hadn't even glanced at the birds and plants around her, let alone stopped long enough to show something to the group.

Alana got her group moving again, and they made the final turn back toward the barn. As she had expected, she saw Tegan hovering near the gate, in the same position where Alana had found her after each of the previous rides. Tegan's watchfulness might have added to Alana's anxiety if she had thought it was due to a lack of faith in her ability, but she knew the truth. Tegan only wanted her to enjoy the rides and to claim the same confidence in herself that Tegan and Chip had in her.

Tegan stepped back as Alana reached down and unlatched the gate to let her riders through to the saddling area, where Chip was waiting to help them dismount. Alana slid off Fitz and landed heavily next to Tegan. She frowned and put her hands on her lower back, arching against them.

"I'm not sure why I'm this sore," she said as she straightened up. "A few laps around the beginner trail at a walk shouldn't be enough to make my back hurt."

"You're riding tense, but you look more relaxed every time you get back here." Tegan moved behind her and encircled Alana's waist with her arms, pulling Alana flush against her stomach. The warmth and closeness of her unknotted Alana's muscles more effectively than any stretches could do. "There are only a couple more groups waiting to go after lunch, and Chip or I can lead them."

Alana sighed, leaning her head back until it rested on Tegan's shoulder. She was tempted to accept Tegan's offer, but she refused to let even her residual fear have any control over her. She had run away once already because of it and she hadn't liked the feeling of giving up—on her responsibilities, on Tegan, and on herself. "No, I'll finish the day. I wouldn't mind some company, though."

Tegan kissed her temple. "You got it. I'll pretend to be one of those sneaky kids who make their horses walk real slow so they have an excuse to trot and catch up to the others. That'll be good practice for you."

Alana turned in Tegan's arms until they were face to face. "I was thinking you could pretend to be one of those helpful trail assistants who keeps watch for dangers like motorbikes and ravenous bears so I can just mosey along and enjoy the trail."

"Fine," Tegan said. She took Fitz's reins from Alana and led him over to the water trough for a drink before taking him to the fence where the rest of the string of horses was tied. "But if I see a bear, I'm just going to shout a warning to you as I run past on my way back here."

Tegan put Fitz's halter over his bridle and tied him in a shady spot. She was glad to see Alana smiling and laughing with her while she loosened her horse's cinch to make him more comfortable until their next ride. She had managed to get Alana out for a few rides on Charm and some of the ranch horses since she had returned from running away, but today was her first time on the trail as a guide. Tegan had worried that Alana would be too afraid to lead her groups, or—even worse—that she would have completely lost all interest in riding and the local environment. She was relieved to hear Alana talking about the trails in an affectionate tone, and to realize that Alana had a healthy concern for the safety of her charges underlying the residual fear she felt from her experience with Michelle.

They walked across the paddock where Dez was leading a tiny boy around in circles on Mouse. Tegan waved at her, feeling a surge of fondness for her assistant. She might be gruff and annoying at times, but she was willing to come out here and help with the children. She had even put her phone away, for once.

"How's it going, Dez?" she called over to her.

Dez sighed visibly. "It'd be better if the woman who forced me into this job actually helped instead of leaning against the gate pining over her girlfriend all morning. But I guess she needs a break to recover from seeing two whole patients yesterday."

"Hey." Tegan put her hands on her hips and glared at her once-again-annoying assistant. "You're conveniently forgetting the three surgeries I did before I saw those patients."

"Oh, please. I did most of the work then, too. *Dez, hand me a scalpel. Dez, run and get some antibiotics from the storeroom. Dez, check the cat's vital signs.*"

"That's called being a surgical assistant."

Alana laughed and grabbed Tegan's hand, pulling her away from the conversation. "Come on, you know she's just messing with you. She really loves working with you, and this is the way she shows her affection."

Tegan softened again as she followed Alana out of the pen. "Do you really think so?"

"Of course," Alana said with a shrug, not meeting her eyes. "Probably. Maybe. I mean, she hasn't quit yet, has she?"

"No, but she's going to be fired on Monday," Tegan said. Alana ignored her comment since they both knew it wasn't true.

They walked hand in hand across the back lawn, stopping to visit with Jennifer who was distributing information to local visitors about the special events the ranch was planning for the summer, and with Gladys and Rosie who were chatting with people about the feral cat rescue group. Tegan had expected the grand opening to be a quiet event, with the ranch's few visitors eating barbecue amidst some understated decorations, but Alana had surprised her, as always. The grounds looked festive with bright red-and-white banners that contrasted sharply with the natural background of pines and bare rocks, creating a carnivalesque atmosphere. Children ran everywhere, playing lawn games and racing to the horse paddock. Alana had managed to entice most of the town to the event, either as visitors or as vendors, so the ranch appeared to be fully booked rather than host to a mere handful of tourists. Every now and again an employee would stop Alana to tell her about a minor crisis, and she handled each one with decisive ease, proving—as if Tegan had needed more evidence—how good she was at her job.

Alana was leading her toward the barbecue pit where Rosie's family was cooking pork shoulders and a variety of peppers over open flames, but Tegan pulled her away and through the ranch's back door. She led them into Alana's office and shut the door behind them.

"What's wrong?" Alana asked, seemingly able to read Tegan's mood change with ease. She brushed Tegan's hair out of her eyes.

"This is great," Tegan said, struggling to express the worry that had crept over her while they walked through the crowds. "This event. It's perfectly planned and it's running smoothly. It's going to attract a lot of business for the ranch. You did a wonderful job."

"Thank you," Alana said, raising her voice at the end as if turning the statement into a question, somehow knowing Tegan had more to say.

"You did this, and you're amazing." Tegan put her hands on Alana's hips, running her thumbs along the top of Alana's jeans and under her shirt, over bare skin. "But there won't be a grand opening to plan every week. And the trail rides might be interesting now, because you're still a little nervous on them, but eventually they'll be routine for you, too."

"And you're worried that I'll get bored here and want to leave," Alana finished for her. Tegan nodded, and Alana shook her head with a laugh. "Please, don't worry. The ranch is far from successful, even though today is going well, and I have plenty more ideas for future events. Hopefully, I'll be more relaxed on the trail rides soon, but that won't stop me from enjoying them."

Alana put her arms around Tegan and walked forward, pushing Tegan back until she bumped into the desk. She perched on the edge of it, wrapping her legs around Alana's thighs and squeezing her close.

"Someday I might get bored and want a change. Maybe I'll find another hotel or resort around here, or maybe we'll talk about moving somewhere else. I don't know. But I can promise you one thing." Alana slid her hand along the nape of Tegan's neck and tangled her fingers in Tegan's hair. "I promise I will never get bored with you. We can change jobs or change cities, but we'll never compromise when it comes to us. Love comes first."

"First, last, and always," Tegan agreed, before giving in to the gentle pressure from Alana's hand and leaning forward to kiss her.

About the Author

Karis Walsh lives in the Pacific Northwest, where she finds inspiration for the settings of her contemporary romances and romantic intrigues. She was a Golden Crown Literary Award winner with *Tales from Sea Glass Inn*, and her novels have been shortlisted for a Lambda Literary award and a Forward INDIES award. She can usually be found reading with a cat curled on her lap, hiking with a dog at her side, or playing her viola with both animals hiding under the bed. Contact her at kariswalsh@gmail.com.

Books Available from Bold Strokes Books

Blood of the Pack by Jenny Frame. When Alpha of the Scottish pack Kenrick Wulver visits the Wolfgangs, she falls for Zaria Lupa, a wolf on the run. (978-1-63555-431-1)

Cause of Death by Sheri Lewis Wohl. Medical student Vi Akiak and K9 Search and Rescue officer Kate Renard must work together to find a killer before they end up the next targets. In the race for survival, they discover that love may be the biggest risk of all. (978-1-63555-441-0)

Chasing Sunset by Missouri Vaun. Hijinks and mishaps ensue as Iris and Finn set off on a road trip adventure, chasing the sunset, and falling in love along the way. (978-1-63555-454-0)

Double Down by MB Austin. When an unlikely friendship with Spanish pop star Erlea turns deeper, Celeste, in-house physician for the hotel hosting Erlea's show, has a choice to make—run or double down on love. (978-1-63555-423-6)

Party of Three by Sandy Lowe. Three friends are in for a wild night at billionaire heiress Eleanor McGregor's twenty-fifth birthday party. Love, lust, and doing the right thing, even when it hurts, turn the evening into one that will change their lives forever. (978-1-63555-246-1)

Sit. Stay. Love. by Karis Walsh. City girl Alana Brendt and country vet Tegan Evans both know they don't belong together. Only problem is, they're falling in love. (978-1-63555-439-7)

Where the Lies Hide by Renee Roman. As P.I. Camdyn Stark gets closer to solving the case, will her dark secrets and the lies she's buried jeopardize her future with the quietly beautiful Sarah Peters? (978-1-63555-371-0)

Beautiful Dreamer by Melissa Brayden. With love on the line, can Devyn Winters find it in her heart to stay in the small town of Dreamer's Bay, the one place she swore she'd never remain? (978-1-63555-305-5)

Create a Life to Love by Erin Zak. When sixteen-year-old Beth shows up at her birth mother's door, three lives will change forever. (978-1-63555-425-0)

Deadeye by Meredith Doench. Stranded while hunting the serial predator Deadeye, Special Agent Luce Hansen fights for survival while her lover, forensic pathologist Harper Bennett, hunts for clues to Hansen's disappearance along the killer's trail. (978-1-63555-253-9)

Death Takes a Bow by David S. Pederson. Alan Keys takes part in a local stage production, but when the leading man is murdered, his partner Detective Heath Barrington is thrust into the limelight to find the killer. (978-1-63555-472-4)

Endangered by Michelle Larkin. Shapeshifters Officer Aspen Wolfe and Dr. Tora Madigan fight their growing attraction as they work together to destroy a secret government agency that exterminates their kind. (978-1-63555-377-2)

Incognito by VK Powell. The only thing Evan Spears is focused on is capturing a fleeing murder suspect until wild card Frankie Strong is added to her team and causes chaos on and off the job. (978-1-63555-389-5)

Insult to Injury by Gun Brooke. After losing everything, Gail Owen withdraws to her old farmhouse and finds a destitute young woman, Romi Shepherd, living in a secret room. (978-1-63555-323-9)

Just One Moment by Dena Blake. If you were given the chance to have the love of your life back, could you ignore everything that went wrong and start over again? (978-1-63555-387-1)

Scene of the Crime by MJ Williamz. Cullen Mathew finds herself caught between the woman she thinks she loves but can no longer trust and a beautiful detective she can't stop thinking about who will stop at nothing to find the truth. (978-1-63555-405-2)

Accidental Prophet by Bud Gundy. Days after his grandmother dies, Drew Morten learns his true identity and finds himself racing against time to save civilization from the apocalypse. (978-1-63555-452-6)

Daughter of No One by Sam Ledel. When their worlds are threatened, a princess and a village outcast must overcome their differences and embrace a budding attraction if they want to survive. (978-1-63555-427-4)

Fear of Falling by Georgia Beers. Singer Sophie James is ready to shake up her career, but her new manager, the gorgeous Dana Landon, has other ideas. (978-1-63555-443-4)

In Case You Forgot by Fredrick Smith and Chaz Lamar. Zaire and Kenny, two newly single, Black, queer, and socially aware men, start again—in love, career, and life—in the West Hollywood neighborhood of LA. (978-1-63555-493-9)

Playing with Fire by Lesley Davis. When Takira Lathan and Dante Groves meet at Takira's restaurant, love may find its way onto the menu. (978-1-63555-433-5)

Practice Makes Perfect by Carsen Taite. Meet law school friends Campbell, Abby, and Grace, law partners at Austin's premier boutique legal firm for young, hip entrepreneurs. Legal Affairs: one law firm, three best friends, three chances to fall in love. (978-1-63555-357-4)

The Last Seduction by Ronica Black. When you allow true love to elude you once and you desperately regret it, are you brave enough to grab it when it comes around again? (978-1-63555-211-9)

Wavering Convictions by Erin Dutton. After a traumatic event, Maggie has vowed to regain her strength and independence. So how can Ally be both the woman who makes her feel safe and a constant reminder of the person who took her security away? (978-1-63555-403-8)

A Bird of Sorrow by Shea Godfrey. As Darrius and her lover, Princess Jessa, gather their strength for the coming war, a mysterious spell will reveal the truth of an ancient love. (978-1-63555-009-2)

All the Worlds Between Us by Morgan Lee Miller. High school senior Quinn Hughes discovers that a broken friendship is actually a door propped open for an unexpected romance. (978-1-63555-457-1)

An Intimate Deception by CJ Birch. Flynn County Sheriff Elle Ashley has spent her adult life atoning for her wild youth, but when she finds her ex, Jessie, murdered two weeks before the small town's biggest social event, she comes face-to-face with her past and all her well-kept secrets. (978-1-63555-417-5)

Cash and the Sorority Girl by Ashley Bartlett. Cash Braddock doesn't want to deal with morality, drugs, or people. Unfortunately, she's going to have to. (978-1-63555-310-9)

Counting for Thunder by Phillip Irwin Cooper. A struggling actor returns to the Deep South to manage a family crisis, finds love, and ultimately his own voice as his mother is regaining hers for possibly the last time. (978-1-63555-450-2)

Falling by Kris Bryant. Falling in love isn't part of the plan, but will Shaylie Beck put her heart first and stick around, or tell the damaging truth? (978-1-63555-373-4)

Secrets in a Small Town by Nicole Stiling. Deputy Chief Mackenzie Blake has one mission: find the person harassing Savannah Castillo and her daughter before they cause real harm. (978-1-63555-436-6)

Stormy Seas by Ali Vali. The high-octane follow-up to the best-selling action-romance, *Blue Skies*. (978-1-63555-299-7)

The Road to Madison by Elle Spencer. Can two women who fell in love as girls overcome the hurt caused by the father who tore them apart? (978-1-63555-421-2)

Dangerous Curves by Larkin Rose. When love waits at the finish line, dangerous curves are a risk worth taking. (978-1-63555-353-6)

Love to the Rescue by Radclyffe. Can two people who share a past really be strangers? (978-1-62639-973-0)

Love's Portrait by Anna Larner. When museum curator Molly Goode and benefactor Georgina Wright uncover a portrait's secret, public and private truths are exposed, and their deepening love hangs in the balance. (978-1-63555-057-3)

Model Behavior by MJ Williamz. Can one woman's instability shatter a new couple's dreams of happiness? (978-1-63555-379-6)

Pretending in Paradise by M. Ullrich. When travelwisdom.com assigns PR specialist Caroline Beckett and travel blogger Emma Morgan to cover a hot new couples retreat, they're forced to fake a relationship to secure a reservation. (978-1-63555-399-4)

Recipe for Love by Aurora Rey. Hannah Little doesn't have much use for fancy chefs or fancy restaurants, but when New York City chef Drew Davis comes to town, their attraction just might be a recipe for love. (978-1-63555-367-3)

Survivor's Guilt and Other Stories by Greg Herren. Award-winning author Greg Herren's short stories are finally pulled together into a single collection, including the Macavity Award nominated title story and the first-ever Chanse MacLeod short story. (978-1-63555-413-7)

The House by Eden Darry. After a vicious assault, Sadie, Fin, and their family retreat to a house they think is the perfect place to start over, until they realize not all is as it seems. (978-1-63555-395-6)

Uninvited by Jane C. Esther. When Acrin McLeary's body becomes host for an alien intent on invading Earth, she must work with researcher Olivia Ando to uncover the truth and save humankind. (978-1-63555-282-9)